THE **SHERL(**
LUCY JA

THE
AFFAIR
OF THE
CORONATION
BALL

THE SHERLOCK HOLMES AND LUCY JAMES MYSTERIES

The Last Moriarty

The Wilhelm Conspiracy

Remember, Remember

The Crown Jewel Mystery

The Jubilee Problem

Death at the Diogenes Club

The Return of the Ripper

Die Again, Mr. Holmes

Watson on the Orient Express

Galahad's Castle

The Loch Ness Horror

The Adair Murders

The Cornwall Mermaid

Miss Nightingale's Gala

The Affair of the Coronation Ball

THE SHERLOCK AND LUCY SHORT STORIES AND NOVELLAS

The Collected Short Stories: Season One

The Collected Stories: Season Two Volume I

The Collected Stories: Season Two Volume II

The Collected Stories: Season Three Volume I

The Collected Stories: Season Thre Volume II

Sign up at SherlockAndLucy.com
to stay up-to-date on Lucy and Sherlock adventures

THE **SHERLOCK HOLMES/ LUCY JAMES** MYSTERIES

THE AFFAIR OF THE CORONATION BALL

BY **ANNA ELLIOTT** AND **CHARLES VELEY**

Typesetting by FormattingExperts.com
Cover design by Todd A. Johnson

PART ONE

CHAPTER 1: WATSON

London, 13th August 1902

It was early on a warm August afternoon, a Wednesday, when my office nurse brought me the telegraph message from Sherlock Holmes.

The message read: *come at once.*

I saw to the needs of my final patient and then quickly set out, taking a cab to 221B Baker Street. I arrived expecting to find Holmes dressed and ready to depart with me on some new case.

Instead, I was surprised to find him in his armchair, sunk in thought, staring at a magazine that lay open on his lap. I drew in my breath in surprise, for I recognised the publication as *The Tatler*, specialising in society gossip, normally the least likely periodical to hold any interest for him.

"Light reading, Holmes?" I asked.

Wordlessly, he handed the publication over to me. The passage, dated 10th August, read as follows:

ROYAL NEED FOR RECUPERATION DISREGARDED
by Lady Whispers

With the royal coronation at Westminster Abbey accomplished, and the royal procession through the city of London now, by the grace of Providence, completed without incident, one would

*expect the wishes of the Royal Family for rest and recupera-
tion to be honoured and respected, particularly after a second
Coronation parade has been postponed until October to enable
His Majesty to recover more fully.*

*Yet, a certain brazenly presumptuous duchess has declared her
intention to host a 'Coronation Ball' at the Savoy on Saturday
the 16th of August.*

*The date, coming so soon after the King's strenuous exertion
during the official events of the Coronation, indicates the lady's
consideration for the King's health is as dimly conceived as her
understanding of royal protocol. One shudders to think what
may be next in her repertoire of gauche antics. Perhaps she and
her tobacco-industrialist husband will exhibit their derring-do
by showering the Royal Couple with common cigars and cigarettes, in a shameless bid for a royal endorsement of the tobacco
products sold by their British and American cronies?*

*We shall be astonished if His Majesty elects to appear any-
where in the vicinity of such an ill-conceived event.*

All England, of course, and indeed most of the English-
speaking world, knew of the serious illness that had so very
nearly ended the King's life. Just before the original day of his
coronation last month, he had collapsed. Emergency surgery
had been performed, alleviating a virulent abdominal infection
that would otherwise have proved fatal.

The pen name 'Lady Whispers' was also familiar to me. I had
dined with the lady herself once or twice following the death of
my beloved wife Mary. She was Eleanor Cavendish, a charming
red-haired writer of novels who supplemented her income with
contributions to periodicals. Holmes knew her as well, for on

several occasions she had provided him with useful background information concerning society figures.

I studied the words of the passage, endeavouring to glean what could have prompted his interest.

Then Holmes handed me the volume of Burke's Peerage that had lain on the side table next to his armchair. "Read the entry on Derrington."

I read as follows:

HINCHCLIFFE, His Grace Daniel, 4th Duke of Derrington, Earl of Marlington, Baron Hinchcliffe of Elmswood

b. 12 July 1847; s. of 3rd Duke and Duchess of Derrington, née Lady Elizabeth Carrington. Educ. Eton and Christ Church, Oxford (MA, Classics). Married 1885, Lady Aline, d. of Zebulon W. Zachary, Esq., of Lexington, Kentucky, USA.

Residences:

- *Derrington House, Belgravia, London, UK*
- *Montpelier Plantation, Saint James Parish, Jamaica*
- *Elmswood Estate, Northumberland, UK*

Career: Founding Member, Imperial Tobacco Consortium, 1890. Director, London Tobacco Board (1892-); Patron, Royal Horticultural Society.

Recreations: Horse Breeding, Polo, Patronage in the Arts and Sciences.

Clubs: White's, Brooks's, The Carlton Club.

Heir Apparent: None; succession to be determined.

"Her comment about derring-do," I said. "It's meant to put knowing readers in mind of this Derrington fellow."

He nodded. "That phrase is what sent me to the entry from Burke's that you are holding. However, I could find no information about the Duchess."

For some reason, my memory strayed to the terrifying moment at the Duchess of Devonshire's Ball, five years earlier, when Holmes, Lucy, and I had killed and captured two traitorous assassins and saved the life of the prince who was now His Majesty.

"Do you foresee danger for the King at this coronation ball?" I asked.

"We have no evidence to go on," Holmes replied. "We do not even know if the King will attend."

"Then I do not see why this article can be of interest to you."

"Inspector Lestrade is also interested in the article."

His tone had hardened. I felt a sense of foreboding, together with that electric excitement that so frequently, for me, preceded the knowledge that a new case was at hand.

He continued, in a kinder tone that somehow increased my foreboding. "We are to meet the Inspector in Hyde Park at four o'clock this afternoon to discuss the matter. It was his call that prompted my telegram to you. I hope you will accompany me."

"Holmes, are you suggesting something has happened to Miss Cavendish?"

"Indeed, old friend. Inspector Lestrade informs me that the body of Miss Cavendish has been found in Hyde Park, with a copy of *The Tatler* in her purse. She has been murdered."

CᕼᗩᑭTEᖇ 2: ᖴᒪYNN

"Quick, hide me!"

For a second, Flynn thought he'd misunderstood the woman who had just hissed those three words at him.

He was at a table at the back of the ham and beef shop on a corner of Bow Street. Mr. Holmes had just paid him for the last job he'd done, so he had money to spare for a hot meal.

The place wasn't fancy. No food shop that would serve a skinny street kid like Flynn—even though he was one of Mr. Holmes's irregulars—was going to be on par with the Savoy or The Carlton. The air was hot and steamy enough to fog up the windows at the front, and it was busy with crowds of customers coming from Covent Garden or Drury Lane. They were loud enough that it was hard to hear anything clearly, too.

The man at the table next to Flynn's was yelling for the waitress to bring him a pot of mustard, and up at the counter, a woman who was trying to buy three pennyworth of brisket had launched into an argument with the shopkeeper about his weights being wrong.

Flynn wasn't even here on a case for Mr. Holmes, which made it even less likely that someone would come to him for help. He had no idea why the woman had just come up to his table.

She wasn't anything extraordinary to look at. She was dressed in a pale grey suit trimmed with black braid and looked to be somewhere in her mid-thirties, with light brown hair, a nose that turned up just a bit, and a wide, generous mouth. The desperation in her eyes, though, was a look Flynn had seen before, and often enough to know that she wasn't fooling.

She cast a quick, scared look over her shoulder towards the door of the shop, then turned back to Flynn.

"Please!"

Flynn barely had time to nod and lift the corner of the white cloth that covered his table. "Under here."

The place was crowded and busy enough that no one was looking in their direction, and besides, Flynn's table was all the way in a back corner of the shop. It was a habit he'd got into while working for Mr. Holmes to always pick a spot where you could see who came in and where no one could sneak up behind you.

The woman ducked around the table and crouched down at Flynn's feet. Flynn let the tablecloth drop back into place, and just in time, too.

A couple of angry-looking toughs shouldered their way in through the front door: a tall, burly man with a fringe of hair around the edge of his bald head, and a thinner, wiry man wearing a chequered cloth cap pulled down low over his forehead. Both were scowling as they came into the shop, and neither of them gave the menu that was written on a board near the door so much as a glance.

Flynn wouldn't have needed Mr. Holmes's training to guess that these were the men from whom the woman was running.

Baldy looked hard at all the tables in the shop and then stomped over to the nearest one, where he asked the two housewives who were sitting there a question. Probably, 'Have you seen a woman in grey who looks like she's running for her life?'

The two women shook their heads, and Baldy moved on to talk to a stooped, white-haired man who barely looked strong enough to lift the roast beef sandwich that lay on his plate. Cloth Cap started in on the tables on the other side of the door, going from customer to customer.

One of the waitresses started towards him as if she was going to ask whether he wanted to sit down. But after he'd shot her a hard glance, she retreated, looking scared.

Flynn picked up his sandwich and gulped down another couple of bites. If he was right about what was likely to happen, he'd be making a fast exit any minute now, and there was no sense in letting food he'd already paid for go to waste.

Baldy worked his way around the whole of the room and finally ended up at Flynn's table, with Cloth Cap arriving just a second or two later. At least that meant that Flynn could deal with them both together.

Baldy planted his ham-sized fists on the table and leaned over Flynn. "Where's the woman who came running in here a minute ago?" he demanded.

Flynn gave him a puzzled look. "What do you mean? What woman?"

"Now, listen here," Baldy jabbed a finger at Flynn and brought his face close enough that Flynn caught a gust of the ale on his hot breath. "We've already asked everyone in the place. That bloke over there and those two women"—he jerked his head at two of the tables behind him—"said they saw her come running towards the back of the shop. You must have seen her. So where did she go?"

"Oh, that woman." Flynn shrugged and took another bite of his sandwich. "Search me. Maybe she went out the back?"

"That's a nice try," Baldy growled. His blunt-featured face darkened. "But there's no door at the back here. So—"

Clearly, the moment had come when it was time to stop trying to talk his way out of this.

Baldy was still leaning over him, with Cloth Cap hovering just behind. Flynn set his hands against the edge of the table and gave it the hardest shove he could manage. It caught Baldy squarely in the midsection, which made him let out a grunt and stumble backwards, straight into Cloth Cap, who tripped and fell over, clutching at Baldy as he tried to right himself. Baldy swore, but his legs had got tangled up with Cloth Cap's, and he went down hard, too.

Flynn turned the table over on top of the pair of them, showering them with tea, crockery, and the remains of his sausage sandwich. Then he grabbed the arm of the woman who was still crouched on the floor at his feet and shouted, "Come on!"

For a second, she stared at the mess he'd just made and at the two men who were thrashing and struggling with the tablecloth. But Flynn had to give her credit; she got over the shock quickly and bolted for the shop door, making it out onto the street with him in what had to be less than five seconds.

Flynn didn't stop running. It was a rule of London that there was almost never a cab ready just when you wanted one. But by some miracle a Hansom was at that moment turning the corner of Bow Street. Flynn didn't even bother to hail the driver, just raced for it and scrambled inside while the wheels were still turning. The woman in grey followed close behind, practically falling across the tufted leather seats as she flung herself inside the carriage.

"Drive!" she gasped to the cabbie. "Please, just drive!"

It took a lot to surprise a London cabbie. This one—a middle-aged man with bushy grey side-whiskers, a plaid tartan scarf, and a clay pipe clamped between his teeth—didn't so much as blink. He urged his horses into a faster trot and steered them into the traffic that was heading towards Long Acre.

Flynn was tempted to look back towards the sandwich shop to see whether Baldy and Cloth Cap were following. But if they hadn't made their way out of the shop in time to see him climb into the cab, he didn't want to risk their seeing him now. So he crouched low in the carriage, keeping his head down. After a block or two, the cabbie opened his mouth around the stem of his pipe and said, "Was there somewhere in particular you were hopin' to go?"

The woman in grey straightened up, drawing a shuddering breath and looking as if she were trying to collect herself. "Yes, thank you. Baker Street."

"*Baker* Street?" Flynn repeated the words before he could stop himself, despite the fact that he didn't generally advertise his association with 221B; he wouldn't be much good as an Irregular if word got round that he worked for a detective.

The woman sat back, her expression mildly puzzled at the surprise in his tone. "Yes, do you know where that is?" She had a quick, decisive way of speaking, and now that she was talking in full sentences rather than breathless one-word gasps, Flynn realised she spoke with an accent that reminded him of Lucy, Mr. Holmes's daughter. Which made her an American. She cast an anxious look out the window, her hands tightening on the worn leather seat of the cab, then added, "I need to find Mr. Sherlock Holmes."

CHAPTER 3: WATSON

"It's a gruesome sight," Lestrade said. His ferret-like features were pinched and tense, but his dark, beady eyes gleamed with determination.

Holmes and I were with the little inspector on the bridle path in Hyde Park, amid a dense green foliage of oaks and lindens on either side. The section of the path nearest us had been roped off. Two uniformed constables stood guarding the area, one on either end. From here, we could barely see several brightly clad boaters drifting on the Serpentine Lake, enjoying their leisure on this late summer afternoon.

The body of Miss Cavendish was curled up behind a rose bush.

"A rider found her just after noon. We haven't moved her," Lestrade continued. He pointed to a disturbance in the dirt and gravel. "She fell there and was dragged into the rose bushes. Notice that swath of soil across the pathway."

"How did you identify her as Miss Cavendish?" I asked.

"Four of her business cards were in her handbag," Lestrade replied. "One of those shoulder-strap affairs. Constable has it."

"You mentioned a copy of the latest edition of the *Tatler*, with her gossip column," said Holmes.

"Oh, yes, when I telephoned you. It was there, but I didn't see anything else unusual. Gloves, a coin-purse, a train ticket, a concert program, as I recall. No powder compact or lip rouge. No cigarettes."

Holmes was now crouching over the body. "Her throat has been crushed by a garrote. Her riding attire—the jacket and skirt—shows signs of a fall. Observe the marks on the elbow, hip, and shoulder, as well as fragments of dirt on the side of her forehead. She was garroted while still in the saddle. The murderer must have been riding with her."

"That should narrow down our field of suspects considerably," Lestrade said.

"Have you checked the stables?" Holmes asked.

"She rented two horses," Lestrade said. "But she didn't reveal the identity of her companion. She paid in cash. The attendant remembered because most of their patrons are upper class and keep an account. Some are slow in settling their debts."

I pondered, "Would there be a connection to the article in the *Tatler* column?"

"We cannot ignore the possibility," Holmes replied.

"Why did you call us?" I asked Lestrade. "Did you know she was an acquaintance of ours?"

"No, I didn't," said Lestrade. "I called because she is the sixth victim to be found here in the park within the past week."

* * *

"So you didn't see her companion?" Lestrade asked. His gaze fixed on the young attendant at the Hyde Park stables who, in his early thirties and neatly dressed, leaned against a wooden partition separating the stalls.

Around us the air was thick with the scent of horses and fresh earth. The horses fed, snuffling and grunting. Amber afternoon sunlight came through the tall windows on the west, lighting up motes of hay-dust in the air and making patches of gold on old timbers and stones that had seen more than their share of Londoners over the years.

"That Miss Cavendish?" the attendant asked. "She came by herself—just took the two horses."

"When?"

"'Twere around eleven. She rode the one and had the other on tether, she did."

"A good horsewoman?" Lestrade inquired, his eyes briefly scanning the row of stalls that led back to the open stable entrance.

"Sidesaddle, you know. But competent."

Holmes asked, "Had you seen her before?"

"A few times."

"And she had rented two horses on the other occasions?"

"Come to think of it, yes, she did. I don't know why." A frown creased the attendant's brow.

"She was a journalist," Lestrade said. "The bridle path would provide a private setting where she could interview someone without being overheard."

"Where are the horses now?" Holmes asked.

The attendant gestured to an enclosed paddock visible through a large opening at the end of the stable. "That one, and the one beside."

"Who returned them?"

"I didn't notice. Just saw the horses come in here. Their reins were down."

"If someone led both horses to the entrance and dropped the reins, would they have come in?" Holmes asked.

"I dunno. I just saw the two of 'em, saw the rent time hadn't run out—she had taken them till three o'clock, you know—so there wasn't no more fee to collect. I put 'em back in their stalls."

"You took off their tack first?"

"'Course. Can't put 'em away wet, you know. We groom 'em down proper," the attendant said with a hint of pride in his voice.

"Where is the tack now?"

"I hung it over there." He gestured towards a smaller room adjacent to the stables, where saddles, bridles, stirrups, and blankets were neatly arranged on hooks and racks.

"Can you show us the bridles for the two horses?" Holmes asked, his gaze shifting towards the tack room.

The attendant led us to the far wall of the tack room. Holmes examined the two bridles indicated by the attendant, his fingers tracing over the steel bits.

"Did you notice anything unusual about the mouth of either horse?" he asked, looking up.

"Little pink, I thought, when I took those bits out. But not bleedin'."

"Thank you," Holmes reached into his waistcoat. He pulled out a half guinea and handed it to the attendant. "Now, is there a room where my friend and I may speak privately with the inspector?"

* * *

"You said Miss Cavendish was the sixth fatality in the area of the park?" Holmes asked Lestrade.

I closed the door to the small stable staff room. Holmes sat astride one of two wooden benches that had been placed along the two longer walls. Lestrade and I sat opposite.

The little inspector nodded. "We're up against a formidable opponent this time. Assuming the murders are linked, of course."

He pulled out his notebook and read aloud in his reedy voice: "The victim found most recently is an elderly man named Samuel Harley, a retired shoemaker by trade. Before him, there was a retired lady's maid, a solicitor, a hotel owner, and a retired church minister. No one of any special power or influence. All ordinary people. Hard to see a motive for all six."

I felt a wave of pity. Six ordinary people, alive one day with their plans and hopes, and then dead the next.

Holmes asked, "Any connection between the victims—other than their being found in the park?"

"None of them seems to have been acquainted with the others and all lived in different areas of the city."

"Were they killed where they were found?"

Lestrade shook his head. "No. This one today is the first. The others had no signs of being dragged. But they were all found near one or another of the park roadways."

"What do you think, Inspector?"

"Easy enough to kill someone and put the body into a cab. That could happen anywhere in London."

"If one owned a cab," Holmes said. "Or had constant access."

"Then dump the body in the park after nightfall," Lestrade added.

Holmes appeared to have made up his mind. He stood. "Can you provide a list of names and addresses connected with the victims?"

"Of course, but my men have already been to each victim's residence. Except for Miss Cavendish."

"I should like the names and addresses of the next of kin."

"Ah. Very well. I have those in the police wagon."

Holmes nodded abstractedly. "We shall proceed in reverse order. Watson and I will attend Miss Cavendish's flat."

Lestrade had a determined look about him, clearly not willing to cede control of the case. "I'll come with you," he said.

Holmes nodded, as if the matter of Lestrade's accompanying him was of no importance. "And to interview the relatives of the next most recent victim—the shoemaker, I believe you said? I shall telephone Lucy James."

CHAPTER 4: FLYNN

"Is anyone following us?" the woman in grey asked.

Flynn was peering out through the rear window of the carriage, scanning the traffic behind them. "Hard to say."

He was keeping an eye on a black carriage three back from their own, but he wasn't ready to say for certain whether it had anything to do with Baldy or Cloth Cap.

He turned around to face the woman sitting opposite him. "You want to tell me who those men are and what they want with you?"

He was betting the answer to that one was *No*. The woman hadn't even been willing to give him her name. But he might as well ask.

She didn't answer right away, just stared at him intently for a second or two. Then she said, "You really can take me to Mr. Sherlock Holmes?"

"I can." That was true enough, although Flynn carefully hadn't yet promised that he *would*.

Her eyes drilled into his for a few seconds more. "I have no reason to trust you."

Flynn shrugged. "No reason to trust you, either. You know how many rum divers and second-story men would love a chance at getting even with Mr. Holmes for landing them in the porridge?"

The American woman blinked. "Rum … I have no idea what you're talking about. What rum? What porridge?"

Flynn nodded. Even before coming to work for Mr. Holmes, he'd had a fairly good idea of when people were lying or not. Living alone on the streets, you survived a lot longer if you could tell who you could trust—there weren't many of those—and who'd steal the clothes off your back without batting an eye. Flynn had seen a lot more of those types over the years, and he'd already been fairly certain that the American woman wasn't one of them.

He also knew real fear when he saw it, and she hadn't been just putting on an act. She was trying not to show it, but Baldy and Cloth Cap had her just about scared white even now.

It wasn't a foolproof test, but the fact that she didn't understand a word of the East End slang that Flynn had used made him more inclined to believe that she wasn't some local gang member's Trouble and Strife, using him as a way of getting to Mr. Holmes.

Not that there weren't American criminals who also had reasons for wanting Mr. Holmes out of the way, but it wasn't as likely that any of them would know about Flynn being an Irregular. The whole reason Mr. Holmes hired boys like Flynn was that nobody knew who they were.

"Rum diver's a pickpocket," he said. "Second-story man's a thief who climbs in windows. And porridge is prison."

"Oh." A line appeared between the woman's brows. "Why?"

"Why what?"

"Why is the word porridge used to mean prison?" The fear in the American woman's voice had been replaced by what sounded like honest curiosity, as though she wanted to know the answer enough that it had almost made her forget about Cloth Cap and Baldy.

"No idea." Flynn had never really thought about it before.

"Hmmm." The American woman drew a small notebook and pencil from her coat pocket and jotted something down.

"What are you writing?" Flynn asked.

"What's that?" She looked up. "Oh, I was just making a note to find out the origin of that particular slang term, if possible."

"Right." Flynn went from thinking that she was probably honest to wondering whether she was a bit batty. But then the carriage he'd been watching pulled up closer to them in the traffic, and he caught sight of a familiar looking bald head through one of the windows. "They're after us."

The American woman turned a shade paler and almost dropped the pencil. "You're certain?"

"That or Baldy's got a twin brother in the cab behind us."

"Baldy? Oh—yes, I see. Him." She nodded understanding.

"I don't suppose you know his real name?" Flynn wouldn't mind knowing more about who exactly they were up against.

The American woman shook her head. She'd put the notebook and pencil away and was sitting with her hands tightly locked together, as if she were trying to stop them from shaking. "I don't know anything about those men at all, except that they've successfully committed at least one murder. And if they catch me, they'll do their utmost to commit another—mine."

Not the answer Flynn had been hoping for, but then no one had asked him for his opinion. He debated asking their driver to try another route, but without knowing what the traffic would be like on the streets up ahead, that could do more harm than good. If they wound up stuck and unmoving in a snarl of cabs and carriages and delivery vans, they'd be fish in a barrel for Baldy and Cloth Cap to come and find.

"Get ready to jump out when I tell you to," he said to the American woman.

They were coming up to Regent's Park, and this was late afternoon, which meant that the park was likely to be crowded with all the amateur cricket players who gathered to play matches and with their friends and family members who came to watch and cheer and lay wagers on who would win. Flynn and the American woman would stand at least a decent chance of being able to lose themselves in amongst all the bystanders. If they could make it into the park without Baldy and Cloth Cap catching them, that was.

Flynn waited, and as their cab slowed down to make the turn from Great Portland Street onto Marylebone Road, he dug into his pocket for the handful of shillings he had left over from what Mr. Holmes had paid him. Not what he'd planned to use the money on, but no one had consulted him about that, either.

He dropped the money on the seat to pay the cabbie for their fare, flung open the carriage door, and shouted, "Jump!"

CHAPTER 5: LUCY

Following Holmes's telephone call, my cab ride to Holloway Prison took me only a few minutes.

The place was, in fact, far less bleak than I had expected. Built within the past twenty years or so, the building had a cheerful exterior fashioned of handsome plaster and red brick, in a style that loosely resembled a Tudor manor house. Inside, the prison was equipped with an on-site hospital, a chapel, and cells that received at least a few hours of direct sunlight every day. There were also workshops, where prisoners might learn skills that would one day help them to gain honest employment.

I found Mariah Todd in one of those workrooms, supervising a group of women who were sewing coal sacks for the Royal Navy. The women were seated at a long, low table, their heads bent over the rough burlap sacks, while Mrs. Todd stood at the head of the table, looking on with an eagle eye. But she agreed readily to spare me a few minutes when I'd explained to her who I was and why I had come.

"First of all, I'm so sorry for your loss," I told her, when we had retreated to a place by the door where we would be out of earshot of the prisoners, but still within sight so that Mrs. Todd could continue to monitor the group for any quarrels or signs of trouble.

"Thank you." Mrs. Todd was a brisk, practical-looking woman of forty or forty-five, with greying hair pulled back into a neat bun. Her face was pleasant without being pretty, her strong jaw and chin showing strength of character and determination, while her brown eyes regarded the world with quiet intelligence in their gaze. At the mention of her father, a pang of sadness crossed her expression. "I don't understand it at all. It seems it must have been the work of some poor deranged madman. Who would have wanted to hurt my father?"

"Had he any enemies that you know of?"

"Enemies?" Mrs. Todd looked almost amused rather than shocked by the idea. "If you'd known my father, you wouldn't have asked that. He was the most even-spirited of men. Mother used to get quite provoked at him at times. She was Irish, with red hair, and she had a temper to go with it. But father would never quarrel with her or with anybody else. He never got riled up or fussed, no matter the cause."

She broke off, her attention focusing on the group of women sewing at the table, and raised her voice to call out, "Smaller stitches, Janet. And you needn't think I didn't see you trying to pocket that spool of thread a moment ago. Put it back in the basket with the others."

Janet, a thin young woman with stringy blond hair and a mouth that fell open slightly over prominent front teeth, looked abashed and replaced the thread spool.

Mrs. Todd nodded stern approval, fixing the girl with a stare as though to imply that she would be watching for any further attempts at pilfering. Then she sighed as she cast a glance at me. "Some of the guards here aren't as honest as one would like, and will sell any little item that the girls manage to pocket for a share in the money. I needn't have come in today," she added in a lower tone. "The warden would have given me the day off from work, on account of my father. But I thought I'd rather keep busy, have something else to think about. At any rate, as I was saying, Mother would come to Father, cross because one of us children had got mud all over the clean laundry, or because the bill from the fishmongers was wrong. And Father would just smile in that gentle way of his and say, *Well, well, my dear, these trials are sent to teach us patience, as the Good Book says.*" Mrs. Todd's voice wavered, and she dabbed at her eyes with a handkerchief.

"He was a shoemaker by trade?" I asked.

"Yes, that's right. He was still in business, right up until this last year or two," Mrs. Todd said. "Then the rheumatism in his hands made it too difficult for him to keep up with stitching the leather. I wanted him to come and live with my husband and me when he closed up the shop. We'd have been glad to have him. But father said that he'd lived his whole life over the shop in Marygold Street—my grandfather was a shoemaker before him, and my father took the business over when his father retired—and he was too old to make a start anywhere else." She wiped her eyes again.

"Mrs. Todd, I'm sorry if these questions seem insensitive or even absurd, but is there anyone who might have benefited from your father's death?"

So far, I could understand why both Lestrade and the murder victim's daughter believed that the killing must have been the work of a madman.

"That's all right, I understand that you have to ask." Mrs. Todd drew a shaky breath to gather herself, but then shook her head. "I honestly can't think of anyone. Father was very successful in his trade. He had a reputation for doing the finest leather work, and several of the gentry used to come to him for their shoes. His proudest moment was when he was asked to make the wedding shoes for Lady Aline Cheverix when she married the Duke of Derrington."

"The Duke of Derrington?" I repeated.

"Yes, the same one who's been in the papers so much lately about his tobacco companies. But this was … oh, it must have been nearly twenty years ago, now, when the duke and duchess were married. The wedding of the London Season, that was. And there was my father, asked to make the bride's slippers." She smiled faintly in reminiscence. "Father used to tell that story often—how delicate the calfskin was, and how he had to take the greatest care to make sure that it didn't tear while he was stretching it and shaping it. He visited her at the hotel where she was staying in London three times, to make sure the slippers would be a perfect fit. And then when the slippers were ready, some women would have sent a servant to go and fetch them. But no, Lady Aline asked that my father deliver them so that she could thank him herself. He loved to remember that story—how pretty Lady Aline was, and how pleasant she had been to him. Wearing a dress that just matched the colour of her eyes, my father always said. And she took the slippers and unwrapped them and said that they were the most beautiful shoes she'd ever seen, and that she'd feel like a princess on her wedding day. Oh, but listen to me rattling on." Mrs. Todd pressed her hands against her cheeks. "That wasn't what you wanted to know about at all."

"That's all right." In my experience, almost the only help for grief besides time was to allow the bereaved party to talk about their lost loved one.

"You asked whether my father's death would have benefited anyone. But despite having always done well with his business, Father wasn't by any means a wealthy man. I suppose that whatever he'd managed to put by over the years will come to me, now, as his only living kin. But—" she bit her lip, looking at me with suddenly anxious eyes.

"That thought never crossed my mind, I promise you," I told her. "Nor will it."

I didn't flatter myself that I was incapable of being duped by an unscrupulous criminal. But I was also certain that if ever I'd seen genuine love and grief, it was now. Whoever had killed Samuel Harley, it hadn't been his daughter for the sake of her inheritance. I'd be willing to stake my reputation and that of Holmes on it.

"Had anything strange or unusual happened to your father recently that you're aware of?" I asked.

"Unusual?" Mrs. Todd paused, reflecting, then shook her head slowly. "I don't think ... no, wait. There was that letter my father received from the newspaper reporter. I suppose that was unusual."

"The newspaper reporter?"

"Yes. It must have been about a week ago. I used to go to see my father every Tuesday and Saturday evening to make sure that he had a hot meal and do a bit of tidying up for him. Well, last Tuesday, he mentioned that he'd had a letter from a newspaper reporter in the morning's post. A lady reporter who asked whether she could interview him for an article that she was writing."

"Did your father agree?"

"Oh no." Mrs. Todd smiled faintly. "I never actually saw the letter myself. My father thought it was just some sort of prank. *Who'd want to read about me in the newspapers?* That's what he said when he told me about it." She blinked fresh tears away from her eyes. "He laughed a bit and said that he'd tossed it into the rubbish bin."

CHAPTER 6: WATSON

"I can't think how this could have happened!" Mrs. Hinchcliffe exclaimed. The landlady for Miss Cavendish, plump and middle-aged, placed her hand over her mouth and stood gasping and whispering to herself, plainly distressed at the spectacle presented by her late tenant's flat.

The room had been searched with a disrespect bordering upon lunacy. Newspapers were strewn across the floor. Books had been tumbled from the shelves and dropped, partially opened, on the carpet. Letters lay opened with their envelopes obscured by feathers from torn-open pillows. The sofa had been upended, as had been the mattress on the small single bed. The wardrobe was lying on its side, the clothes and their hangers in an untidy heap. The drawers in the writing-desk and clothing chest had been pulled out and their contents unceremoniously dumped. The oriental rug had been turned up and folded back on one side, exposing a bare wooden floor.

Only the far side of the room, with a small dressing-table, seemed undisturbed. A jewel box and a pocket watch lay on its varnished wooden surface.

"You saw no one enter? You admitted no one?" Lestrade asked.

"Certainly not!"

"Have you been here all day?"

Mrs. Hinchcliffe hesitated. "I did go out shopping around noon. I had lunch as well."

"You returned when?"

"About three."

Holmes and Lestrade exchanged glances, and I realised that Miss Cavendish had been killed only a short time before the room had been ransacked.

"Whatever were they looking for?" the landlady cried.

"We don't know," Lestrade said.

"Why was she was killed?"

"We don't know that either."

She clasped her hands as if in prayer. "Oh, Lord, it's a blessing I was out. They likely would have killed me!"

Holmes asked, "Can you think of anyone who might have wished to harm Miss Cavendish?"

She shook her head. "I didn't know any of the people she knew."

"But her job required her to write about gossip," Holmes said. "Her writings might have embarrassed people, whether she knew them or not."

"I never read anything she wrote," the landlady said.

Holmes moved to the dressing table, glancing up at the mirror and then tilting it on its swivel frame to look at the back side. I could see nothing other than the back of an ordinary oval mirror. "Did Miss Cavendish wear facial makeup?" Holmes asked. "Rouge, powders, that sort of thing?"

"I didn't really notice, but I don't think so. I never asked her about it, of course."

"Did you clean her room?"

"Oh, yes, once a week. Swept and dusted."

"And when you dusted the dressing table, it was free of makeup products?"

"Why, yes. I don't remember otherwise."

"Did you notice the bench beneath this dressing table? Was it always pushed back underneath?"

She paused, leaning forwards and sidewise, bird-like, bending slightly to see the bench, which was pushed back against the wall. "Why, yes, come to think of it. The bench was always pushed back, out of the way. I suppose because she didn't use makeup. She didn't have to sit and look at herself in the mirror."

Holmes had pulled the bench out from beneath the dressing table, lifting it up onto the rug.

"Something pasted underneath?" Lestrade suggested.

Holmes tilted the bench upwards to expose an empty underside. Then he set the bench down. "It is a piano bench," he said. "The seat is a lid. Music is stored beneath the lid."

He lifted the lid. We stepped forwards to see what was inside.

There was only a newspaper.

"*The Evening Standard*, opened to the obituaries page," Holmes said. He scanned the paper and then handed it to Lestrade. "I believe we have learned all we can from this visit," he said.

Taking his cue from Holmes, Lestrade turned to the landlady. "Mrs. Hinchcliffe, we thank you for your cooperation. Please telephone if you learn or recall something that you believe may be useful."

Outside, I said, "Do you think the intruders were interrupted?"

"The undisturbed dressing table would indicate as much," Holmes said.

Lestrade said, "I recognised one of the obituaries."

"The retired minister," Holmes said. "Reverend Wyatt."

"What now? Shall we retrieve his case file from the Yard?"

Holmes shook his head. "First, we visit the offices of the *Tatler*. It is on our way to the mortuary."

* * *

The editor on duty at the *Tatler* was a waspish, grey-haired chap by the name of Fenshaw, with shrewd dark eyes glittering behind his octagonal spectacles. He was just closing up his office, but he gave us a knowing smile when Lestrade told him the purpose of our visit.

"The late Miss Whisper, eh? Not surprised she's dead. Thought it would happen before this."

"Why?"

"She had a way about her, sly and insinuating, and a nose for mean-spirited gossip. Bad for her, but it sells newspapers."

"What was the last piece she did for you?"

"Let's see." He turned to a shelf, took down a ledger book, and opened it. After turning a few pages, he said, "We last paid her two weeks ago, for a piece about the Countess of Calloway."

"What about the one in yesterday's edition—about this coronation ball that's supposed to be given at the Savoy?"

"We didn't pay her for that one." He closed the ledger book and shoved it back onto its shelf.

"Why not?"

"We didn't see the benefit of that particular article. Usually our readers like to puzzle out which lord or lady is being referred to and what goings-on might embarrass them, if you know what I mean. But in this case the matter was out in the open. A straightforward statement. There was to be a ball at the Savoy. Miss Whisper thought that the timing of the event was in bad taste. Nothing to discover, really, except the name of the hostess, and that would be readily apparent as soon as the ball was announced."

"Yet you ran the article."

"She paid us."

"Isn't that unusual?"

"Sometimes it happens. Our contributors like to keep their names before the public. We didn't see the benefit of that particular story, as I said, but we were willing to print it as a form of advertisement for Miss Whisper." He paused, thoughtfully. "Do you think this had anything to do with her death?"

"It's too soon to know," Lestrade said. He left his card with the editor and we bid our farewells.

Outside, we hailed a cab for the mortuary. On the way, Lestrade said, "I'll have my men investigate Miss Cavendish's bank records. See if we can find out if someone was paying her."

"Which bank?" Holmes asked.

Lestrade pursed his lips.

"You did not find a cheque-book in her handbag, I believe you said?"

"I don't think so. I would have noticed it, I think. We'll have to ask at the Yard."

"I did not see a cheque book in her flat."

"Perhaps that was what the thieves were looking for," I said.

"Perhaps they found it," Holmes said.

CHAPTER 7: LUCY

The trip from Holloway to Middleton took less than a quarter of an hour, which meant that within thirty minutes of leaving Mrs. Todd I was introducing myself to Mrs. Freda Goodspeed, widow of the late Martin Goodspeed.

The hotel that the couple had established and run together was located on a small side lane that branched off from Middleton Mews Street: near enough that any hotel guests could easily visit the exclusive haberdasheries and dressmakers' shops while still avoiding all the rush and bustle. The hotel itself was a deceptively plain building, a simple square of whitewashed brick standing in a row of other similar houses. The sign over the door that proclaimed it the Colonnade Hotel was a small, modest affair, gilded and clearly of the best quality, but without seeking to attract any undue notice.

Inside, though, was an entirely different matter. The carpets were thick Orientals, the drapes that covered all the windows and blocked out the noise and dirt of the outside world were of heavy velvet. The furniture, from the chairs and small tables that dotted the lobby to the front desk itself were all dark mahogany and brocade upholstery.

The entire place seemed designed to instill a feeling not just of comfort, but also of one's own importance. Here, everything seemed to say, you could expect to find both a respite from the outside world and the luxury which you so clearly deserved.

"A private inquiry agent." Mrs. Goodspeed looked down at the card I'd given her and read the words as though tasting them for the first time and finding that they had a slightly rancid flavour.

She was a tall woman with a head of frizzy red hair, sharp features, and the most aggressively refined voice I had ever heard.

"Well." Holding my card by the tips of her fingers as though to avoid contamination, she set it carefully down on the desk that stood between us then returned her gaze to me. "I'm sure I don't think we've ever had such a thing in this establishment."

I smiled pleasantly. First, because refusing to take offense is a handy trait in any investigation. And second because I was imagining how entertained Jack and Becky would be tonight at the dinner table when I gave them an account of Mrs. Goodspeed's conversation. "I just had a few questions about your husband's death, if you don't mind. I know it must be painful for you to talk about, but some new information about the case has come to light."

"New information?" Mrs. Goodspeed's expression was not so much pained as extremely nervous, mingled with a look that I identified as distaste. "Well." She darted a look around the hotel lobby, which was deserted save for an elderly grey-haired gentleman dozing in an arm chair by the fireplace. "I suppose I might spare you a moment or two, if you will step into the office." She indicated a door with frosted glass marked *private* that stood directly behind the front desk. "I would not wish to disturb any of the guests."

The inner office proved to be furnished on a less luxurious scale than the lobby, with a large, utilitarian-looking desk dominating most of the space, and a row of cabinets set against one wall. Mrs. Goodspeed settled herself behind the desk. She didn't, I noticed, ask me to sit down in one of the two wooden chairs that faced her, but I did anyway.

Mrs. Goodspeed pressed her thin lips together. "You say that you have new information about Martin's …" She paused, clearly searching for a more refined way of saying *death*, and eventually settled on, "… *departure?*"

"Nothing definite, I'm afraid. But we believe it's possible that your husband's death might be linked to the murder of another man, an elderly shoemaker by the name of Samuel Harley."

"A shoemaker?" Mrs. Goodspeed's lips pinched even more tightly together. "I don't see how Martin could have anything to do with a person from that occupation."

Her tone implied that she would take it as a personal affront if her husband had managed to be killed in such a way as to link himself with anyone who performed manual labour.

"You don't recognise the name Harley at all? Your husband didn't, for example, ever buy a pair of shoes from his shop? Mr. Harley's business was in Marygold Street."

"No." Mrs. Goodspeed gave a decisive shake of her head, setting her frizz of red curls bouncing. "No, he most certainly did not. Martin always bought his shoes from Boules, in Bond Street."

"Could Mr. Harley have been a guest of the hotel at any time?"

I was fairly sure that I already knew the answer, but I had to ask for the sake of being thorough.

"A guest!" Mrs. Goodspeed looked horrified. "Certainly not! We cater to a *very* exclusive clientele here at the Colonnade. For over twenty years, we have offered accommodations to those members of the aristocratic classes who wish to avoid the scrutiny of the public eye. The larger hotels like the Savoy are positively crawling with reporters from the society papers, eager to report on who has been seen with whom." She gave a virtuous sniff. "Here at the Colonnade, we offer discretion and privacy from all that sort of attention. Just last month, we had the younger son of Lord Rutherford as a guest here, as well as the Duke of Simsbury. But a *shoemaker*?" Mrs. Goodspeed raised her eyes to the ceiling, as though inviting heaven to bear witness to the effrontery of the very idea.

"I see." I hadn't really expected that the two murder victims would know each other; that would have been too easy.

"Is that all?" Mrs. Goodspeed asked. "It's very inconvenient that Martin was killed just now. I've been left to cope with the running of this hotel all on my own, and during one of our busiest weeks of the year. And to make it all worse, since it was murder, I've had the police here from morning until night, looking here and there and asking questions and causing no end of disruptions. One of the inspectors even insisted on questioning the guests who were staying with us on the night of Martin's death." She shuddered.

"Very upsetting," I agreed solemnly. "You mentioned reporters a moment ago. I don't suppose that any newspaper people had been in contact with either you or your husband shortly before he died? Had anyone written to him with a request to interview him, by any chance?"

"Oh, I've no doubt that a good many of them would love to have tried." Mrs. Goodspeed looked venomous. "I can't tell you the number of times I've had one of the brazen creatures come sidling in here and offer to pay five pounds in exchange for confirming a story about one of our gentleman guests who was here with a lady other than his wife. I soon send them away with a flea in their ear, I can tell you! And Martin would have known better than to speak to anyone from a newspaper."

Would he, though? Unlike Samuel Harley, I had no real picture of the type of man Martin Goodspeed had been. Except that his wife seemed to feel more irritation than grief at his murder, and the stuffy, self-consciously rarefied air of his hotel gave me the same feeling of claustrophobia as being trapped in an underground cellar.

"Is that a photograph of your husband there?" I asked, gesturing to a framed print that hung on the wall. Somewhat ironically, considering everything his wife had just said, the photograph looked as though it had been cut from a newspaper, the paper thin and beginning to turn yellow with age. The picture showed a man in one of the striped suits that had been fashionable during the 1880s. His dark hair was slicked down with pomade and parted in the centre, and he stood behind a desk I recognised from the hotel lobby outside, his hands planted on the surface. The photograph was clearly staged, but a smile that looked genuine curved his mouth, and his dark eyes crinkled at the corners. Whatever the ensuing twenty years had brought him, Martin Goodspeed had been happy when the picture was taken.

Mrs. Goodspeed barely glanced at the photo. "Yes, that was taken the year that Martin opened the Colonnade. The same year that he and I were married. Lady Caroline Thurston was one of London's most fashionable debutantes, and she and her mother came to stay here for the Season. That attracted the attention of several other debutantes and their mothers and chaperones, and it became *chic* to stay here. Especially when one or two of the girls married quite well and had their names printed in all the society papers. Although of course," Mrs. Goodspeed hastened to add, "it was really the superior service we offer here at the Colonnade that established us firmly in the sphere of London's most exclusive hotels."

"Of course. Well, thank you, Mrs. Goodspeed, you've been very helpful," I told her. "Now, one last thing. Would you mind looking over this list of names and telling me whether any of them looks familiar?"

Mrs. Goodspeed looked distinctly long-suffering, but she put out her hand, and I gave her the list of murder victims that I had copied down from Lestrade.

- *Samuel Harley*
- *The Reverend John Wyatt*
- *George Pennythwaite, KC*
- *Emma Thompkins*
- *Martin Goodspeed*
- *Eleanor Cavendish*

Mrs. Goodspeed's gaze flicked over the page, and after a moment's pause, she shook her head with decision. "No. Apart from Martin, I've never heard of any of these people before."

CHAPTER 8: WATSON

The London police morgue never failed to remind me that we were always dealing in matters of life and death.

The air was thick with the antiseptic scent of carbolic acid, sprayed by the staff in a feeble attempt to mask the more morbid odours that lingered beneath. As Holmes and I made our way along dimly lit corridors, we passed familiar rows of dark wooden doors lining the hallway, each leading to a chamber wherein had lain many silent occupants, many of which I remembered. The faint echo of our footsteps on the stone floor mingled with the distant, muffled sounds of London outside, where people were oblivious to the sombre proceedings within these walls.

We were greeted by an attendant, a gaunt figure in a wrinkled and stained brown laboratory coat. "We are here for Reverend Wyatt," Holmes said.

The attendant's fatigued expression showed a flicker of hope. "Come to claim him, 'ave you?"

"We need to see the examiner's report. And the body."

With a shrug, he led us through the maze of corridors to the chamber where the body was kept. "Been 'ere three days now," he said.

The room we entered was starkly utilitarian, illuminated by the harsh, unforgiving light of electric lamps that cast long shadows against the cold, tiled walls. A solitary table stood at the centre, its marble surface gleaming dully beneath the light, awaiting the next occupant with an air of grim inevitability.

The attendant gave a sombre nod towards a door marked *cold chamber*. "In there," he said. "Are you going to take him?"

Holmes said nothing.

"What will become of him, if we do not?" I asked.

"Potter's field, most likely," the attendant replied, a trace of resignation in his tone. "Or we'll reach out to his parish. They might have a vacant plot in the churchyard."

Holmes said, "The medical report, if you please."

The document was in a rack alongside the cold chamber door. Holmes quickly scanned it, his eyes pausing at the critical details on the cover sheet. "Cause of death appears to be a blow to the right temple. The temporal plate is badly fractured, with temporal lobe tissue visible. A powerful blow." He paused. "Now, we shall view the body."

The attendant gave a baleful gaze towards the cold chamber. "I must warn you, it's not been as cold in there as it ought…"

"Nonetheless," I said.

He rolled out the body from its chamber on a wheeled trolley. The acrid air that accompanied the movement was unmistakable, and I braced myself against the wave of it. I knew that the state of the body could offer clues not evident in the medical report alone.

As the sheet was drawn back, the reality of what lay beneath struck me with an unsettling force. The head was, as I had anticipated, virtually unrecognisable after three days in the unforgiving grip of the August heat. Yet, it was essential to confirm the lab report's findings with our own eyes, and, having seen the body of Miss Cavendish, I knew why Holmes had insisted.

"The neck is unmarked," I observed aloud, my voice steady despite the grim tableau before us.

Holmes nodded, his expression unreadable as he replied, "Then we have seen enough."

CHAPTER 9: BECKY

The pounding on the kitchen door made Becky jump. She was in the kitchen because Mrs. Hudson had gone out to do the weekly marketing and had asked Becky to take a batch of raisin scones out of the oven when they were done. Becky had promised faithfully that she wouldn't let the scones burn, so she'd been sitting at the kitchen table, eating an apple and reading the chapter on tonsillitis in one of Dr. Watson's old medical school textbooks.

Her heart tried to leap up into her throat even before she turned to look at the kitchen door, because no delivery man would hammer like that, and of course for Mrs. Hudson to pound on her own door would be out of the question. Then she caught sight of Flynn through the glass window. He was dripping wet, his jacket and trousers covered with some sort of greenish scum, and he was accompanied by a woman dressed in a grey walking suit that didn't look much better than Flynn's clothes.

"What on earth—" Becky began as she opened the door and allowed the two of them to tumble inside.

"Pond at Regent's Park." Flynn spoke between gasps for air, shivering a little, despite the warmth of the day. "We were hiding in the reeds. She fell in." He jerked his head at the woman with him.

The brown-haired woman gave a rueful nod. "I'm afraid I'm out of practice at cloak and dagger operations." She spoke like an American, which wasn't entirely a surprise. Becky had been trying to employ Mr. Holmes's methods of observation, and she'd already noticed that the woman wore an American style of high-button leather boots.

What *was* surprising was that her face looked familiar to Becky somehow. As Becky studied her, trying to recall where and when she could have seen the woman before, Flynn nodded towards the kitchen door and said, "Better lock that."

Becky snapped the lock shut immediately. There were at least a dozen questions crowding onto the tip of her tongue. But none of them was quite so important as the most obvious one:

"Does whoever was chasing you know that you ran in here?"

"Maybe," Flynn said. "We tried to lose them in Regent's Park, like I say. But they spotted us just as we were turning onto Baker Street."

"Also my fault," the American woman said, looking down at her ruined clothes and the puddle forming at her feet. "Falling into a pond doesn't exactly make one inconspicuous, especially on a public thoroughfare."

"You'd better stay out of sight," Becky said. She crossed to the kitchen windows and quickly jerked the curtains shut. Although it was probably wasted effort. Dr. Watson's stories had become popular enough that 221B Baker Street was arguably the most famous address in London, with the possible exception of Buckingham Palace. If whoever was chasing Flynn and the American woman had seen them turn onto Baker Street, they wouldn't wonder which house the two of them had gone into for very long.

"You'd better come upstairs," she said. "I'll try to find you both some dry clothes and then I'll telephone Jack at Scotland Yard."

CHAPTER 10: LUCY

Emma Thompkins, former lady's maid, had spent the final years of her life in one of the 'Model Lodging Houses' constructed in Saint Giles by the Society for Improving the Conditions of the Labouring Classes. Built in the 1840s, the houses had been the Society's attempt to improve the neighbourhood and offer an alternative to the disease-ridden and overcrowded slums that were all so many in Saint Giles could afford. It was a well-meant thought, and in their earliest days, the twelve foot by eight-foot rooms that the lodging houses offered had probably been a blessedly safe, warm, and comparatively clean refuge to the widows and poor women who could apply to live there.

Now, though, sixty years later, the lodging house was as bleak and cheerless a place as I'd ever seen. The worn linoleum in the hallway squeaked underfoot as I made my way to the end of the first-floor hall where Emma Thompkins had resided. The walls were a dull grey, the paint flaking in spots, and the air smelled strongly of weak cabbage soup. I knew already that I wouldn't be able to get a look at number 3, Miss Thompkins' room.

Emma had been killed less than a week ago, but there was always an abundance in London of poverty-stricken individuals with no home and nowhere to go for help. Emma Thompkins' room had already been allotted to another elderly woman in straightened financial circumstances, which meant that the best that I could hope for was to talk to the women who had been Emma Thompkins' neighbours.

Accordingly, I knocked lightly at the door to room number 4. There was a silence from within, followed by shuffling footsteps, and finally the door was opened by a tiny, white-haired lady who wore a grey shawl over a blue woollen dressing gown, and had a pair of pince-nez perched on the end of her nose.

She peered at me inquiringly. "Yes?"

"Hello." I smiled. "I was wondering whether I might speak to you for a moment about Miss Thompkins, the lady who used to live at number 3?"

"Who?" The woman had an age-cracked voice, but the eyes behind her pince-nez were surprisingly sharp. "Oh, you mean Emma." She looked at me more closely, her gaze narrowing. "What's this about, may I ask?"

"I'm a private inquiry agent, hired to look into the circumstances of Emma Thompkins' death."

I gave her my card, which she studied with the same intense scrutiny with which she'd observed my face.

"Well. A lady private investigator." She looked up at me. "I confess that I've never heard of such a thing, but then I've always said that there's no reason a woman can't do a job as well as a man—and better, in some instances. I was a governess, before I retired. But if my father had been willing to pay for me to continue my education—which most weren't, back in my young days—I should have liked to have studied mathematics. I always knew that I would be far better suited to developing mathematical theorems than trying to cram a lot of eminently useless information into young minds that would vastly prefer to forget everything I taught them. But ah well," she said briskly.

"What can't be cured must be endured, as they say. Would you like to come in?"

She stepped back, allowing me to enter her room. The walls were the same depressing grey colour as the hallway outside, but a patchwork quilt and a knitted blanket covered the bed, and a brightly coloured wool work cushion with a design of birds and flowers adorned the single rocking chair. A braided rag rug brightened the worn linoleum floor, while against the wall opposite the bed, a small card table held a spirit lamp, a copper tea kettle, and a pair of Blue Willow cups and saucers. Everything was worn, threadbare and even shabby, but also spotlessly clean and orderly.

"I can offer you a cup of tea," my hostess said, with a gesture to the table.

"That's very kind of you, Miss …"

"Selfridge. Katherine Selfridge."

"Thank you, then, Miss Selfridge, but I won't trouble you." I hated to deplete whatever supplies of tea and sugar she had managed to put by. "But I would be happy for anything that you can tell me about Emma Thompkins."

"About Emma? Or about her murder?" Miss Selfridge asked shrewdly. Unlike Mrs. Goodspeed, she didn't try to dress up the mention of death with more palatable terms.

"Either," I told her. "Although I imagine that the police have already asked you for anything you might know about how Miss Thompkins died."

"They did indeed," Miss Selfridge agreed. "And I will say that inspector who came to see me—Lestrade, I believe he said his name was—was far less of a fool than I would have expected."

It was a shame, I reflected, that Inspector Lestrade hadn't

enough of a sense of humour for me to pass that ringing endorsement on to him.

"Not that I could tell him very much," Miss Selfridge went on. "I didn't even know that Emma had gone out until the police came the next morning, asking me to identify the body."

"She had no family, then?"

"She had a sister in Kent who died last year. And then I believe there was a cousin in Australia. Emma would receive the occasional postcard from her at Christmas. But no, she was entirely alone in the world."

Most of the women who were poor enough to qualify for a place in one of these tiny cubicles probably were.

"Miss Thompkins was found in Hyde Park," I said. "Was it a habit of hers to go walking there?"

"Not that I'm aware of. Emma went out very little. She would step out now and then to buy tea or a package of biscuits. But I never heard her mention a visit to Hyde Park. Her being killed there of all places is nearly as inexplicable as the fact that she was killed at all." Miss Selfridge fixed me with another searching gaze. "I had thought it mere random violence—a sign of these depraved times in which we live. But your being here would seem to suggest that there might be more to it than that?"

"There might be," I said. "I've no proof just yet, though. Only theories, and the fact that Emma Thompkins' murder was one of a string of killings that happened in the park."

I'd come up empty-handed with Mrs. Goodspeed, but I drew out the list from Inspector Lestrade again and handed it to Miss Selfridge. "Would you be able to tell me whether any of these names is familiar? Was Miss Thompkins acquainted with any of them?"

Miss Selfridge adjusted the pince-nez on her nose and peered at the sheet of paper. "George Pennythwaite, KC." She tapped the space next to his name with the tip of a finger. "I believe that I remember reading of his death in the newspapers a few days ago. It caught my eye because he was a barrister, and it reminded me of that rather macabre quotation from Shakespeare: *The first thing we do, let's kill all the lawyers.* Henry VI. But if you're asking whether any of these names is familiar to me personally, the answer is no. Nor can I recall that I ever heard Emma speak of any of them."

"What sort of person was Miss Thompkins?" I asked.

Miss Selfridge opened her mouth, then appeared to change her mind and gave me a conspiratorial smile. "Well, I was about to say, *wooly-headed*. But considering that she has passed on, perhaps it would be kinder to say, *chronically sentimental*. She lived very much in the past. She was forever telling stories about the ladies she'd served—the dresses and furs and jewellery they wore, the gentlemen they danced with at this or that society ball, the wedding clothes that they'd ordered directly from Paris and that Emma herself had charge of pressing. Poor soul, I suppose she'd little enough glamour or romance in her own life, so she had to make do with what glimpses she got through the eyes of her ladies, as she called them."

"Do you remember the names of any of the ladies whom she'd served?"

"Hmmm." Miss Selfridge considered. "Lady Penelope Warwick was one, I know that. Before she went out to join her husband in India. And I think there was an Adeline? Or was it Eileen? I'm sorry." She gave me an apologetic smile. "The truth is, I only ever listened to about one word in ten that Emma said.

There's only so much prattling on about chiffon dresses and Flanders' lace that I can manage to absorb."

"What about just before her death?" I asked. "Did Miss Thompkins seem worried or upset in any way? Or had anything unusual happened?"

I asked the questions without much hope of learning anything useful. But to my surprise, Miss Selfridge regarded me for a long moment, her head a little on one side. Then she nodded as though coming to a decision.

"I believe you ought to come with me."

She opened the door to her room and led the way out into the hall, stopping in front of the door across from her own. She rapped sharply, and then, when that produced no immediate result, she called out, "Harriet? You haven't fallen asleep again, have you?"

The door was opened at last by a woman who reminded me a little of the dormouse in Alice in Wonderland, if that character had been a plump elderly woman instead of an animal. She was round and red-cheeked, wrapped in a paisley shawl and wearing a black lace cap and fingerless black mitts, and she blinked at us with a look of sleepy confusion in her watery blue eyes.

"I beg your pardon." She stifled a yawn. "I believe that I must have nodded off."

"Hardly surprising, Harriet." Miss Selfridge fixed the other woman with a censorious eye. "If you will continue to over-indulge in too many sweets. They sap all one's strength and energy."

"I'm sure you're right, Katharine." Harriet ducked her head meekly and cast a quick, guilty look behind her to where I could see a tin of Turkish delight sitting on a card table that was much like the one in Miss Selfridge's room.

"Well, never mind that," Miss Selfridge said. "This lady here has some questions for you about Emma. I want you to tell her what you took from Emma's rooms."

"Oh." Harriet's mouth dropped open and she put a hand to her throat, looking at me in some alarm. "Oh dear. Will I have to give it back, do you think? I didn't mean any harm—and it wasn't like stealing, was it, because poor Emma was dead?"

"No, I'm sure it wasn't," I said soothingly. I still wasn't sure why Miss Selfridge had brought me here or what Harriet was talking about, but I added, "Emma Thompkins didn't have any family to leave her things to, so I'm sure she would have liked her friends to have them after she was gone."

"Yes—yes, exactly!" Harriet agreed with me eagerly. "Everything else she had was just swept up by the Matron here and given to the charity shop on the corner, so it really wasn't—"

"That will do, Harriet," Miss Selfridge interrupted firmly. "No one is accusing you of anything dishonest. But show us what you found in Emma's room the morning after she died."

"Oh. Oh, yes, of course." Looking flustered, Harriet turned around, disappearing into her room for a few moments and then returning with something cupped between her two hands. "It was after the police had come to tell us that poor Emma was gone. They'd looked through her rooms already and locked up behind them. Only I had a key, because you see once or twice Emma had asked me to water her plants while she went to visit her sister in Kent. Emma liked to grow mint plants in a pot on the window-sill in her room. She'd use the leaves to brew herself a cup of tea, and she didn't want them to wilt while she was away. Of course, that was before she died. Emma's sister, I mean."

Harriet's manner grew a shade more flustered, her words tripping over one another.

"We quite understand, Harriet," Miss Selfridge said in a tone of marked patience. I thought she must have been a formidable figure as a governess, despite her small stature. "Now show us what you found."

"Well, it was this." Harriet opened her cupped hands to reveal a small china figure clasped within them: a shepherdess, dressed in the style of the 17th century. Tiny blue and pink painted rosebuds adorned her china skirts, and golden blond china curls spilled out from beneath her blue china bonnet. Her face was delicately moulded, her lips curved in a smile and painted pale pink.

I stared at the figure, startled. "That's Dresden china, surely."

I was no expert, but I would guess the shepherdess to be from the Meissen factory, manufactured at least a hundred years ago. Finding it in the bleak and shabby Model Lodging Houses was like discovering a rose bush blooming in an otherwise barren field.

"Was it some sort of family heirloom?" I asked. "Something she could have inherited from her sister? Or a gift from one of Miss Thompkins' employers?"

I could imagine one of the ladies whom Miss Selfridge described making a careless gift of the shepherdess to her personal maid, and then Miss Thompkins cherishing it for years afterwards.

But both Harriet and Miss Selfridge shook their heads.

"Her sister didn't leave her anything at all, poor soul," Miss Selfridge said. "Emma had to spend her last few coppers just to see that her sister wasn't buried in a pauper's grave. She'd been ill a long while, and the doctors' bills had taken what little money she had."

"And I've never seen it amongst Emma's things before," Harriet said. "She had very little of her own. And nothing so fine as this."

"She might have kept it locked away in a trunk or a box?" I suggested.

"She might. But then why would she have taken it out now?" Harriet cradled the small figure lovingly. "It was standing up on the table by her bed when I went in after she was gone, and it had gone a bit dusty, like. So I picked it up, just meaning to give it a bit of a polish. But then … well …" She trailed off and looked up at me anxiously. "I hope I didn't do wrong by keeping it. It just seemed such a shame to think of anything so lovely being carted off to the charity shop."

"I'm sure Emma would have wanted you to have it to remember her by," I said.

Harriet looked slightly relieved, but then bit her lip, looking apprehensive once again. "There's something else. Something else I found after Emma died, I mean."

"What's that?" Miss Selfridge frowned. "You never told me about finding anything besides the statuette."

"No. I wasn't sure what it meant. Or whether Emma would have wanted me to show anyone. But if you'll wait just a moment, I'll fetch it." Still looking unhappy, Harriet retreated once more into her room and then returned holding out a single sheet of paper. "I found this. Not in Emma's room, though," Harriet added. "I found it when I was emptying my rubbish bin." She glanced at me. "There's a bin in the courtyard at the back for everyone to use, and then the bin man comes twice a week to collect—"

"Not important, Harriet," Miss Selfridge interrupted in the same quelling tone.

"No—no, of course not," Harriet stammered. "Only you see this paper had fallen out of the bin outside and onto the ground, so I picked up—thinking only to toss it in with the rest of the rubbish, you see. But then I recognised Emma's handwriting, so I read it, and … well."

She handed the paper over to me. It had clearly been crumpled up and smoothed out again. The words looked to be a draft of a letter, the sort of thing one would write out to get the ideas and the spelling clear, then copy over when it was ready to be finalised. The lines were written in pencil in a shaky, uneducated hand, and here and there a misspelled word had been crossed out and corrected. But the letter was perfectly legible, all the same.

I find myself in very reduced circumstances, and I was hoping as how you might see your way to lending some assistance, especially given that I knew—

The letter broke off there, as though the author had decided to scrap the attempt and try again.

I looked up. "You're certain that this is Emma Thompkins' handwriting?"

Wordlessly, Harriet nodded. "You can see, can't you? It sounds … well, it sounds as if Emma was asking someone for money."

It did indeed.

"Have you any idea to whom she could have been writing?" I asked.

Harriet shook her head again. Miss Selfridge, looking rather shocked, echoed the movement. "No. No, I haven't the least idea," she said slowly.

"Did you show this to the police?" I asked Harriet.

It was the note's final line, *especially given that I knew,* that was uppermost in my mind. Of course, Emma Thompkins might have intended an entirely innocent ending to the sentence: *Especially given that I knew your late mother.*

But I doubted it. If the bin man came to collect the rubbish here twice a week, then the note must have been thrown away very shortly before Harriet found it outside. And if that were true, Emma had been murdered just a day or two after writing these words.

"The police?" Harriet repeated. She looked shocked by the idea. "No, I didn't. They'd already been here and gone by the time I found the note, you see."

And suggesting that she ought to have called them back or gone to turn in the note herself at Scotland Yard would be pointless.

Jack ran into this sort of attitude often when canvassing for witnesses: at best, women like Harriet believed it was not-quite respectable to have any dealings with the police force. At worst, they thought police were the enemy.

"May I take the note with me now?" I asked.

"Yes, of course." Harriet looked relieved as she nodded, happy to have handed the responsibility for it off to someone else. Then she hesitated, an anxious frown puckering her brows. "What about the shepherdess?" She had set it down on the table behind her when she went to fetch the note, and now cast a quick look over her shoulder. "Do you need to take that, too?"

"I don't think so. I can come back if I need to look at it again. But I think it's safe enough with you here."

I doubted that the china shepherdess statue could tell us anything. Any fingerprints would be long since gone, obliterated by Harriet's careful handling. And it looked to me as though

Harriet had little enough beauty in her life that I needn't deprive her of this one small bit.

"Just one more question," I said, turning to include Miss Selfridge in the query. "I was wondering whether you happen to know which employment agency Emma used, when she was working as a lady's maid?"

It seemed unlikely that either of them would, but once again, Miss Selfridge surprised me. "Westaway's," she said immediately. "On Tottenham Court Road. I remember Emma speaking of them—with some bitterness, too—because after her last posting ended, the woman who runs the place claimed that Emma was too old to be seeking employment, and refused to help her find another position."

"Westaway's." I nodded. "Thank you. Oh. One last question. Do you know whether Miss Thompkins had been in contact with any newspaper reporters lately? Had she had a letter from one of them by chance?"

I wasn't really expecting an affirmative reply, but to my surprise, Harriet and Miss Selfridge glanced at one another.

"Do you think ..." Harriet began.

Miss Selfridge nodded. "Quite possibly." She looked at me. "Emma received a letter, shortly before she died. We were both of us surprised, because she scarcely got any mail here, particularly after the death of her sister. But I saw a letter in Emma's slot in the common mail room. I noticed it particularly, because it was a proper letter, not just a postcard or a sales circular or something of that kind."

"Did you ask her what the letter was about?"

Miss Selfridge looked severe. "She never mentioned it to me, and I would not have wished to pry."

Harriet looked slightly guilty, as though she would have had far less compunction about prying into the subject of Emma's correspondence. But she shook her head. "I never had the chance to speak to her about it. It was only a day or two before she died that it arrived."

"I don't suppose either of you knows where the letter is now?"

Both ladies shook their heads. "It wasn't in amongst Emma's things in her room," Harriet said. "At least, I didn't see it when I went in."

"Nor did I," Miss Selfridge confirmed. "I had the job of sorting through Emma's possessions and deciding what could be sent to the charity shop and what ought to be thrown away. I didn't find any letters of any kind." Her brow puckered. "A newspaper reporter, you say? I wonder what one of them could have wanted with someone like Emma."

CHAPTER 11: WATSON

Lestrade looked up from behind his desk in his sparsely decorated office at Scotland Yard. "You've seen Wyatt's body, then?"

Holmes nodded. "Now, could you please send for the case file?"

"Jack Kelly's been handling the case," Lestrade replied. "I'll bring him."

We waited, each on one of his wooden chairs. Presently, Lestrade returned with Jack, accompanied by Lucy.

"The Hyde Park victims," Jack announced as he placed a stack of files on Lestrade's bare wooden desktop. "Thought it might be as well to look for connections."

Holmes gave an approving nod. Lestrade sat behind his desk. Lucy took the remaining chair, next to Holmes.

Jack continued, "I interviewed the retired Reverend Wyatt's housekeeper. He didn't have family. Never married, no brothers or sisters, parents both deceased. Had the same little room and housekeeper for nearly forty years. Never had a parish house of his own. Always a junior clergyman."

"So, no family money?" Lestrade inquired.

"None. The housekeeper didn't know anyone who might bear a grudge against him, either."

Holmes raised his eyebrows. "The housekeeper must have had some insights about him, after forty years."

"I was coming to that. She mentioned the Reverend hadn't been himself the past couple of weeks."

"How so?"

"He seemed preoccupied. And she mentioned hearing him muttering something about the greater god, or maybe it was the greater good. She couldn't tell, and she didn't want to let on she'd been listening."

Holmes asked, "Anything else about the Reverend?"

"Nothing else stands out."

"Then Watson and I can add that the Reverend's cause of death was a blow to his right temple, likely delivered from behind by a cosh."

"So, a right-handed person, possibly?" Lucy interjected.

Holmes nodded. "You made some inquiries as well?"

"I'll be brief," Lucy said. "I asked after the shoemaker, the hotelier, and the lady's maid. The lady's maid seems to have been a blackmailer."

Holmes's eyebrows raised in inquiry.

"She had a china sculpture far too expensive for her to have come by on her own. And she was writing a letter asking for money." Lucy handed Holmes a wrinkled scrap of paper from her reticule. "One of her fellow boarding house roomers found this."

Holmes glanced at the writing. "She saw something, received the expensive statuette in return for her silence, but wanted more. We need to find out where she worked and any visitors she might have overheard."

"I plan to visit her employment agency."

"What about the others?"

"The hotelier's widow had little regard for him and was

unaware of his connections to any of the other victims. Said he had no enemies."

"And the shoemaker?"

"Serviced the carriage trade. Known for beautiful leather-work, but no visible connections to the other victims or known enemies."

Lucy had been perusing the stack of files, taking out a single sheet of paper from each. "The cause of death," she said. "Each of these victims died from a blow to the temple."

"With one exception," I said. "The file of the latest victim, Miss Cavendish, is not yet here. She had no head wound. She was garroted."

"Yet she was connected," Holmes observed. "We found a clipping about Reverend Wyatt secreted in her room, away from the searchers."

"Where does this leave us?" Lestrade asked.

Holmes gestured at the files. "We should map out the locations, the positions in the park where they were found. We may deduce something from that."

"Except for the body of Miss Cavendish," I noted. "She was riding on horseback when she was killed, and likely she was riding with her murderer."

PART TWO

CHAPTER 12: FLYNN

"So there's no one else here?" Flynn asked. Becky had unearthed an old and tattered jacket and a pair of corduroy trousers that she wore when she was pretending to be a boy. They were big on her, which made them a bit too short in the arms and legs for Flynn, but at least they were dry.

He'd changed in Mr. Holmes's dressing room, and now they were in the 221B sitting room, waiting for the American woman to put on the spare clothes of Lucy's that Becky had found for her.

"No one besides us," Becky said. She picked up the telephone receiver. "Dr. Watson and Mr. Holmes are looking at a dead body—a murder victim that Inspector Lestrade wanted a second opinion on. Lucy went to interview the murder victim's daughter, I think she said. She's a wardress in the female wing of Holloway Prison. The daughter, I mean. That's why I wasn't allowed to go along with Lucy to interview her—no children are permitted inside the prison. So unless Mrs. Hudson comes back early from her marketing, we're on our own."

Flynn didn't scare easily, but he also didn't love the sound of that. "Not good news."

"No. But I have worse news," Becky said.

"What's that?"

"The telephone is out of order."

"Oh." Flynn tried to take in just what that meant. "That is worse."

"I know." Becky set the receiver down. She didn't like admitting that she was frightened any more than Flynn, but he saw how tense her shoulders had grown. "I was going to telephone Jack, but—"

The American woman came into the sitting room in time to hear Becky's last words. "Who exactly is this Jack?"

"My older brother," Becky told her. "He's a police sergeant at Scotland Yard. But with the telephone out of order, I'm not going to be able to reach him or anyone else."

The American woman's face blanched as she looked at them. "What are the odds, do you think, that the telephone just happens to be out of order now?"

"My guess would be zero to none," Becky said. She left the telephone and went to one of the sitting room windows. She'd pulled the curtains shut as soon as they got up here, but now she lifted one just a fraction so that she could look down into the street below. "Who am I looking for?"

"Two men," Flynn told her. "One big and bald. The other one's not so tall, and he's wearing a checked cloth cap."

She frowned, squinting through the glass, but then shook her head. "I don't see anyone like that—which most likely just means that they're around the back of the house."

"They'd have to be, to have cut the telephone line," Flynn said.

Becky looked at him. "How long do you think it will be before they force their way in here?"

"Not long enough."

The American woman interrupted. "Why don't we just leave? If those men are around the back, we can get out through the front door, can't we?"

"Too dangerous," Flynn said. "If they're around back, it's

a solid bet that they've left someone out in front of the house to nab us if we come out. Baldy and Cloth Cap don't strike me as being amateurs."

"Who *are* you?" Becky asked the American woman. "And how on earth did you get Flynn mixed up in all of this?"

"By hiding underneath his tablecloth in a sandwich shop," the woman said. She swallowed, casting a quick, nervous glance towards the sitting room door, as though expecting to see Baldy and Cloth Cap come bursting through at any moment. "As for the rest, I'll admit that the two of you deserve answers. But perhaps now isn't the best time—"

"Wait a moment!" Becky was staring at the American woman with a look of dawning realisation. She snapped her fingers. "I *do* know you! That is, we've never met before, but I've seen your photograph in the newspapers. You're the reporter! Nellie Bly."

CHAPTER 13: BECKY

"Who?" Flynn looked blank; the name Nellie Bly clearly meant nothing to him.

"She writes stories for the newspapers," Becky said. Despite their current predicament, she couldn't help feeling a small spark of excitement at her realisation of who the American woman really was. "She reported on the political situation in Mexico, and then she went undercover in a lunatic asylum—pretended to be a patient there, so that she could write a piece exposing how cruelly the women inside were being treated. And she travelled all the way around the world in 80 days, just like the book—"

"Technically speaking, I finished the journey in just 72 days," Nellie Bly interrupted. There was a brief flicker of amusement in her gaze, but that vanished instantly as a crash sounded from somewhere downstairs. She jumped. "That sounds as though they've managed to get inside."

"They must have broken one of the kitchen windows," Becky said. Her heart was jumping wildly against her ribcage, but she forced herself to sound steady as she looked at Flynn. "Do we run? Or try to fight?"

A thump of heavy footsteps sounded from the bottom of the stairs.

"They're between us and the door," Flynn said. "Doesn't look like we've got much choice."

Becky ran to the sitting room door and snapped the lock shut. That wouldn't hold the men downstairs for long, but it would buy them a moment or two. Her mind was skipping through the possibilities. There were the glass vials and beakers on Mr. Holmes's chemistry bench—some of them like sulfuric acid could easily serve as weapons—but she hadn't been working with Mr. Holmes on any experiments lately, so she didn't know exactly what was there. Dashing a beaker full of something harmless like bromelain or calcium citrate into an attacker's face wouldn't be any help.

She looked at Flynn. "Up."

"Up?" Flynn looked skeptical. "I wouldn't have said 'up' was the direction we should be heading right now."

"We can get out onto the roof from Dr. Watson's room."

Dr. Watson occupied a bedroom at the top of a short flight of stairs at the back of the sitting room. The stairs were usually screened by a hanging curtain, and Flynn and Becky had perfected the art of hiding behind it when they wanted to listen in on a conversation the adults were having. Since that only worked if the adults had no idea that they were even inside the flat, they would use a ladder to get into Dr. Watson's upstairs room, and then creep down to sit on the stairs.

They just had to accomplish that in reverse now, with the additional step of getting from Dr. Watson's room up onto the roof.

Becky led the way, racing up the stairs two at a time. Flynn and Nellie Bly followed, although she heard Nellie ask Flynn in a low, breathless voice, "Does she have some sort of plan for how we're going to get down from the roof safely?"

Becky's pulse was hammering in her ears, but she still heard

Flynn answer, "I learned a long time ago not to ask questions like that."

He reached the top of the stairs last and slammed the door of Dr. Watson's room shut behind them, throwing the bolt shut. He looked at Becky. "Do you think Dr. Watson took his revolver with him?"

"Maybe not. If they were only going to look at a dead body," Becky said. She felt slightly guilty about rifling through Dr. Watson's things, but anyone who'd read his stories knew that he kept his old service revolver in his desk.

She could hear the repeated *crash crash* of the intruders trying to break down the door of the sitting room. How long until they managed to get it open? A minute? Thirty seconds?

Flynn yanked open the top drawer of the writing desk that stood against the wall in the corner of the room. "Here." He scooped up the revolver and thrust it in his pocket.

Becky ran to the window and threw up the sash, then put her head out, twisting to look up at the rooftop. Somehow the distance seemed far less when all they had to do was swing down from the roof and in through the window.

"There's a drainpipe, anyway." Flynn had joined her in looking out and didn't sound nearly as daunted as Becky felt. But then, he was used to getting in and out of upper-story windows when Mr. Holmes sent him to search a suspect's house. "Should be easy enough."

Only if you're a spider monkey. Becky didn't say it, though. Two years ago, a nasty customer had grabbed her and dangled her out of a second-story window just like this one, threatening to drop her if Mr. Holmes didn't do as he was told. Becky didn't like admitting even to Flynn that sometimes she could still feel the man's rough hands gripping her arms and her feet dangling in empty space.

Instead she turned to Nellie Bly. "Do you think you can manage the climb?"

Nellie looked slightly pale as she eyed the window. But she said, "Since it's considerably better than the alternative of being caught, I'll just have to, won't I?"

"You go first," Becky told Flynn.

He scrambled unhesitatingly out the window, grabbed hold of the drainpipe, and shimmied up as easily as though he was part monkey. Then he turned back to look down at her and Nellie Bly.

"Come on."

Becky swallowed. "Wait a moment." Dr. Watson's room was almost as much a jumble of odds and ends as Mr. Holmes's sitting room. Medical textbooks and journals, stethoscopes and other doctor's instruments, curios that he'd brought back with him from Afghanistan, stacks of the newspaper printings of his published stories, a gramophone and a stack of records. But in amongst it all, Becky had seen a dog's collar and lead hanging on a hook beside the wardrobe.

The bull pup that Dr. Watson had kept for a pet when he'd first come to London had been long since gone by the time that Becky first visited 221B. But apparently he hadn't bothered to get rid of all the dog's equipment.

She snatched the lead off the wall just as she heard the splintering crash of the sitting room door giving way. Leaning out the window, Becky tossed the end of the lead up to Flynn, who was on the roof now, leaning over the low stone parapet at the edge.

"Catch!"

Flynn caught the leather strap on the first try and wrapped it once around his wrist. Not perfect, but it was better than having only the drain pipe to hang onto. Becky considered telling Nellie Bly to go first, but that would be cowardly, and besides, Nellie was heaviest of the three of them. If she needed help, Becky and Flynn together would have a better chance of pulling her up onto the roof than Flynn alone.

If Becky made it to the roof, and didn't wind up smashed on the paving stones below.

She blew out a hard breath. Thinking like that never helped anything.

Becky climbed up onto the window sill and stepped out.

The drainpipe was cold and slippery under her clammy palms and her legs cramped as she tried to brace her feet against the brick wall. She held tight to her end of the dog's lead, tilting her head just enough that she could look up at Flynn.

"Don't let go."

"Oh, really? You think?" Flynn's expression was unusually grim, but he braced himself against the low parapet and held the lead taut, allowing Becky to use it to haul herself upwards. It felt like an hour, but it probably wasn't more than a minute or two before she managed to scramble the last foot or two up and with Flynn's help pull herself onto the top of the roof. Every part of her wanted to lie down flat on her back and let her heart stop trying to pound its way out of her chest. But instead she tossed the lead back down to Nellie Bly and called out, "Come ahead."

Up here, with the noise of the wind and the traffic from Baker Street down below, Becky couldn't hear anything from inside the flat. But the men chasing them wouldn't be far behind, and it wouldn't be much longer before they broke down the door to Dr. Watson's room.

Not many famous people lived up to their reputations, but Nellie Bly didn't hesitate. She set her jaw and clambered out the window, pulling herself steadily upwards. A minute later, and she landed on the roof beside them, exhaling a shaky breath.

"I can't believe we made it. Now what?"

Becky was saved from having to admit that she hadn't come that far yet by a shout from down below them. The men who'd been chasing Nellie and Flynn were inside Dr. Watson's room, probably looking out the window.

CHAPTER 14: FLYNN

Flynn couldn't entirely hear what Cloth Cap and Baldy were shouting, their voices were too muffled by the noise of the street traffic for him to fully make out the words. But he got the gist. Cloth Cap was calling to someone in the alley to ask whether they'd seen anyone climb down from the window, and whichever gang member was down below—there seemed to be at least four of them, including Baldy and Cloth Cap, which wasn't good news—was saying they hadn't seen anyone.

Becky had heard, too. They were sitting crouched down below the level of the parapet, with Nellie Bly in between them. Becky looked across her to say to Flynn, "Three guesses how long it will be until they decide that we must have gone up, not down."

"I don't need three guesses. Baldy and Cloth Cap may not be the brightest, but even they can figure out that we must be up here on the roof," Flynn said. "We need a way down from here that doesn't walk us straight into their arms."

"I know, I know." Becky rested her forehead against her raised knees, squeezing her hands against her temples. "Just let me think." She glanced at him. "And don't say that it was my thinking that got us into this mess in the first place."

"I wouldn't."

Becky raised her head and gave him another look. "Yes, you would."

"Well, all right, maybe," Flynn admitted. "But not now." Especially not when he was the one who'd brought Nellie Bly to Baker Street and roped Becky into this, too.

He turned to Nellie Bly. "Do you know whether Baldy and Cloth Cap have weapons?"

He hadn't intended the question to be an upsetting one. No more upsetting than being stuck up on a roof while a pair of thugs were trying to bring you down, anyway. But Nellie's face turned even paler and she looked a bit sick, her eyes unfocused, as if she were remembering something.

"I'd say that it's a virtual certainty that at least one of them is carrying a gun."

By now, Flynn was used to getting answers exactly opposite to the ones he was hoping for.

"We can't let them come even close to getting up here, then," he said. Nellie had said that they wanted her dead, not captured, which meant that they had no reason at all to leave Flynn and Becky alive if either of them got in the way.

Flynn tugged Dr. Watson's service revolver out of his pocket.

"What are you doing?" Nellie Bly gasped. She'd kept her nerve very well until now, but her voice sounded like she was on the verge of panicking. "I can't let you kill anyone to protect me!"

"I'm not going to kill anybody." Flynn cocked the revolver and pointed the muzzle at the sky. "Not if I can help it, anyway. I need to call in some reinforcements."

CHAPTER 15: WATSON

"I expect Westaway's has already closed for the night," Lucy finished, "so I intend to visit their office tomorrow."

We were sharing a cab ride back to Baker Street, wending our way through the heavy traffic of Piccadilly Circus. Lucy had just finished giving us an account of her recent activities while Holmes and I listened attentively.

"I know it's a long shot," Lucy went on. "But the note that Harriet found in Emma's handwriting is the nearest thing we've uncovered that could offer a motive for her death."

"You are thinking of blackmail," I said.

"Emma herself probably wouldn't have thought of it in quite those terms," Lucy said. "By all accounts, she sounds to have been the sort of woman who would have told herself that she was just asking for a present in exchange for keeping something a secret. But yes. Whoever got that note probably surmised that Emma intended blackmail and was threatening to expose something that someone wanted hidden. So then we need to find out to whom Emma was writing. We need a list of the people she knew. I don't know how long Westaway's keeps its records, but there's just a chance that they might still have names of her former employers."

"Indeed." Holmes had been listening with his eyes closed, seemingly impervious to the jolts of the carriage as it rolled over rough cobblestones. "It would be interesting to know, would it not, whether Samuel Harley ever made a pair of shoes for one or more of the ladies who employed Emma Thompkins as a lady's maid."

Lucy nodded, seeming to understand precisely the lines upon which Holmes's thoughts were running. Even I was beginning to get a glimmer, such that I was not surprised when Lucy went on, "And whether Martin Goodspeed and his delightful wife ever hosted anyone who knew either Emma Thompkins or Samuel Harley at their hotel?"

"As you say." Holmes opened his eyes and gazed out the window at the fine equipages and shabby growlers, mail-phaetons and curricles that crowded the street all around us. "The common thread—the only visible common thread—in the lives of these three murder victims seems to have been that in one capacity or another they were employed by members of the wealthiest classes: Harley as a shoemaker, Miss Thompkins as a lady's maid, and Goodspeed as the host of an exclusive hotel."

"What of the other victims?" I asked. "George Pennythwaite, the lawyer, and the other man … What was his name? John Wyatt."

"We must look into them, of course," Holmes agreed. "However, the sudden appearance of a piece of valuable Meissen china amongst the possessions of an otherwise impoverished elderly servant is suggestive. It smacks, to my mind, of a bribe. And a bribe from a very particular class of person, at that."

"Which would fit in with Miss Cavendish's involvement," I put in. "She might have been acquainted with our hypothetical killer—or have mentioned him in one of her society gossip articles. Somehow, she got wind of the killings, started to investigate, and—"

"And became the killer's most recent victim," Lucy said. "And you're right about the class of society to which our murderer most probably belongs. I'd say it's someone with a title, or at the very least an old family name going back to the days of the Conqueror. Only someone with that type of background would think to pay off a blackmailer using Dresden china. Nearly anyone else would have simply given Emma Thompkins cold hard money."

"True. Although I believe that is not the only clue that can be gleaned from our aristocratic blackmail victim's choice of a gift," Holmes said.

Lucy gave him a quick, searching glance, but Holmes said nothing more. Lucy looked thoughtful, but we were interrupted at that juncture by Holmes abruptly stiffening and leaning forward in his seat. His eyes were still fixed on something out the window, but his expression had taken on the look of keen attention which I knew so well.

"What is it, Holmes?"

We had turned onto Baker Street by now, but were still about a block away from 221B.

Holmes answered without turning away from the window. "That street sweeper who just passed us by. He was moving with unusual speed for a man who should be tired out and nearing the end of his workday. And his hands were remarkably clean and entirely uncalloused."

Lucy sat up straighter, suddenly alert as well. "Meaning that either he hasn't been a street sweeper for very long, or else—"

"Or else he is merely playing the part of one." Holmes turned to Lucy. "I believe young Becky was spending the afternoon with Mrs. Hudson while you visited Holloway Prison?"

I very rarely—if ever—saw Lucy frightened or even shaken, but her face turned a trifle paler now. "Mrs. Hudson had some shopping to do, so I said it would be perfectly all right if she left Becky alone for a short while."

Our cab had slowed to a near halt, blocked by a farmer's cart and an omnibus that were vying for space to make a turn. Without another word, Lucy pushed open the door to the carriage and jumped out. Her feet had scarcely touched the pavement when I heard the explosive clap of a gunshot ring out above the noise of the street.

Lucy started to run.

CHAPTER 16: BECKY

The echoes of the shot Flynn had fired still hung in the air, but so far as Becky could tell, the traffic in the street down below seemed to be moving on just as normal. Most people would probably have assumed the noise came from the backfire of one of the new automobiles that had begun to appear on the London streets.

Becky looked at Flynn. "How long until they find the ladder, do you think?"

Mrs. Hudson kept a rickety wooden ladder in the small tool shed at the back of the house. The shed was locked, but it wouldn't take more than a second or two for their pursuers to kick the door down the same way they'd broken through into the sitting room.

"Not long enough, probably," Flynn said. They were all three of them crouched down out of sight of anyone below. But now Flynn raised his head a little, scanning the roof in all directions. "They'll probably come at us from the back of the house."

"We have the gun," Becky said. "And if they're using the ladder, they'll have to come up just one at a time."

She still didn't relish the thought of trying to defend their rooftop position from attackers—

Her thought snapped off as a thump sounded against the side of the roof, followed by a pair of male hands that appeared at the edge of the parapet. Flynn leaped forward and smashed the butt of the gun against the knuckles of the right hand.

The man gave a yell of outrage and let go of the rooftop. But he also hauled himself far enough up to seize hold of the shoulder of Flynn's jacket.

The man was big and bald-headed. Becky saw that much in the split second when time seemed to hang suspended. He yanked Flynn towards him, hard enough that despite having dug in his feet, Flynn stumbled. The gun went flying out of his hands, sailing over the side of the rooftop and vanishing, as far out of their reach as though it had landed on the surface of the moon.

Becky's stomach dropped, but she flung herself forward. Her first thought was to try to drag Flynn out of the bald man's grasp, but Nellie Bly was there before her, wrapping her hands around Flynn's other arm—at least until the bald man backhanded her across the face.

Nellie stumbled back with a sharp cry, and the bald man lifted Flynn up so that his feet were an inch or two off the roof.

Fear closed off Becky's throat and scrambled around inside her chest as for a second she stood frozen, transported five years back in her memory, to those moments when she'd been the one dangling in the air outside of an upper-story window. But this time she wasn't actually being held captive; she was free to move.

The big man's feet were still planted on the top rung of the ladder he'd used to climb up onto the rooftop. Becky darted forward, coming in from the side where the bald man was holding Flynn and wouldn't be able to reach her as easily. Instead of attacking him or trying to grab Flynn, she ducked and threw herself hard against the top posts of the ladder, shoving them away from the wall.

The ladder rocked, tilting back and carrying the bald man with it. His eyes widened in an almost comical look of alarm and he dropped Flynn as he tried to make a grab for the edge of the roof to steady himself. It didn't work. He fell, carried in a wide backwards arc by the ladder, and ended up crashing into the clothes line and a pile of Mrs. Hudson's washing that had been strung across the back courtyard.

Becky exhaled a hard gust of air as she watched him struggling to untangle himself and get back up again. Despite the fact that they were still stuck up on the roof, she was glad that she didn't have to decide whether or not to feel guilty over killing the bald man.

Then she didn't feel glad anymore. The bald man had allies now. Two more men ran to help him up, while a third, in the cloth cap that Flynn had described, started to set the ladder back upright.

Four men, all ready to climb up the ladder to get them.

The bald one was staring straight at her, eyes blazing, and plainly wanting to get even.

And Dr. Watson's revolver—their one weapon—was currently lying somewhere on the ground far below.

As though he knew what she was thinking, Flynn looked at her and said, "We're not dying here today."

"How do you know that?"

He glanced over his shoulder at Nellie Bly. "Because if I die before I find out who those men are and what this is all about, I'm coming back to haunt someone."

Becky almost laughed, although she would have felt better if the top rungs of the ladder hadn't thunked against the side of the roof at that moment.

But then what was probably the most welcome sound she'd ever heard in her life split the air: the shrill blast of a police constable's whistle coming from down below in Baker Street.

CHAPTER 17: LUCY

"You'll have to pay Mrs. Hudson a bonus this month to make up for the state of her kitchen," I told Holmes.

We were standing together by the window in the sitting room, and Mrs. Hudson was downstairs, already energetically sweeping up the broken glass on the floor and taping butcher paper over the shattered window until a workman could be found to mend it.

"She has always been remarkably patient with such events," Holmes said. He was looking out at the street below us with a keen gaze. "But I shall endeavour to offer suitable recompense, yes."

"Do you see anyone trying to keep a watch on us?" I asked.

The men who had tried to break into the flat had all fled at the sound of the police whistle, which was a mixed blessing. Flynn, Becky, and the woman who appeared to be our new client, were all safe and unharmed. But we also didn't have any leads that would help us unravel the mystery of where the four men had come from and who had paid them.

"Not so far," Holmes said. "Which is in and of itself interesting." He turned away from the window to where Nellie Bly was sitting on the sofa between Becky and Flynn. Watson—having returned his service revolver to its proper place in his desk drawer—had already examined the bruise on Miss Bly's face and pronounced it only a minor injury.

"And now, Miss Bly," Holmes said, "perhaps this would be a suitable moment for you to explain what has brought you to our door."

Nellie Bly set down the teacup from which she'd been sipping. Before she'd set to work cleaning the kitchen, Mrs. Hudson had insisted on providing us with a tea tray, despite all our combined efforts to persuade her not to bother.

"I confess that it's a little strange to hear that name again," Nellie said. Despite the angry mark on her cheek and the shadow of weariness about the corners of her eyes, she seemed to have recovered well from her recent ordeal. "It's been several years since I resigned from newspaper work, and it was only ever a pseudonym. I was christened Elizabeth Cochrane, and since I took my husband's surname on our marriage, my name technically speaking is Elizabeth Seaman." She smiled faintly. "But by all means, continue to call me Nellie Bly, if you wish. Perhaps it will help me to re-adjust myself to the present circumstances and remember some of the skills I thought that I had put away when I hung up my newspaper reporter's pen."

She took a deep breath and surveyed the room. "To begin with, though, I must apologise to everyone here. First, for the damage that was done to your property. And second, for putting these two in danger." She looked at Becky and Flynn. "I would never have come here if I had known that would be the result."

Becky's expression turned a shade indignant at that, although she didn't speak.

Holmes made a dismissive gesture. "You need not blame yourself. They have both proven remarkably adept at getting both into and out of danger without assistance from anyone else." He eyed Becky and Flynn, and though his expression did not change, he added, "You both acted with commendable courage and resourcefulness today."

"Thank you." Becky seemed somewhat mollified; Flynn shifted position and looked embarrassed, as he did when anyone tried to offer him praise.

"Well, then." Nellie locked her hands together in her lap. "To begin with, I should say that although I've not been in the business of reporting for the past several years, I do still have friends on the staff of several of the most prominent newspapers, both in America and in Europe. Three weeks ago, one of those friends—her name is Eleanor Cavendish—sent me a telegram, asking me to come to London as soon as could possibly be arranged."

Watson started at the name. Even Holmes looked at her, his brows edging upwards.

"And the reason for her summons?"

"I don't know." Nellie looked up at him and said, "I had to arrange passage on a steamer across the Atlantic. It was late in the day yesterday evening when I finally arrived in London. I telephoned the number that Eleanor had given me, but there was no answer. So this morning, I went to the flat where she lived."

She stopped speaking, studying all of our faces, and then said, "She's dead, isn't she." Her tone made it a statement rather than a question. "I can see that you recognise Eleanor's name. Will you tell me what happened?"

Holmes knew when to answer bluntness with equal bluntness. "I'm sorry to tell you that she was found this morning in Hyde Park," he said. "She had been murdered."

Nellie's face blanched at the news, but she nodded. "I knew

it. I knew that Eleanor wouldn't have summoned me like that unless she was in danger. And I knew she wouldn't have disappeared without leaving me any word as to where I could find her."

She paused, looking down at her own hands a moment, then said, "If you know my name, you're probably aware that my *around the world* series of articles made me quite famous." She spoke entirely without conceit, a mere statement of fact rather than bragging. "Those articles also began something of a trend that I think of as stunt reporting. Girl reporters did sensational things for the sake of writing about them in the newspapers. Some were decent journalists. Most weren't. But Eleanor was different. I met her in Washington, D.C. when we were both covering the second inauguration of President Cleveland. The London *Times* had sent her over."

She paused, turned one hand palm up, and then continued, "I know she'd begun writing silly, vapid little pieces for the society gossip pages in the past few years. She had to, to pay her bills. It's hard to make a decent living at being a reporter, and Eleanor was supporting her elderly mother on what she earned, right up until her mother died a little less than a year ago. But she truly loved newspaper work. And she had an absolutely fearless commitment to discovering and reporting the truth."

Holmes rarely allowed himself to demonstrate his surprising capacity for sympathy. But now he said, "I, too, was acquainted with Miss Cavendish. She occasionally provided me with information concerning society figures. I can imagine no more fitting epitaph for her than your words."

Nellie's expression had been as hard as her voice until this, but at Holmes's remark she blinked away a sheen of moisture from her eyes. "Thank you," she said again. "At any rate, to give you the full story, I went to Eleanor's flat—she had a place in Chelsea—and found the door to the place unlocked. I went in. I realise now that probably wasn't the wisest course of action, but if I'd been uneasy before, I was truly frightened. I thought I might find Eleanor inside. Instead, I found those two men, the ones who chased us here."

"They were searching the flat?"

"I think they must have been. I didn't realise that they were there at first. I went in and found the sitting room empty. I was just beginning to look through the papers on Eleanor's desk when they came out of the bedroom. I only just managed to escape without them catching me."

Holmes's grey eyes had sharpened with a familiar look of focused intensity. "Which tells us that the death of Miss Cavendish by no means settled whatever is behind this affair. Someone, somewhere, is acutely afraid of what she might have been able to reveal—or of what she might have had in her possession. You have no idea what sort of story she was working on?"

"None, I'm afraid. That is, not really."

Holmes leaned forward, immediately alert. "Then there is something?"

"Perhaps. Although I may be mistaken," Nellie said. "It's this way. I'd barely set foot inside the door to Eleanor's flat when I had to run for my life. But I went to her desk first. It was in the front room. And before those two men came charging out of the bedroom, I happened to see an entry in Eleanor's appointment book for last week. Ordinarily, I wouldn't have expected that to mean anything to me. I scarcely know anyone in London, nor am I familiar with Eleanor's acquaintances. But this name was one that I recognised. Or thought that I recognised. As I say, I barely had time to glance at it before I had to run."

"And the name was?" Holmes asked.

"Granby. George Granby. I recognised the name because I interviewed him for a story … oh, it must have been seven or eight years ago, now."

The name meant nothing to me, but Holmes appeared to find it familiar. He nodded, then glanced at the rest of us and said, by way of explanation, "Mr. George Granby is a wealthy American tobacco baron. Indeed, it would not be entirely an exaggeration to say that he is *the* wealthy American tobacco baron. His company controls most of the business interests of the new world's tobacco farmers."

I turned back to Miss Bly. "Can you think why Eleanor Cavendish would have been meeting with him?" I asked. "Is he staying in London?"

"If it's the same George Granby whom I met years ago, then yes," Nellie Bly said. "The address in Eleanor's appointment book for their meeting was the Savoy Hotel."

"The Savoy," Holmes repeated. His expression flattened into the remote, austere look that meant that his mind was at work, rapidly sorting through possible theories and explanations. He voiced none of them, though.

"Is that all?" he asked Nellie.

"I think so. Those men tried to catch me. I made my escape. Although obviously it wasn't an entirely successful escape, since we all wound up here, with them battering down the door." Nellie made a wry face.

Holmes put the tips of his fingers together and studied her a moment. Then he turned to focus on Flynn. "Can you describe the two men who pursued you today?"

Flynn answered promptly. "The big one was bald, heavyset. Brown eyes. Had a scar like he'd been burned on the back of his hand. I saw it when he grabbed hold of me up on the roof top. The smaller one—"

Holmes held up a hand to stop him. "That will be sufficient. Thank you."

I looked at Holmes with interest. "I take it you recognise the description?"

"I believe so. The evidence we saw where Miss Cavendish died in Hyde Park was suggestive, but Flynn's added detail about the mark on the hand clinches the matter. Watson, if you will be so good as to pass me the volume of my files pertaining to the letter *B*?"

Watson moved at once to comply, handing over a leather-bound volume that bristled with the odd scraps and sheets of paper that Holmes had put in over the years.

"Now, then." Holmes turned the pages, running his finger down the column of names until he came to the entry he was seeking. "Ah yes. Here we are. William Brasher, known to his associates as the Butcher because in addition to serving as a thug for hire to whomever will pay him, he also runs a butcher's shop in Blackfriars Lane, which doubles as a front for his less-savoury avenues of business. Contrary to his nickname, he favours garroting as a means of execution when he is hired to commit murder. The identifying mark on his hand, incidentally, is from an accident with a paraffin lamp during his youth." Holmes paused and shut the book.

Nellie straightened in her seat. "So we know who he is and where to find him. If only we could go straight to this butcher's shop and see that he's arrested. But I suppose it's not that easy."

"I fear not." Holmes gave a shake of his head. "We could certainly find Mr. Brasher in Blackfriars Lane. We might even be able to have him charged with assault or attempted kidnapping based on your testimony. But we have no evidence as yet that would tie him to the death of your friend Miss Cavendish. Nor do we know who hired him. Brasher is merely a pawn in a larger game, a puppet dispensed to do the dirty work of an individual who does not wish to soil his hands with anything so ugly as murder. Nor do I imagine that arresting Brasher on a minor charge and questioning him as to the name of his employer would lead to anything but a wall of silence or perhaps a string of ready lies. He is not the sort of man to fear a temporary spell of incarceration, and without any proof that he is responsible for Eleanor Cavendish's murder, we cannot threaten him with anything more severe than a few months' residence at Millbank or Newgate Prison."

"Oh." Nellie looked discouraged. "What can we do, then?"

"When hunting rats, it is a common practice among rat catchers to introduce a ferret into the rat hole to drive the animals out." Holmes turned to me. "Do you think that Jack would be available for a brief excursion from Scotland Yard this afternoon?"

"To play the role of ferret?" I nodded. "Yes, I'm sure that he would be happy to."

"There was just one other thing," Nellie said. "Although I don't know that it's at all pertinent to the case of Eleanor's death. But before Brasher—if that's his name—chased me out of the flat, I'd picked this up off the top of her desk, and I accidentally came away with it clutched in my hand."

She reached into a pocket and drew out a newspaper cutting. It was crumpled and damp—I remembered Nellie's account of falling into the water with Flynn during their escape from Brasher and his associates—so she had a difficult time in unfolding it. But when she'd spread the scrap of newspaper out, I could read the headline:

Body of West End Hotelier Martin Goodspeed
Found in Hyde Park

CHAPTER 18: WATSON

Holmes regarded the newspaper headline with an impassive face. If his thoughts were racing along the same lines as mine, he gave no sign of it.

After a brief moment's silence, he looked up. "Thank you, Miss Bly. And now we ought to discuss precautionary measures as regards the matter of your safety."

"My safety?" Nellie Bly's chin lifted. "I can assure you that I'm not going to be frightened off by those thugs who chased after me today."

"Far be it from me to suggest otherwise," Holmes replied. "However, I believe this investigation—and any contributions which you care to make—will proceed far more smoothly without Brasher and his friends in constant pursuit."

Nellie Bly gave him a wary look. "What exactly are you suggesting?"

"Brasher and his associates chased you with an eye to eliminating you as a witness. I wish merely to give them the impression that one of them succeeded."

"Succeeded?" Nellie Bly's mind was clearly very quick. It was scarcely a moment before she caught Holmes's meaning. "You mean that you want me to fake my own death?"

"The act need not be quite so elaborate as that. But if a police officer were to pay a call on Brasher, seeking to question him in relation to the death of an American tourist who had recently arrived in London—"

Lucy, too, took Holmes's meaning without his having to explain any further and jumped up. "Of course. I'll call Jack straight away and tell him."

"Very good. Miss Bly, you can remain here for the time being. There is a flat downstairs—221A—which we have used on occasion. You will be quite comfortable."

Nellie Bly continued to look a trifle wary. "For how long? I didn't come all this way just to sit on my hands. Eleanor was a friend."

"And quite naturally, you wish to ensure that those responsible for her death do not remain unpunished," Holmes said. "However, you, Miss Bly, to put it crudely, have a target affixed to your back. You need only remain out of sight long enough for whoever pinned that target in place to be informed that you are no longer a threat."

Nellie Bly seemed to struggle a moment, but then finally gave an unwilling nod. "I'll stay here. Temporarily, mind you," she added.

"That is all that I ask," Holmes answered. "First, though, I believe we might just create some photographic evidence."

"What evidence?" Miss Bly asked.

"To enhance the story which Jack is planning to tell."

CHAPTER 19: BECKY

August 14

"You don't have to worry about Jack," Flynn said the next morning. "He'll be all right."

"I'm not worried," Becky told him. Which might have been true, depending on what you meant by 'worried' and 'not.' She knew her brother could take care of himself, and that he'd faced down worse criminals than William Brasher before this, or at least ones who were just as bad.

She just didn't like having to wait while not knowing what could be happening to him. A minute or two ago, she'd watched him push open the door of *Brasher's Butcher's Shop*, a small, dingy-looking little clapboard place sandwiched in between a pawn shop and a toy-maker's.

Now he was probably talking to Mr. Brasher, who would be armed with knives and cleavers and all the other sharp tools of a butcher's trade.

"So we're thinking that Eleanor Cavendish was looking into the Hyde Park murders? And that the same person who killed her also killed all the other Hyde Park victims?" Flynn asked.

Becky knew he was just trying to distract her, but she decided to let him. It was better than thinking about Brasher and Jack.

"I'm pretty sure that's what Lucy and Mr. Holmes think.

That's why Lucy's gone off to Westaway's Employment Agency this afternoon to look into Emma Thompkins."

And that was why they were here at Brasher's shop. Jack was the ferret that they were putting down the hole, and Becky and Flynn's assignment was to wait until the rat—Brasher—left his shop.

If he ever did leave.

"How long do you think it's been since Jack went in there?" Becky asked.

Flynn looked at her and then sighed. "Come on."

"What do you mean?" Becky asked. "We're supposed to be keeping watch from over here on the other side of the street."

They'd both changed clothes. She was wearing a blue dress with a crisp white pinafore and a flat straw hat that shaded her face. Flynn was looking—for him—very respectable in a brown tweed knickerbocker suit and a matching tweed cap, although what was most important was that Brasher wasn't likely to recognise either of them, so long as they kept their distance.

"Sure, but if you keep looking like a long-tail cat in a room full of rocking chairs, someone's going to notice us and wonder what we're up to." Flynn nodded to the toy maker's shop across the street. "That's probably better cover anyway. You can pretend to be looking at all the fancy dolls in the window. Brasher's got a side window open, too. There's a chance we might be able to hear what he and Jack are saying."

Becky's lip curled slightly at the suggestion that she'd want anything to do with the row of ridiculous-looking dolls with lacy dresses and bonnets and smirking expressions on their painted china faces. But Flynn had a point about the open window.

"All right, come on."

She dodged a book binder's cart and a man selling umbrellas and darted across the street to press her nose against the toy shop window. Flynn followed. Blackfriars Lane was busy, and there was enough noise from the traffic all around them that it took a moment for Becky to pick out the sound of voices coming from inside the open window of Brasher's Butcher's Shop. But then she caught Jack's voice.

"—just a few questions in connection with the recent death of a woman by the name of Eleanor Cavendish. She was found dead in Hyde Park this morning." He was using his most stolid, official-sounding policeman's tone.

"What? Never 'eard of 'er." Becky hadn't heard the voice of the big bald man who'd chased them up onto the rooftop, but she could picture the rough growl as belonging to him.

"She was a reporter for the *Tatler*," Jack said patiently.

"And wot's that to me?' Brasher growled. "I don't 'old with women taking men's jobs. Maybe if she 'adn't, she wouldn't 'ave ended up with her throat cut."

Becky gave Flynn a quick look, and he nodded back.

Jack hadn't mentioned Eleanor Cavendish's throat being connected with her death. But although Brasher's slip wouldn't hold up in a court of law as hard evidence, it was enough to raise the fine hairs on the back of Becky's neck as she pictured Brasher's hands drawing the garroting cord around Eleanor's neck.

"So you're certain that you've never met Miss Cavendish?" Jack asked.

If this had been a real interrogation, he would have never let Brasher's temporary slip pass by, but now Jack was going on, doggedly, asking questions with the same slow, plodding determination of a street constable walking his beat.

Lucy would be proud of him. Jack didn't go in for acting very much, but right now he was doing a good job of living up to the idea most people—criminals, especially—had that the police weren't very bright.

"Did she ever come here as a customer, maybe?" he went on.

"And 'ow would I know that?" Brasher demanded. "People come in here wanting to buy a bit of chipped beef or a rasher of bacon and I take their money and 'and 'em over the goods in return. I don't ask 'em for their name and address. Why?" Becky couldn't see Brasher, of course, but she pictured him studying Jack with narrowed eyes. "Is someone saying they saw this Cavendish woman come in 'ere?"

"I'm afraid I'm not at liberty to say," Jack said, still sounding stolid and a bit pompous. "What about this woman?"

"What?" Brasher might be a nasty customer, but he wasn't very good at dissembling. Even standing outside, Becky could tell how the pitch of his voice had changed.

Jack, she knew, would have just showed him one of the photographs that Mr. Holmes had staged of Nellie Bly and then developed himself using his own chemistry apparatus. In the pictures, Nellie Bly lay sprawled lifelessly on the Baker Street floor with a neat round gunshot wound—courtesy of Mr. Holmes's theatrical makeup—in the centre of her forehead.

"She's dead?" Brasher demanded. Then hastily added, "Who is she, anyway?"

Jack wouldn't have let that slip go by, either, if this interrogation had been real. But all he said was, "She was an American tourist who was found dead in Baker Street yesterday."

"And wot's that got ter do with me?" Brasher demanded. His tone of voice still wasn't very convincing.

"You've never seen her before?" Jack asked.

"Never clapped eyes on 'er."

There was a silence from inside the shop. Then Jack said, "Well, if you've nothing more that you can tell me, thank you for your time, and I'll say good day."

Becky kept her eyes fixed on the toy shop window, staring in at a doll with golden hair and trying to pretend that she was hoping to get it for a Christmas or a birthday gift. Out of the corner of her eye, she saw Jack come out of the butcher's shop next door. He didn't pause or so much as glance in their direction, just turned and strode away down the street, heading towards Blackfriar's Bridge.

There was a minute or so of silence from inside the butcher's shop. Then Brasher's voice ground out, "Hello? Hello!"

Becky raised her eyebrows at Flynn and whispered, "Telephone?"

Flynn nodded back. "The thuggery business must be paying well."

Not very many butcher's shops would be able to afford telephone service.

"Something wrong?" Brasher's voice was so loud that Becky didn't even have to strain to make out the words. "I'll say there's something wrong! I've just 'ad the police 'ere. That's right, the police. One good thing, the American woman's dead. That's right. Found shot in Baker Street, according to the copper. One of the lads must have popped her and not realised the bullet struck 'ome. It was a right circus there at the end, when the police started swarming all over the place, and we 'ad to scarper. But the copper wot came here wasn't just asking about the American. 'E was wanting to know about the Cavendish woman. What's that? No, I don't know what put them onto me. The policeman didn't say. But I don't like it, I'll tell you that—"

Brasher broke off and seemed to listen to the other end of the conversation for a few seconds.

"All right. All right, fine. But you'd better make it worth my while, understand?"

Becky heard the clatter of the telephone receiver being hung back in its cradle, followed by a shuffle of movement from inside the shop. Then, a moment or two later, Brasher himself appeared at the front door.

Becky had to tense against the impulse to run. New clothes or no new clothes, Brasher was bound to recognise them if he looked closely.

But he didn't. As Becky stared fixedly at the dolls in the window and Flynn crouched down a little as though to get a better look at a toy train, Brasher flipped the sign on the butcher's shop door from open to closed, shut it with a bang, and locked it using a bunch of keys that jangled from his belt. Then he, too, strode off down the street, although he wasn't heading towards the bridge and the river. Instead, he turned his steps towards Fleet Street.

CHAPTER 20: FLYNN

Flynn watched Baldy—Brasher—stomping along a little over a block ahead of them. So far he hadn't looked behind him even once, but Flynn and Becky were hanging back and following at a distance all the same.

"Where do you think he's heading?" Flynn asked.

They'd been walking for about a quarter of an hour, and he was wondering where exactly Baldy was headed.

"I don't know." Becky squinted at one of the street signs up ahead. "But that's Leather Lane he's about to turn onto. Not a bad place to meet someone anonymously."

That was true enough. Despite the name, Leather Lane wasn't actually a place that specialised in leather goods. But you could buy almost anything else that you could think of, and for cheap, from the costers' stalls that lined the road on both sides. Flynn knew from experience that a penny in Leather Lane would get him a glass of sherbet or a handful of leathery oranges or a stoneware jug or cup. Or you could spend a bit more and get anything from eels and eggs to brass-tagged boot-laces, smoked haddocks, and Dutch dolls.

They watched as Brasher turned in at the stall of the watercress vendor on the corner. Then they picked up the pace and ran to turn onto Leather Lane, too, so as not to lose sight of him.

It was getting on into the later afternoon, with dusk settling in and shadows falling, but the street was still crowded. He saw mothers with kids clinging to their aprons, a couple of soldiers in uniform, street loafers lounging in the doorways and smoking pipes. The fish vendor was shouting, "Mackerel all alive! Fine silver mackerel, six a shilling!" The man was selling shrimp, too, because he had a ring of them decorating his hat band like a wreath of roses, and from time to time he bellowed, "Shrimp! Penny a pint!"

It took Flynn a second to pick Brasher out of the crowd, but then he saw a domed bald head just turning into a narrow alley-way that ran alongside a shop with an Italian name over the lintel and statues in plaster and terra-cotta in the windows. He nudged Becky, and together they pushed their way through the lines of shoppers and vendors to keep him in sight.

"Do we go after him?" Flynn peered down the darkening passage that ran between the Italian place and the building next door. It was barely even an alley. He could put out his hands and touch the walls on both sides, and the ground was clogged with piles of vegetable peelings and broken bottles and all the other rubbish that accumulated in such places.

Already there was no sign of Brasher, so he must have turned onto one of the other alleyways that Flynn could see branching off on either side.

Becky shrugged. "We're not going to find out who hired Brasher by standing out here."

That was true, but it didn't argue away the tense, expectant feeling that Flynn had in the pit of his stomach. He knew that feeling, and it meant trouble every time. But he started forward, picking his way through the mounds of trash. An alley cat jumped out at them from one pile and probably took a year off his life, but they didn't see anyone human.

They reached the first of the turns Brasher could have taken and peered into the gloom. "Doesn't look like he went this way," Flynn murmured.

There was a pile of old bed springs near the corner that Brasher would have been almost bound to have tripped over and knocked apart if he'd passed through this way.

Becky nodded. "Keep going."

They passed by another alleyway that had a couple of drunks sleeping in doorways and snoring loudly.

"Think we've lost him?" Flynn asked.

Becky shook her head. "He can't be that far ahead of us. We just have to keep looking."

The next alleyway they peered down was darker than any of the others. For a second, Flynn thought the figure sprawled across the muddy ground was another drunk who'd had one too many glasses of gin to even manage to find a doorway.

Then Becky sucked in a quick breath, and Flynn realised that the man on the ground was big and bald and that his eyes were staring sightlessly up at the narrow sliver of darkening sky visible between the rooftops on either side.

Brasher.

Becky ran forward and crouched down to feel for the pulse in Brasher's neck, but Flynn could have told her it was already too late. The hilt of a knife that was sticking out from between Brasher's ribs was enough to make him certain of that. The expression on Brasher's heavyset face looked a bit surprised, as if he hadn't been expecting to die this afternoon.

Becky shook her head and stood up, looking in all directions. "Do you think whoever did this is still around?"

"Doubt it." Flynn moved to join her in standing beside the

body. "Whoever it was that knifed him probably got away as fast as possible."

Up ahead, the alleyway broadened out into a courtyard at the back of a square of brick houses. Yellow light spilling out of the windows showed a shared water pump standing in the centre of the yard, with a grey-haired woman pumping water into a bucket.

"Doesn't look like there was much blood," Flynn said. "But he could have washed his hands off at the pump over there and gone on his way with no one the wiser."

"We should ask that woman whether she saw anything," Becky said.

"We can try it," Flynn agreed. "Half a crown says that she didn't notice, though."

The woman hadn't even noticed them or Brasher's body, although granted their alley was probably too dark for her to see them clearly.

Becky started to answer, then gave a small wordless exclamation and stooped down again to point to something clutched between the fingers of Brasher's right hand. "Look at that. He's holding something."

Flynn bent to look. The dead man's fingers clutched a small scrap of paper, torn at the edges. "Looks like part of a bank note."

"A ten-pound note. You can just make out the marks there." Becky gingerly detached the torn scrap from the dead man's hand and picked it up.

"Shouldn't you leave that for the police?" Flynn asked.

Becky waved that aside. "I can always put it back." She wrinkled her nose. "Does it smell like anything to you?"

Flynn put his nose closer to the torn piece of bank note and inhaled. A musky, powerful aroma tickled in the back of his throat. "Tobacco?" he said after a second.

"That's what I thought, too."

"So maybe our murderer smokes a pipe?"

"Or cigars." Becky's brows drew together as she went on, clearly thinking out loud. "So after Jack left, Brasher telephoned to whoever hired him to kill Eleanor Cavendish. That person told him to come out here for a meeting—probably promised him extra money in exchange for lying low for a while, maybe closing his shop so that the police wouldn't be able to find him if they came looking again?"

"Makes sense," Flynn agreed. "We heard Brasher say on the telephone that whoever he was talking to had better make it worth his while. So he met the man who hired him here, got a fistful of ten-pound notes as payment—and while Brasher was counting them, the other fellow stuck a knife into him."

Becky didn't scare easily, but she shivered. Flynn couldn't blame her. He had a nasty cold feeling crawling the length of his spine, too. "You're saying it was a man who met Brasher here," Becky said. "But it could have been a woman."

Flynn tilted his head. "You think a woman would have had the strength to overpower a big hulking brute like Brasher?"

"That's just the point, though," Becky said. "She wouldn't have had to overpower him. Just distract him long enough that she could catch him off guard." Becky was looking down the alley but her eyes had gone unfocused, as if she were imagining how it all could have happened. "It doesn't take so very much strength to drive a knife into someone, as long as the blade is sharp enough." She looked down at Brasher again for a long moment. Then she said, "Come on. You're right that we need to tell the police about what's happened."

CHAPTER 21: LUCY

"So Becky and Flynn are all right?" I asked Jack.

"Safe, unharmed, and annoyed that they weren't allowed to investigate the alley where Brasher's body was found," Jack said.

While Flynn and Becky were discovering dead bodies, I had paid a visit to Westaway's Employment Agency. The proprietress was something of a dragon in human form, but I had miraculously persuaded her to let me make a copy of the file she had kept on Emma Thompkins. Actually, that the file still existed at all, several years after Emma's retirement from service, had to be a miracle.

I had stopped by Scotland Yard on my way home to see whether Jack was ready to leave for the day and to hear how his visit to Brasher's shop had gone. Now we were walking along the embankment under the glow of the street lamps. Ahead of us in the distance loomed the delicate grey stone spires of Westminster Abbey, while the dark, swiftly moving Thames stretched out alongside.

Jack had just finished telling me about Flynn and Becky's adventures, which on second thought shouldn't have surprised me. Where Flynn and Becky went, mayhem inevitably followed.

"I sent them back to Baker Street to wait for us," Jack said. "And Mrs. Hudson's promised not to let them out of her sight for so much as a second," he added, before I could ask. "Although

I think even Flynn and Becky may have had enough danger for one day."

"I'll believe that only when I see it, but I suppose we can hope. It's unfortunate about Brasher's murder, though." From what I'd seen and heard, his death wasn't exactly a staggering loss to humanity. But he had been our best lead in terms of finding out who had killed Eleanor Cavendish and why.

Jack shrugged. "Like your father says, sometimes a crime scene talks louder than a suspect. We've got Brasher's death to investigate now, and the murderer's bound to have slipped up and left some evidence behind. They always do." He spoke with the quiet, matter-of-fact confidence of a police officer who's investigated countless murders before. "What about your visit to Westaway's?"

"I was able to find the names of all of Emma Thompkins' former employers, going back twenty years," I said. I brought out the slip of paper on which I'd written down the list of names. "Now comes the tedious part—comparing it to lists of Samuel Harley's customers and the guests who stayed in Martin Goodspeed's hotel. I suppose I'll have to find a way to look through a list of George Pennythwaite, KC's clients, too, although that's bound to be fraught with difficulty. I doubt the other partners in his legal firm will take kindly to my rooting through their confidential papers. And I've no idea how the Reverend Wyatt fits in."

"You'll get there." Jack still spoke with calm confidence. "If we're absolutely sure that the two cases are linked, that is?"

He was just being thorough, another trait of an excellent policeman. I nodded. "I'm sure. I know that newspaper cutting about Martin Goodspeed's murder that Eleanor Cavendish was keeping isn't sufficient evidence. But I've got two other reasons for thinking that her death and Lestrade's rash of killings are connected. First, Holmes and I both spotted a man on Baker Street pretending to be a street sweeper. He wasn't Brasher or the other man whom Flynn and Nellie Bly described. He was disguised, waiting on Baker Street, and running *towards* 221B before we even knew that Nellie Bly and Flynn had taken refuge there."

"So he was someone who'd been assigned to keep an eye on the neighbourhood and report on what your father might be doing," Jack said slowly. He paused for a moment to look out over the river. "And he somehow got wind of what Brasher was up to and decided to lend a hand."

"Exactly. And the only case my father has taken lately is this one for Lestrade. If someone has decided to invest in keeping my father under surveillance, it's almost certainly because he's looking into the string of murders."

"And the second reason?" Jack asked. He'd lowered his voice a bit.

"I imagine you've already noticed the second reason." I spoke quietly, too. "Considering that we've stopped here."

"Right." Jack's gaze was still fixed out across the night dark waters of the Thames, as though he were watching the bright yellow lamps on a barge making its way up the river. But I knew he was focused on whatever he could glimpse out of the corner of his eye. I knew, because I was doing exactly the same.

"About a hundred yards back behind us?" Jack murmured. "Tweed coat, cloak, muffler, hat pulled down low over his eyes?"

"Or her eyes. It's hard to tell anything, even whether it's a man or a woman, under that many layers."

The cloak and hat and muffler were what had first drawn my attention to our follower. The August night air was a bit chilly, but not nearly cold enough to warrant wearing quite so many concealing layers. That might have had an innocent explanation—a hypochondriac, deathly afraid of catching a chill. But for the past five minutes, the figure had also been keeping pace with us—slowing and speeding up as we did—while always maintaining the same distance behind.

Now the figure was standing awkwardly beside a street lamp, ostensibly enjoying a view of the river, too.

"So what do we want to do about it?" I asked. I risked a quick, appraising glance in the muffled figure's direction. "There are two of us and only one of him." I was leaning towards the figure's being male. Based on where the top of the head reached on the lamp post, his height had to be nearly six feet, and few women were that tall. "We could probably overpower him if we work together."

One side of Jack's mouth lifted in a brief smile. "True. But I'm not sure that *We could probably overpower him* counts as a plan. Especially if he's armed."

"All right, I suppose. What's your idea?"

Jack grinned and offered me his arm. "He's having such a good time following us. I say we let him keep on with it for a bit."

The area around the embankment was nearly always thronged with pedestrians and other traffic, especially at this hour, when people were hurrying home to supper after a day's work. Jack and I led our mysterious follower up busy streets and down narrower lanes, circled Westminster Cathedral, walked past the National Portrait Gallery, and finally after so many twists and turns that even Holmes might have lost count, we fetched up outside the British Museum.

"Brings back memories," Jack said, as we paused to look up at the marble columned entrance.

"It does." Jack and I had met for the first time just outside the British Museum. I'd been knocked unconscious by a criminal whom my father was investigating, and Jack—who'd been just a patrolling beat constable then—had stopped to find out whether I was dead or merely intoxicated.

"Is our uninvited companion still following us?" I asked.

"Still about a block behind," Jack confirmed. "You have to credit him for perseverance if nothing else."

We hadn't really been trying to lose our mystery follower, despite the circuitous route we'd taken. If we had, he wouldn't still be behind us now; both Jack and I knew how to lose a tail, especially one who wasn't terribly experienced in avoiding being seen. What we had been trying to accomplish was to wear our follower out and frustrate him with the difficulty of keeping us in sight on a succession of busy streets.

Most people, when tired and frustrated, will slip up and get careless. And nothing about our pursuer said that he was experienced in the art of surveillance. People who knew how to blend in and stay anonymous didn't dress as though embarking on a polar expedition.

Jack glanced at me. "Do you have your Ladysmith?"

"I do."

I'd slipped the revolver into my handbag when I left Baker Street. I don't always carry a weapon, but given today's earlier events, I hadn't been willing to risk going out alone without taking suitable precautions.

"Time to embark on phase two?" Jack asked.

"I believe so."

We turned and walked briskly around the side of the British Museum, turning from Great Russell Street onto Montague Street, where we continued our brisk pace until we reached Russell Square Gardens. Then we stepped onto one of the tree-lined paths that criss-crossed the square of parkland. Here, with night having fallen, there were far fewer pedestrians. Jack and I were alone as we stepped behind the towering stone base of the statue of Francis, Duke of Bedford, that graced the park.

We didn't have long to wait. Hurried footsteps approached, slowed, hurried forwards again, then paused once more.

I could picture our follower looking out from under the brim of his hat, peering anxiously in all directions, trying to determine where we could have gone.

He seemed to remain unmoving for an impossibly long time. Long enough that Jack looked at me and grinned again. He didn't say anything, but I knew he was reacting with amusement to my impatience—which he no doubt could sense without *my* having to say anything. Jack, of course, was waiting with perfect, still-muscled control: ready to spring into action at any moment, but at the same time entirely calm.

I rolled my eyes, then stiffened as the footsteps approached the base of the statue once again. He'd be about ten feet away, judging by the sound. Eight feet … seven …

When I estimated that our pursuer was about five feet from us, Jack stepped smoothly out from one side of the statue's base, while I emerged from behind the other.

Jack had already grasped the muffled figure by the collar by the time I was fully out in the open. I was in time to point my revolver at the stranger's chest, though, and say, "Don't move."

But the stranger wasn't struggling in Jack's grip. He stood

motionless, whether frightened or simply dumbfounded, I couldn't tell. Only the narrowest sliver of his face was visible between the muffler that covered his nose and chin and the hat brim that shadowed his eyes. But then he spoke.

"I beg your pardon." His voice was polite and surprisingly educated, with the unmistakable accent that marked him as a member of one of England's oldest—and quite probably wealthiest—families. "I must apologise for troubling you this way, but I wasn't sure where else to turn. I'm quite desperate, you see. You are an associate of Mr. Sherlock Holmes, are you not?"

I didn't lower the revolver, but I did say, "I am."

The stranger let out a shuddering breath. "Thank heavens for that. My name is Daniel Hinchcliff. But you may know me as Derrington."

My brows rose. When I'd pictured confronting our follower, I certainly hadn't anticipated this. "You are the Duke of Derrington?"

The stranger made a bow, taking off his hat in the process. "At your service. I have come to you because I do not know where else to turn."

Jack eyed him. I knew that he was taking in every detail of the stranger's appearance, just as I was. Evaluating the weave of the silk muffler around his neck, the obviously expensive tailoring of his cloak and the quality of his boots. I wouldn't recognise the Duke of Derrington by sight, despite the recent newspaper articles. But I was inclined to believe that this man was who he claimed to be. Anyone could wear expensive clothes and even put on a posh accent, but it was very, very hard to do it convincingly enough and effortlessly enough that you looked as though you were truly born into them.

"Seems like you could have saved yourself some trouble—and shoe leather—by paying a call in the ordinary way," Jack said. "Or by using the telephone rather than following us all around London."

"I'm sorry about that." The duke gave us an apologetic smile. He was a younger man than I'd first thought, certainly no more than forty-five, with sandy hair beginning to turn grey at the temples and an attractive, square-jawed face. His eyes were blue, with lines of good humour gathered around the corners. "I realise the melodrama of my approach. But I felt that I had to find a way of contacting you in absolute secret. Without any of my household—family or servants—getting wind of what I was about. Not to mention the newspapers that seem to dog my footsteps wherever I go."

I lowered the revolver. The longer we stood here, the more likely it was that someone would happen to walk by and see me holding a man at gunpoint. And if we were wrong about the duke, Jack could still overpower him.

"What can we do for you, Your Grace?" I asked.

The duke waved a hand. "Please. Don't bother with titles. I had to tell you who I was so that I could make you understand the need for secrecy. But I have very few opportunities for informal conversation."

Despite his tailored clothes and polished manners, there was something almost forlorn about the way he said it.

"Go on," I told him. "What is it that you need from Sherlock Holmes?"

The duke drew an unsteady breath and passed a hand across his eyes before answering. "It's my wife, you see. Aline."

He stopped and was silent so long that I finally asked, "Is your wife the Duchess unwell?"

A spasm of pain twisted the duke's face and he laughed harshly. "I only wish she were. No. No, she is not unwell, unless you define the term to include diseases of the mind and spirit." He heaved a breath and squared his shoulders as though bracing for an unpleasant task, then met my gaze. "I believe that my wife is guilty of the murders of at least four people. And that she is putting on this wretched coronation ball as part of a plot to assassinate our king."

CHAPTER 22: LUCY

"It all started when I missed some money from the top drawer in my desk," the Duke of Derrington began.

He had, after some persuasion, consented to return to Baker Street with us and, in the interests of secrecy, be smuggled in through the back door. Introductions to Holmes and Watson had already been made. Now Watson sat in his usual armchair, while my father stood by the mantel, listening as the duke began his story.

"I always keep a sum of ready cash in my desk," Derrington went on. "For the running of the household and any incidental expenses that may crop up during the month."

Night had fully fallen outside, and the sitting room curtains were closed against the darkness. A fire leapt and crackled in the grate, the noise covering the occasional rustle from Flynn and Becky, who were, I was certain, listening at the keyhole on the landing outside the door. Holmes no doubt knew that they were there, as well, and so did Jack, but none of us had bothered to order them back downstairs to the kitchen. Some battles weren't worth fighting, and besides, at least this way we knew exactly where they were and what they were doing.

Derrington wrapped both hands around the cup of tea that Mrs. Hudson had brought for him, displaying a gold signet ring on his left hand. He kept speaking. "I always keep the same amount. That is to say, at the beginning of each month, I always withdraw enough from the bank to ensure that is the amount I have on hand. Then, whatever portion of the money has been spent throughout the month, I withdraw the required amount to return the balance to two hundred and fifty pounds."

He was stalling. I recognised the technique from other witnesses whom we had interviewed: the tendency to spend time over-explaining trivial details in order to put off having to reveal whatever part of the story they were dreading having to say out loud.

Holmes evidently thought the same, because he said, with more patience than usual, "And you say some of this money went missing?"

"Two weeks ago. Yes." The duke's throat bobbed as he swallowed. He raised the cup of tea to his lips, then lowered it again without actually drinking. "I realised that I had one hundred pounds which was unaccounted for. A smaller amount and I might have thought that I had simply made an error in counting, or paid out the money to cover a bill which I had forgotten to note down. But such a large sum—" he shook his head. "My first thought, of course, was that perhaps one of the servants had taken it. But the drawer to my desk is kept locked, and only I am in possession of the key. Also, my servants are one and all old family retainers, all of them intensely loyal. None have ever given me the slightest cause to believe them dishonest before."

Holmes tamped tobacco from the Persian slipper down in his pipe. "Go on."

"I asked my wife whether she had taken the money. At first she denied it." The duke swallowed again. "But then, when I pressed her on the matter, she broke down and confessed. I was shocked.

I give Aline a very generous allowance, nor have I ever balked at paying her dressmaker's bills or refused to buy anything that has caught her fancy. Before our marriage, my wife was the heiress of a wealthy American tobacco industrialist. She grew up accustomed to luxury. I understand that, and I have never denied her anything that she has wished for. I asked her what reason she could possibly have had to take such a large sum—why she had not simply come to me and asked me to buy her whatever it was for which she needed the hundred pounds."

The duke paused, his eyes on the carpet. Then he seemed to force himself to look up. "Mr. Holmes, she could give me no adequate explanation. All I got in answer to my question was a tissue of lies that would not have persuaded a child of five. She claimed first that she had a friend who had run into debt gambling at bridge, and that she had made her friend a gift of the money to settle the debt. I responded with no small degree of surprise. Aline has many acquaintances, but few close friends. I could not imagine one for whom she would be willing to steal from me. I pressed her for a name. And her story changed. She claimed that this friend must remain anonymous, because it was not after all a matter of gambling debts, but blackmail. The friend had written compromising letters to a man who was not her husband, and now this man was threatening to reveal all unless he was paid a sum of one hundred pounds in cash."

Holmes took the pipe from between his teeth. "I take it that you were skeptical of that story, as well?"

"Indeed. Not that such affairs are by any means unheard of in the circles in which Aline and I move. Indeed, they are regrettably commonplace. But all of my wife's friends are ..."

He paused and seemed to search for words.

"Likewise accustomed to a life of luxury?" I suggested.

The duke's smile was both rueful and deprecating. "It sounds rather pretentious to put it that way. But I must admit that is the case. Any friend of Aline's would be bound to have jewellery which she could easily sell or pawn in exchange for money, if need be. If she were truly desperate to keep the affair for which she was being blackmailed a secret, why bring another party into it by requesting Aline's help?"

"And did you express these doubts to your wife?" Holmes asked.

"I did not."

The duke stopped and was silent. At last Holmes said, "Since I can think of a wide variety of explanations for your wife's behaviour that fall short of an accusation of murder, I assume that there is more to the story, Your Grace?"

"There is." Derrington spoke heavily. "Mr. Holmes, I am not proud of what I have done. But it seemed to me my only course of action if I wished to learn the true purpose for which Aline had purloined the money from my desk. I pretended to accept her explanation at face value. Then, when next she left the house, I followed her. This would have been somewhere about ten days ago."

"You followed her yourself?" Jack asked. He had been quiet until now, simply sitting beside me on the couch and listening to Derrington's account. But I knew what he was thinking: if the duke had employed the same techniques while following his wife as he had done tonight while following us, then either Aline knew quite well what her husband had done, or else she was remarkably unobservant.

"I did." Derrington's shoulders sagged. "I did not know what to think, but I suppose in the back of my mind I had suspicions that it was my wife who had either run into gambling debts or become the victim of a blackmailer."

"Have you known your wife to gamble before this?" Holmes asked.

"No. She finds card games in general tedious, and even when we have travelled to the casinos at Monaco, she has had little interest in the roulette wheel or any other games of chance."

"And your marriage has been a happy one?"

Again a quick twist of pain passed across Derrington's expression. "I have always believed so. Until two weeks ago, I should have said that we had no secrets from one another at all."

Holmes inclined his head. "Go on. You followed your wife. What then?"

"Imagine my shock and surprise, Mr. Holmes, when I saw her enter a butcher's shop."

Holmes was more adept than anyone I knew at concealing his private thoughts. But I still caught his slight start of surprise, followed by a sharpening of the interest with which he was regarding our visitor. "A butcher's shop, Your Grace?"

"I know." Derrington gestured helplessly. "It sounds absurd, does it not? What has my wife to do with such a place? We have a cook and a housekeeper who between them see to all the ordering of our meals—and from places of far better quality and reputation than a dingy, mean-looking place on Blackfriars Lane. I could not imagine what my wife could be about! The place was small enough that I did not dare to follow her inside. She would have been bound to see me. But I crept around to the side of the shop where there was an open window."

I nodded. Flynn and Becky had already given us an account of listening outside that same window.

"My wife was conversing with a man whom I presumed to be the proprietor of the shop," Derrington went on. "I could see him through the window: a big, bald-headed, rough-looking fellow. I could not overhear everything that was said between him and Aline. But one scrap of conversation reached me quite plainly: Aline said, 'The man's name is Martin Goodspeed.'"

CHAPTER 23: WATSON

At the duke's words, even Holmes's brows edged upwards a fraction. "I see. And you overheard nothing else?"

"Nothing of value. I thought that Aline and this butcher fellow seemed to be haggling over the price for something—although the price of what, I could not at the time imagine." The duke stared into his teacup for a moment, then went on, "I returned home in considerable agitation of mind. On the surface, there was nothing illegal in the errand which I had observed my wife perform. Odd, certainly, but not overtly sinister. But I could not rest easy all the same. Something about the whole affair seemed to fill me with the deepest sense of apprehension and alarm."

"Did you confront your wife about what you had seen?" Holmes asked.

"I did not. Perhaps I should have done. But I was certain that she would not tell me the truth as to what she had been about, and I thought that I would stand a better chance of learning the real facts of the affair if she still believed me to be ignorant."

"And you took no steps to find this Martin Goodspeed of whom you heard your wife speak?"

"I did go so far as to look in the telephone directory under 'G'. But in a city the size of London, do you know how many Goodspeeds are listed? And the directories only give a man's surname, not his Christian one. Besides, I had no assurance that this Martin Goodspeed was even on the telephone, when the majority of Londoners are not. Or that he even lived within the metropolis of London. I myself had never heard the name, nor had I ever heard my wife mention him, of that I was certain. But beyond that ..." Derrington spread his hands in a gesture of helplessness.

"I quite understand," Holmes said. "And were you illumined when you saw the notice of Martin Goodspeed's death in the newspapers several days ago?"

 But Derrington shook his head. "No. I know now that the fellow is dead, of course. But at the time, I had no idea. I seldom read the newspapers, beyond the racing pages and perhaps a glance at the front headlines for stories relating to my business interests. And the death of a middle-aged hotelier was hardly front-page news material. No, after my wife's visit to Brasher's Butcher's Shop, I was uneasy, as I say. But for the next day or two, we settled down into a state that I can best describe as the calm that comes before a storm. My wife had conceived the idea of hosting a coronation ball at the Savoy, in order to facilitate a business enterprise that currently engages me."

"Enterprise?" Holmes sounded disinterested, though I knew from the glitter in his grey eyes that this was far from the truth.

"A business merger, so to speak. An understanding between the major tobacco companies of America and those of Britain. It will be profitable for both groups, and for the economies of both nations."

"How would this be affected by a coronation ball?" I asked.

"Americans frequently feel slighted by British aristocracy, as you no doubt are aware," he said. "Inviting all those involved to mingle at what would be one of the elite occasions would induce a feeling of satisfaction, and prompt cooperation. At least, that is how Aline explained it. She has spoken to the wives of the Americans and they are most eager to attend. She thinks the plan will succeed in calming what might be troubled waters during the final stages of negotiations."

"Do you?" asked Holmes.

"I think it can do no harm. Provided that the ball succeeds, of course. If it fails, well, of course then there will be disappointment among my American colleagues, which would make the negotiations more difficult."

"And was your wife optimistic about the event?"

"Until recently, she seemed quite happy and cheerful. It was only once or twice that I would catch what I thought was an odd expression on her face, when she was unaware that she was being observed. But, of course, that may be hindsight. Despite my sense of foreboding, I had some hopes that whatever had been the matter was behind us, and that my wife and I could move forward together with a return to normalcy between us."

The duke's brow furrowed, and he seemed to gather his thoughts before going on. "The first inkling I had that such was not to be the case was three days ago. I had gone out for a ride in Hyde Park, as is my custom on fine mornings. My wife typically joins me. She is an avid rider, as well. But on this particular morning, she claimed to be feeling a trifle unwell, and so remained at home to take breakfast in bed. Upon my return from the park, I thought to look in on her to see how she was feeling." Derrington paused. "Upon entering my wife's room, I found her kneeling before the fireplace, feeding a sheet of paper to the flames."

"Extraordinary," Holmes remarked.

"It was—it was indeed. I did not know what to think!" the duke said. "The mere act was odd enough, but when she saw me, she gave a start of surprise and stared at me with a look of the utmost guilt upon her face before thrusting the paper deeper into the flames."

"Did you ask her what the paper contained?"

"I did. She said that it was a letter from a newspaper reporter. A woman by the name of Cavendish, who was requesting an interview with her. Aline said the Cavendish woman had written a nasty, spiteful column in a society gossip magazine about Aline's upcoming coronation ball, and then had the cheek to ask Aline for an interview."

"A plausible explanation," Holmes said.

"Indeed. Were it not for the other events of these past two weeks, I might have believed Aline to be speaking the truth. As it was, I left my wife's room in considerable agitation of mind. I determined to go out for a walk, in an attempt to calm my nerves. But scarcely had I set foot outside my front door when I observed a carriage driving past." The duke paused again to draw a steadying breath. "Mr. Holmes, in the driver's seat was the butcher—the great, rough-looking fellow with whom I had seen my wife conversing a few days previously."

"Another extraordinary development."

"You may well say so." Derrington took out a handkerchief and mopped his forehead. "The carriage was driving around the side of the house, as though it had come from the alley that runs between our row of houses and the mews behind. My wife's dressing room, I may say, overlooks that same alley."

"I see. You believe that your wife had some sort of communication with Mr. Brasher by way of this window?"

"I thought it possible—I … I hardly know what I thought. I felt as though I were trapped in a fantastical nightmare! But I determined to follow this man Brasher to whatever his destination might be. My horse had not yet been rubbed down and put away after my morning ride. Accordingly, I mounted and was in time to follow the carriage as it moved towards Hyde Park."

"Was Brasher aware of your pursuit?" Holmes asked.

"I believe that I can say with some degree of certainty that he was not—for reasons which will become plain in a moment." A twist of something like sickness crossed Derrington's expression as he went on. "I followed Brasher into the park to a secluded spot near Kensington Road. He stopped the carriage near to a thick clump of trees, climbed down from the driver's seat, and removed what looked like a large, unwieldy bundle of clothes from inside, which he deposited behind the trees." Derrington swallowed. "It was as he was carrying the object that I saw that it was not, in fact, a mere bundle of clothes. It was a body—the body of an elderly woman."

He paused, clearly expecting us to react with shock, but no one spoke. Jack and Lucy remained on the couch, unmoving. Holmes still stood by the hearth, one hand resting on the mantle.

Derrington gave Holmes a puzzled frown. "Mr. Holmes, you do not appear to be surprised by what I have told you."

"I was made aware," Holmes replied, "of a rash of killings that have either occurred or been discovered in Hyde Park. Including the murder of an elderly former lady's maid by the name of Emma Thompkins."

Derrington nodded jerkily. "Thompkins. Yes. That was the name. Not that I knew it at the time, you understand. I was dumbstruck—frozen in horror as I observed Brasher leave the body and then return to his carriage. I suppose the whole business had not taken more than a minute or two at most."

"And you did not report the matter to the police?" Holmes asked.

There was no judgment in his tone, but the colour rose in Derrington's face all the same. "To my eternal shame, I did not, Mr. Holmes. You must understand that I was watching from quite a distance—screened by a row of trees, so that Brasher would not see me. I stood there, deliberating on what to do. On the one hand, my duty to report what I had seen to the proper authorities was clear. On the other …" His voice grew husky and he cleared his throat.

"You had your wife to think of, of course," I said. "It was a wrenching position for any man to be in."

Derrington threw me a grateful look. "You understand, I see. I have loved and esteemed my wife for nearly twenty years of marriage. Despite my suspicions, I could not quite bring myself to cast her into the middle of a police investigation. At least, I could not in that moment. As I stood there, wrestling with my own conscience, I observed a pair of bicyclists heading in the direction of the shrubbery where I had seen Brasher leave the woman's body. I knew at least that she would be found and the crime reported." The duke exhaled a heavy breath, then squared his shoulders. "Blame me, Mr. Holmes, as you will—as indeed I blame myself—but I left the park and returned home. But this time, I was not content to let the matter drop."

"No?"

"No. My wife had gone out when I arrived home. She told her maid that she was doing some shopping. Whether that was actually the case, I have my doubts, but I do not know for certain. I know only that her absence gave me the opportunity for which I sought. I entered my wife's room and conducted a search of the ashes in the fireplace."

"And was your search successful?" Holmes inquired.

"That depends upon what you mean by *successful*." Derrington's lips tightened in a pained grimace. "If you are asking whether I found something, the answer is that I did. I found this." Reaching into his pocket, Derrington produced a scrap of charred paper on which a few scrawled words were just barely legible. He handed it across to Holmes, who read it aloud.

"Die Krönung." He paused and looked up. "That is German."

"I know. The words mean, *the coronation*," Derrington said. "I do not speak German myself, but I looked them up."

Holmes returned his attention to the paper and continued to read the partially charred words. "*König muss sterben*. The king must die."

"I know that, too," Derrington said He looked wretchedly unhappy, his shoulders slumped and his head bowed.

There was silence in the room until at last Holmes said, "We will save time, Your Grace, if we speak plainly. You fear that your wife is enmeshed in a German plot, and that the plot concerns the coronation and threatens the life of the king?"

Derrington's head lifted. "Believe me, Mr. Holmes, if there is an innocent explanation that would account for both the words you have just read and my wife's strange behaviour, no one would be a happier man than I. But what other explanation can there be? My wife has no German friends, no one who would be corresponding with her in that language. And even if she had, why the secrecy? Why burn the letter in order to keep it from my eyes? Why visit this ruffian Brasher and pay him to … to …"

The duke stopped, unable to complete the thought.

"To kill both Martin Goodspeed and Emma Thompkins and deposit their bodies in Hyde Park?" Holmes finished for him.

"More than just those two." Derrington's tall frame sagged again. "After witnessing Brasher deposit the elderly woman's body in the park, I searched the evening edition of the papers. I wanted to know what the police had made of the case and whether the woman's identity had been learned. I found a newspaper article mentioning the woman's death and giving her name as Miss Emma Thompkins. The article implied that her death might not otherwise have been newsworthy, save that four other murder victims had been discovered in Hyde Park within the past week. The newspaper hinted at all the usual sensational explanations, as you might expect—another Jack the Ripper, or a return of that same fiend. But the bare facts were nonetheless plain, and were damning enough."

Holmes was silent for a long moment, his eyes half-closed. Then at last he said, "The facts, as you have narrated them, certainly paint a very convincing picture. Save for one missing piece: do you know what motive your wife can have had for orchestrating the murders of the six Hyde Park victims?"

"Six?" Derrington's head lifted. "I thought that there were only five, counting Emma Thompkins."

"Six. Another victim was discovered just yesterday. A newspaper reporter by the name of Cavendish. The same woman, in fact, who penned the disparaging lines about your wife's upcoming coronation ball."

As he listened, the duke's expression changed from shock to horror to a kind of miserable resignation. His posture sagged once again. "You have your motive, then."

"Perhaps in the case of Miss Cavendish, yes. Although an insult in the society gossip pages is not generally taken as cause for murder. But as for the other murder victims … it remains unclear what motive your wife would have had for wishing the deaths of as disparate a collection of people as a retired lady's maid, an elderly shoemaker, a lawyer, and a clergyman. Or how persons from those walks of life could possibly be embroiled in a plot to assassinate the sovereign."

Derrington gestured helplessly. "Mr. Holmes, I am as baffled as you are. And yet the evidence is plain. What else am I to believe?"

"What else indeed, Your Grace." Holmes's expression, though tinged with grimness, was also not without sympathy. "For answers, I believe that we must speak to the duchess herself."

"But—"

Holmes waved away Derrington's incipient protest before the duke could say any more. "I do not propose to allow your wife to know that she is under investigation. Can you think of a pretext which would allow us to interview her?"

Lucy spoke out before Derrington could offer anything in the way of suggestions. "I could pay her a call as a newspaper reporter—one wishing to write a more favourable piece for the society pages than the one written by Miss Cavendish."

Holmes glanced at the duke. "Do you think your wife would be amenable to giving such an interview?"

"Yes. Yes, I believe that she would."

Holmes nodded. "Good, then. The hour grows late to accomplish such a visit tonight. Tomorrow, though, ought to be soon enough."

"Are you sure?" Anxiety creased Derrington's forehead.

"Surely we ought not waste any time, with the ball being held tomorrow evening—"

Again, Holmes interrupted. "I can assure you, Your Grace, that Mr. Brasher will commit no more murders. But we must have certainty, and if there truly is to be an attempt on the life of the King ..."

Holmes let his voice trail off, but the duke grasped the implication. "We would have to cancel the ball, of course," he said, "if that were needed to prevent an attack. My American colleagues would be disappointed, but they would no doubt understand that higher forces were at work."

"Whereas," Holmes added, "if they were present during an assassination attempt, whether successful or not, your colleagues would come under suspicion and the effect on your business relationships would be disastrous."

"Do you know if the King will attend the ball?" I asked.

The duke still looked worried, but he gave a dubious inclination of the head. "No."

"Go home, then," Holmes said. "Get whatever rest you may, and Lucy will call upon your wife in Belgravia first thing tomorrow morning."

CHAPTER 24: BECKY

August 15

Derrington House was a huge, three-story mansion built of white marble, with white columns supporting a terraced balcony that ran across the whole front of the building. If Becky hadn't known any better, she would have assumed that any place this big had to be a hotel, and if Flynn were here, he would have said that you could practically smell the money. Becky might not have put it quite like that, but she did wonder, looking up at the place, what the duke and duchess did with so many rooms.

"They don't even have any children," she murmured out loud.

Lucy turned to look down at her. "No, they don't. Although according to the duke, they do have a young niece of his staying with them at the moment."

"Is that why you let me come along?" Not that Becky was complaining. If Lucy hadn't agreed to let her visit Derrington House, she would have been wracking her brains to think of a way to get here anyway.

Lucy started up the marble front steps. "I let you come along because it seemed unlikely that you'd be kidnapped, shot at—or forced to jump off a roof to avoid being kidnapped or shot at—during our visit here. But also because I thought you might be able to get the Duke of Derrington's niece to talk to you while I'm interviewing the duchess."

Their ring at the front doorbell was answered promptly by a stiffly upright, grey-haired butler who informed Lucy that Lady Aline was expecting her, and led the way into a sitting room that opened off the marble tiled entrance hall.

It was a pretty room, Becky decided, less fussy and grand than she would have expected based on the outside of the house. The walls were painted a cool, pale green, and the furniture was made in the simple style that reminded Becky of the drawings she'd seen in history books about ancient Greece. Curtains patterned with leaves and birds hung at the windows.

Still standing as though someone had replaced his spine with a metal rod, the butler cleared his throat and announced, "Miss Lucy James to see you, Your Grace."

Since Lucy was pretending to be a newspaper reporter, she hadn't used her married name.

A blonde-haired woman looked up from the couch where she'd been sitting, poring over what looked like note cards that were all spread out before her on the coffee table.

"Oh yes, the reporter from *The Daily Telegraph*, isn't that right?" she looked at Lucy.

Lady Aline, Duchess of Derrington, was a tall, pretty woman who looked as though she belonged in the pleasant, green-painted room. Her high, broad forehead and oval-shaped face gave her an intellectual air. She wasn't very young; Becky would guess that she was somewhere close to forty. But her features were still mostly unlined. Her hair was a deep shade of golden blond, and she had hazel brown eyes framed by thick black lashes. She was wearing a pale blue chiffon tea gown trimmed with lace at the cuffs and collar, and she was smiling as if she were genuinely happy to see them.

Her eyes moved from Lucy to Becky, and she smiled again. "And who do we have here?"

"This is Becky, a young cousin of mine who's visiting me while her parents are travelling." Returning the duchess's smile, Lucy put a hand on Becky's shoulder. She was speaking as if she'd been born here in London, rather than letting her real accent, the one that marked her as American, come through. "She wants to be a newspaper reporter herself someday, so I said that she could come along with me today. I hope that's all right with you, Your Grace," Lucy added.

"Oh yes, of course."

If what her husband suspected was true, then Lady Aline was guilty of ordering Brasher to murder six people. And what about Brasher himself? For a second, Becky felt a bit queasy as she remembered the knife sticking out of Brasher's chest and his wide, surprised-looking eyes, and wondered if Lady Aline was somehow responsible for that, too.

But it was hard to picture the woman in front of them murdering anyone. Her voice was sweet and warm, and she gestured for them both to sit down on the settee opposite her own.

"It's always nice to see a bright young face," the duchess said with another smile at Becky. "I'm afraid we're terribly dull here. Isn't that right, Emmeline?"

She turned to a girl who was sitting in one of the needlepoint chairs near to the window.

"My husband's niece, Emmeline Hinchcliffe," she told Lucy. "She's come to stay with us for the coronation ball we're holding. But I'm afraid that till then we'll be boring her horribly."

When Lucy had mentioned the duke's niece, Becky had pictured someone closer to her own age. Instead she saw a young woman of nineteen or twenty with silvery blond hair and a face that would have been pretty if she hadn't had what looked like a permanently petulant look stamped across her features.

She was flipping through the pages in a lady's fashion magazine, and she barely even glanced up at the duchess's words. She also didn't bother to answer Lady Aline or acknowledge the introductions. But she did give Lucy a curious glance.

"What newspaper did you say you were from?"

Lucy smiled. Becky had seen her intimidate hardened murderers, but she was also very good at looking like someone you would immediately want for a friend.

"*The Daily Telegraph.*"

"Oh." Emmeline didn't return the smile, just studied Lucy more closely, her eyes narrowing a bit. "I thought I knew the names of all the reporters who write for the *Telegraph's* society pages. I don't remember ever seeing your name."

Lucy had far too much experience with playing a part to let someone like Emmeline throw her off-stride. "I use a pseudonym, of course," she said smoothly. "Nearly all of us do, in the newspaper business. We wouldn't have very many friends otherwise. Everyone we met would worry that we were gathering material for a story."

"Of course," Lady Aline said. "Now—"

Emmeline interrupted before she could go on. "What do you think of these for the bridesmaid dresses, Aunt Aline?"

She held up a page in the fashion magazine she'd been looking at, one that showed a drawing of a tall, willowy woman dressed in a rose-coloured taffeta gown. The dress was pretty if you liked that sort of thing, Becky had to admit, but the expression of annoyance that crossed Lady Aline's face at the interruption was decidedly not. She only looked annoyed for a second or two, though, before she managed to wipe all trace of the look off her face.

Smiling once more, the duchess gave Lucy an apologetic glance. "You'll have to excuse us. Emmeline is engaged to be married to young Lord Stuart Kildare next month. Which means we're simply up to our eyeballs in wedding planning at the moment, and of course shopping for Emmeline's trousseau."

"And you're hosting the coronation ball, as well," Lucy said. "That must be quite an undertaking."

"It is, of course," Lady Aline agreed. "I wasn't really anxious to take on the planning of another event, but my husband was so eager to celebrate the king's return to health. That's what I was working at when you came in—trying to choose the menu cards for the supper tables." She gestured to the squares of paper spread out before her.

If Lucy was surprised to hear that Lady Aline's story didn't at all match up to the duke's, she didn't show it. Before she could ask another question, though, Emmeline huffed out an exasperated breath and said, rattling the fashion magazine, "The dresses, Aunt Aline? What do you think of them?"

This time, Lady Aline didn't look so much annoyed as tired, as if she'd not only exhausted her patience but she'd also given up all hope that Emmeline would improve. She turned and looked at the drawing of the woman in rose taffeta. "Very nice, dear. But if you mean to have Magdalena Nicol as one of your bridesmaids, the pink colour will clash with her red hair."

"I hadn't thought of that. I suppose that's true. And of course Magdalena will see that I'm never invited to another ball or supper party again if I don't have her for one of my bridesmaids." Looking even more sullen, Emmeline tossed the illustration aside, paused for a second to admire the huge diamond ring on her left hand, and then picked up another fashion magazine from the stack by her chair.

"I'm sorry," Lady Aline said to Lucy. "As I said, we're positively drowning in wedding details at the moment. But we needn't bore you with all of that. Can I offer you tea or some other refreshment?"

"Oh no, please don't trouble yourself," Lucy said. "I don't want to take up too much of your time when you're in the midst of such a busy season. And I know our readers will be so interested to hear all about the upcoming wedding. If it's all right to mention your engagement?" she asked Emmeline.

Emmeline had opened up her magazine, but at that question her head jerked up and she gave Lucy a suspicious look. "What kind of article were you thinking of writing?"

"Oh, just a short human-interest piece about the flowers you've chosen, the menu for the wedding breakfast, that sort of thing."

"I suppose that would be all right," Emmeline said grudgingly.

"Wonderful." Lucy was also very good—when she wanted to be—at ignoring other people's rudeness. She smiled as sweetly as though Emmeline had just given her a birthday gift and said, "Perhaps we can talk for a few minutes after I've finished speaking to your aunt. For now, though." Lucy turned back to Lady Aline. "Do you think you could give me the background information on you and the duke? How you met, how long you've been married?"

"I—well, I suppose." Lady Aline looked somewhat taken aback. "But surely that doesn't have anything to do with the coronation ball?"

"Oh, readers always like to have the full picture—or what they think is the full picture. They want to feel that they really know you," Lucy said.

"I see. Well." For the first time since they'd arrived at Derrington House, Becky thought that Lady Aline looked less than her usual poised self. She seemed almost uncomfortable. But then she gathered herself and went on, "I … well, there's not very much to tell. I grew up in Kentucky, and lived there until I was seventeen. My father was a horse breeder, and he also raised tobacco. That's how he and my husband met. Daniel was in America buying up contracts for tobacco supply."

Becky got up from the sofa and went across the room to sit down next to Emmeline. "Would you mind if I looked at your magazines?" she asked in a whisper.

Emmeline shrugged, but at least she didn't outright refuse. Becky picked one of them up and tried to look interested in the pages and pages of lady's fashionable walking suits and tea gowns and evening ensembles, all while trying to think up a plan for getting Emmeline to talk to her.

"That's a lovely ring," she murmured.

It was big, at any rate. Becky couldn't remember ever having seen a bigger diamond. It looked a bit like a lump of rock salt on Emmeline's finger. But she'd picked the right opening for a conversation, because Emmeline actually smiled just a bit and said, "Yes, isn't it?"

With half an ear, Becky listened to Lucy and the duchess's conversation, wondering how Lucy was going to work the Hyde Park murder victims into the conversation. So far, she seemed to be still focusing on what Lady Aline had said about her upbringing.

"So you're American, then?" Lucy brought out a notepad and pencil and wrote something down. "How interesting, I hadn't realised."

Lady Aline tucked a loose strand of hair behind her ear. "Yes. I went to boarding school in Paris, though. That's where I learned to speak without the American accent."

"And was that before you met your husband or afterwards?"

"Oh. After. Daniel is an avid rider and hunter, and so was my father. They became friends, and Daniel visited our house often. Of course, I had no thought of marriage at that time, I was so young. But I thought him very handsome."

"How romantic!" Lucy made another mark on her notepad. "But then your father sent you away to school?"

"At Lady Claudine's in Paris. Yes, that's right. Of course, I was thrilled at the opportunity."

"She's lying," Emmeline said under her breath.

"What?" For a second, Becky was certain that she hadn't heard right.

But Emmeline jerked her shoulders again and said, still in the same soundless murmur, "Well, she's not telling the whole truth, anyway. My mother met a woman who was at school with Aunt Aline years ago. She and her husband were on holiday in Baden-Baden, where my father always goes every winter for his gout, and my mother happened to strike up an acquaintance with her. Penelope Travers was her name. Well, according to Penelope, Aunt Aline didn't want to go off to boarding school in Paris at all."

"Really? Why did she go, then?" Becky whispered back.

Emmeline cast a quick glance in her aunt's direction and lowered her voice even more. "She'd been mixed up with some local boy who worked on her father's plantations—I don't know his name, but of course he was quite unsuitable."

By which Emmeline probably just meant, *poor*. But Becky didn't say that out loud.

"Aunt Aline's father was absolutely furious," Emmeline went on. "He insisted that she break things off and shipped her over to Paris straight away to get her away from the local boy."

Becky studied Lady Aline's delicate, pretty face. She'd come here only thinking about how they were going to get proof that Lady Aline was guilty of getting Nellie Bly's friend killed. But right at this moment, she found herself feeling almost sorry for the duchess.

She had missed the last part of whatever Lady Aline and Lucy had been saying to one another, but she must have been telling the story of how she and the duke had married, because she said, "My father had inherited land, in Carolina and in Virginia and Pennsylvania, and the Pennsylvania land included mineral rights. He used to worry a great deal over what would happen to all his holdings when he was gone, since he didn't have a son to take over the running of the business. Only me. He wasn't in the best of health, you see. He had heart trouble. So he was quite pleased when Daniel asked his permission to marry me. Father knew that I would be in good hands and that he could leave the land and business holdings to Daniel in his will. Daniel, as I said, understood the business side of things, because he was a tobacco industrialist himself, although his plantations were all in Jamaica. He had already suggested to my father that they form an alliance, of sorts. So it was a happy ending all around."

Lady Aline's expression didn't alter as she said it, her softly composed voice didn't show the slightest bit of regret or sadness.

But Becky still had to clamp her mouth shut to avoid saying that it sounded to her as though Lady Aline's father had bribed the duke into marrying her. And as though the duke had been perfectly content to be bought.

"It must have been a great weight off your father's mind to know that you were so well provided for," Lucy agreed.

Only because Becky knew her well, could she tell that Lucy's private thoughts were much more along the lines of Becky's own.

"So you were married shortly after you left Lady Claudine's?" Lucy asked.

"Yes. The wedding was in Paris. My father sailed to France so that he could attend. And then we left on our honeymoon."

"How lovely!" Lucy made another note in her book. "Where did you and His Grace go?"

"To Italy. And then to the Caribbean. Daniel wanted to show me his estates. That was when—" Lady Aline's voice faltered. "That was when we received word that my father had died. His heart had finally given out."

"Oh, I'm terribly sorry," Lucy said. "What a dreadful way to lose him."

"Yes. I suppose it was." Lady Aline looked away for a moment. Her voice had lost colour, sounding almost toneless. But then, a lot of people sounded that way when they were trying not to cry or give away how they were really feeling.

Becky was so wrapped up in listening to Lucy and the duchess that she didn't even realise that Emmeline was speaking to her again until Emmeline poked her in the arm and made an irritated hissing sound.

"I'm sorry. Did you say something?" Becky asked.

Emmeline's temper hadn't been improved by being ignored.

She gave Becky a vexed look, but then she whispered, "I *said*, 'How much can you trust your cousin to actually write a favourable newspaper piece about Aunt Aline?'"

"Lucy wouldn't break a promise," Becky said. "And she would never write a nasty article about Lady Aline, I'm sure."

She wasn't likely to write any kind of article at all, but Becky wasn't about to mention that.

"All right." Emmeline sounded both relieved and sceptical, as if she didn't entirely believe Becky but was hoping to be convinced. "She'd just better not, that's all."

"Really? Why?"

"Because Stuart was terribly angry about the first article. The one that hinted that Aunt Aline's good breeding and manners weren't what they should be. He thought it might reflect badly on him, because he and I are engaged. Another article along those lines—and in the *Daily Telegraph*?" Emmeline shuddered. "I don't know what he might do, I really don't. What if he were to break off our engagement?"

If he did, Becky thought privately that Emmeline would have had a lucky escape. But she didn't say that out loud, either. Actually, it sounded to her as though Emmeline and Lord Stuart—whoever he was—thoroughly deserved each other.

"Do you remember your aunt and uncle's wedding?" she asked instead.

Emmeline shook her head. "I was only about a year old at the time. My mother still talks about it, though. She was angry with Uncle Daniel for running off to Paris and getting married without even bringing Aunt Aline to meet our family first. Her mother—my grandmother—was furious, as well. My mother says she refused to even call on Aline for more than a year after the wedding."

"But they came around eventually?" Becky asked.

"Well, I suppose. Mother and grandmother like Aunt Aline well enough now."

"How lucky for her." This time, Becky didn't quite manage to catch herself before saying it out loud. But luckily for *her*, Emmeline didn't appear to notice the sarcasm in Becky's tone.

"They were probably relieved that he was safely married to a woman of good breeding. Even if she is American." Emmeline lowered her voice. "Uncle Daniel was quite wild in his youth, or so I've heard. At one time, they were afraid that he was going to marry a bar maid. Or maybe she was an actress. Some perfectly impossible profession, at any rate."

"Impossible," Becky echoed.

This time, Emmeline gave her a suspicious glance, but Becky countered it with a look of wide-eyed innocence.

She hesitated, wondering whether to risk asking another question. She didn't want Emmeline to get suspicious, but she also didn't want to let Lucy down by wasting this opportunity to learn something.

"Did you and your aunt go to the Duchess of Marlboro's luncheon party Wednesday?" she asked.

"The Duchess of Marlboro's?" Emmeline frowned.

"Yes." Becky had chosen the first name she'd thought of from the copy of Burke's Peerage that Mr. Holmes had. She braced herself for Emmeline to say that the Duchess of Marlboro wasn't even in London right now, much less giving luncheons.

But instead Emmeline's cheeks flushed a deeper shade of pink and her eyes narrowed. "I *knew* that wretched Magdalena Nicol didn't like me! She probably saw to it that I wasn't invited. Just wait until I see her again."

Becky felt a small pang of guilt for causing trouble for the unknown Magdalena. Then again, if Miss Nicol was anything like Emmeline, feeling guilty really wasn't necessary.

"So you didn't go?" she asked.

"No! We had an unutterably dull afternoon." Emmeline's cheeks were still flushed with temper. "My uncle was at his club, and Aunt Aline went out riding, so I was stuck here all on my own."

Out riding.

Becky came instantly alert. Maybe this wasn't going to be a wasted opportunity after all. Could she safely ask where Aunt Aline had gone riding on the day Miss Cavendish had been murdered? The questions sprang into her mind. *Oh, really? Riding? I love riding, don't you? Is it Hyde Park where your aunt rides?* After all, Becky had been introduced as Lucy's niece, hoping to be a reporter someday.

But would even a girl who wanted to be a reporter someday ask a question like that?

Becky hesitated.

Then she saw that Lucy and the Duchess were standing, saying their goodbyes.

PART THREE

CHAPTER 25: FLYNN

The office of *The Tatler* was on Fleet Street, along with many of the city's other newspapers.

Flynn knew most of them; he'd pretended to be a paper boy from one newspaper or another often enough. People streamed in and out of the advertisement office of the *Daily Chronicle*, which stood beside the office of the *Daily Telegraph*. *The World* had a bronze statue of Atlas in front of its offices and, located in the same court—which led to St. Brides church—was the office for *Punch*.

All of those offices meant that this area of London was always busy, especially mid-morning, as it was now. Flynn barely had to think about blending in and staying inconspicuous as he kept the main entrance to *The Tatler* in sight. He could have been carrying a baton and leading a brass band, and no one would have spared him much more than a passing glance.

He also wasn't entirely sure what he was doing here. Becky and Lucy had gone off to speak to the Duchess of Derrington, but Mr. Holmes had assigned Flynn to keep watch on the office of the *Tatler*, and in particular on the managing editor of the paper, a man called Fenshaw.

That was all. Flynn didn't know whether Mr. Holmes thought Mr. Fenshaw was guilty of something or whether he thought Mr. Fenshaw was in danger of becoming the killer's seventh victim, after the death of Miss Cavendish yesterday.

Flynn shifted his weight from foot to foot. Fleet Street ended at Ludgate Circus, where at the beginning of Ludgate Hill, the bridge of the London, Chatham and Dover Railway crossed over the road. A train rattled past, showering fragments of coal onto the carriages and the people down below.

Pigeons landed on the dome of St. Paul's Cathedral, which Flynn could also see in the distance.

"Flynn!"

If Flynn hadn't had Mr. Holmes's training to fall back on, he would have jumped at the sound of someone whispering his name right behind him. As it was, he spun around and saw Nellie Bly.

He got his heart working again and asked, "What are you doing here?"

Nellie Bly was wearing a big floppy straw hat that shaded her face and a green and white dress that Flynn recognised as one of Lucy's. Her eyes were covered by smoked glasses, of the kind that people wore when they were getting over a bout of scarlet fever and too much sunlight hurt their eyes.

"I overheard Mr. Holmes giving you your assignment this morning," she told him. "So I thought I'd tag along."

"That's not what I meant. You're supposed to be dead!"

"I am. As far as Brasher and whomever he spoke to yesterday on the telephone are concerned. But that doesn't mean I have to cower inside of 221A Baker Street forever, not when I can help."

A couple of years ago, Flynn would have told her flatly that he didn't need any help. He was still temped to, but this time it was probably Becky who was rubbing off on him. She was always telling him he needed to have better manners, especially when they were on a job.

But apparently keeping his mouth shut didn't stop his face from showing what he was thinking, because Nellie said, "You're wondering what help I can possibly offer. Well, for one thing, I know the editor of *The Tatler*—Mr. Fenshaw—by sight. I can point him out to you if he does come out of the offices."

"Mr. Holmes told me what to look for," Flynn said. "Thin, grey hair, dark eyes, octagonal spectacles."

Nellie didn't look at all discouraged. Flynn supposed you didn't travel around the world or do all the other things she'd done by being easily put down.

"Also, I have an appointment at the Savoy for later. With George Granby."

"The American tobacco fellow?" Flynn remembered a second too late that he wasn't supposed to know that name, given that he and Becky had been eavesdropping outside the door when Nellie had told Mr. Holmes about Granby. Nellie didn't seem to notice, though.

"That's right. I used the telephone at Baker Street to reach him at the Savoy. He is in fact staying there as a guest. And he's promised me an exclusive story about his business here in London. Which gives me the perfect cover to ask him about Eleanor."

That might be, but it didn't erase the bad feeling in the pit of Flynn's stomach. "I still say it's dangerous for you to be here."

"I'm in disguise."

It wasn't much of a disguise, if Flynn had recognised her right away. But he didn't get the chance to say that.

"I can …" Nellie started to say, but then broke off, her gaze lighting on a young man in a chequered suit and black bowler hat who was striding along the pavement on the opposite side of the street. "I know him, that's Charles Lightwood," she said. "I gave him an interview for the *Daily Mail* when I was on my round the world trip. Charles!"

Before Flynn could stop her, she was darting across the street, continuing to call out. "Charles!"

Flynn blew out a gust of air and followed, arriving on the other side of the street just as the man in the bowler hat turned at the sound of his name. He looked puzzled for a second, but then his expression cleared.

Charles Lightwood looked to be somewhere around thirty-five, with wavy dark hair, dark eyes set under thick dark brows, and an amiable, square-jawed face. "Why … why, it's Miss Nellie Bly!" he said. "What brings you over to this side of the Atlantic? Aiming to break another record for world travelling?"

"Nothing so exciting as that, I'm afraid." Nellie smiled. "I'm just here on a visit, looking up old acquaintances. I was hoping to meet up with Eleanor Cavendish; have you seen her recently?"

Flynn stayed behind Lightwood, blending in with the crowd and out of the reporter's line of sight, so that he wouldn't be noticed. But he was easily able to stay close enough to hear everything that was said. He knew that the news of Miss Cavendish's death hadn't been announced yet in the papers, so he wasn't surprised when Charles Lightwood didn't react except to say, "Not in the past day or two. I saw her … I suppose it must have been somewhere around a week ago, now." He shook his head. "It's a shame."

"What is?" Nellie asked.

"A reporter with a nose for a story like Eleanor, reduced to writing a lot of drivel about Lord X being seen in the company of Lady Y, and the Countess of B snubbing the Duchess of D by not inviting her to tea. Although mind you," Lightwood added, "I think Eleanor is hoping to change that."

Flynn saw Nellie barely stop herself from startling. "Really? How do you mean?"

"She didn't say, not exactly," Lightwood said. "But the last time that I saw her, she seemed excited about something. Could barely stop to talk to me, said she had to rush off to speak to a source. I asked her what was so important, whether she'd heard that Lord Windemere had bought himself a new monocle. Just pulling her leg a bit, you know," he added. "But Eleanor looked mysterious and would only say she wasn't going to be writing Miss Whisper pieces for the society gossip pages for much longer, because she was on the track of a first-class story, real front-page stuff."

"Really? Did she tell you anything else besides that?" Nellie asked.

"Not to speak of. I asked her how she'd got hold of something like that, and she said that it just went to show that every noble family had a skeleton or two in the closet. And that the king himself would be interested if this particular skeleton came tumbling out."

"The king?" Nellie repeated. "She really said that?"

"She did," Lightwood confirmed. "Although it may be she was exaggerating. You know what reporters are." He winked. "Well, I must be getting on. It's nice to have seen you, and give my regards to Eleanor if you do happen to meet up with her. See whether she can be persuaded to tell you about this front-page story of hers."

Flynn saw Nellie swallow, then force a smile. "Yes, I'll do that. Thank you, Charles."

CHAPTER 26: LUCY

"What did you think of the Duke of Derrington's household?"
I asked Becky.

We were walking along Belgrave Place, about to cross through
Eaton Square Gardens, which was clean, lovely, and perfectly
maintained. Sunlight slanted through the trees up ahead, casting
a patchwork of shadows on the perfectly mowed green lawn
and the immaculately weeded and tended flower beds. Ladies
carrying white parasols strolled along the gravel paths.

People who were rich enough to live in Belgravia didn't like
being confronted with anything so ugly as a dead flower or a weed.

Becky had been quiet and thoughtful ever since we'd left
Derrington House. Now she said, "It reminded me of Alice in
Wonderland. You know, the line where the Cheshire Cat says,
We're all mad here? Except instead of *mad*, substitute, *Horrible*."

I laughed. "Did you think Lady Aline was unpleasant?"

"No," Becky said slowly. "No, I didn't really mean her.
I was talking about Emmeline and her fiancé and the Duke
of Derrington's mother and sister. They weren't there, but
Emmeline told me all about them and how they refused to speak
to Lady Aline for a full year after she and the duke were married
because the duke hadn't asked their permission before marrying
her. Oh, and Emmeline says that Lady Aline didn't really want
to go off to boarding school in Paris at all. She was involved with

a boy her father didn't approve of, so he shipped her out of the country to make sure that she never saw him again."

"Emmeline told you that?"

"Yes. I told you she was awful. She'd barely even exchanged two words with me, but she couldn't pass up the chance of sharing a piece of spiteful gossip about her aunt."

"Do you think she dislikes the duchess?"

We passed by a stone table where a pair of elderly men were playing chess in the shade of an oak tree. They both nodded and smiled in our direction.

Becky tilted her head, considering my question. "No. I don't think she dislikes Lady Aline any more than she does anyone else. She just enjoys spreading malicious rumours about people. That doesn't mean what she said isn't true, though."

"No, it doesn't."

"There's one other thing I found out from Emmeline," Becky said. "I asked her where she and Lady Aline were Wednesday afternoon—because of Miss Cavendish being killed sometime around then, you know. Emmeline told me that she was stuck at home all day because her aunt had gone out riding."

"Riding in Hyde Park?"

"She didn't say. But didn't the duke already tell you that's where he and Lady Aline are accustomed to riding?"

"He did." I tapped my upper lip. "So Lady Aline doesn't have any alibi for the time of the murder. On the contrary, it would seem she was very likely near to the scene of the crime."

"And we already know that Brasher didn't kill Miss Cavendish, don't we?" Becky said. "The timing is all wrong. At the time of Miss Cavendish's murder—or near enough—Brasher was ransacking her apartment and then chasing after Miss Bly and Flynn."

"True."

Becky frowned and was silent, watching a small red squirrel leap from branch to branch in the trees along our path. Then she said, "Lady Aline as good as said that her husband had only married her because it was good for business."

"She said her father was relieved that the duke could take over all of his estates and business affairs, since he understood the tobacco trade. Not that the duke married her for the sake of her father's money and estates."

Becky gave a snort of disbelief. "What did you tell me that they say in America? *If you believe that, I'd like to sell you a bridge in Brooklyn?*"

"I wasn't necessarily disagreeing," I said mildly. "Just pointing out that Lady Aline may not entirely see it that way."

"If she doesn't, then she's not very bright. And she didn't strike me as being stupid," Becky said.

"No, nor me."

As we passed out of the gardens and turned onto Lyall Street, I thought back over my own conversation with Lady Aline. Like Becky, I wouldn't have called her unpleasant, and I certainly wouldn't have said that she was unintelligent. But I also hadn't quite known what to make of her, which in itself puzzled me. If Lady Aline was no mere social butterfly but was, as her husband suspected, conspiring with Germany in an attempt to assassinate the king at the coronation ball, then it made sense that she would be extremely good at playing a part.

But even so, I'd investigated hundreds of people over the course of working on criminal cases with my father. Very, very rarely did I find that I couldn't read someone during an interview. But I'd been hard pressed to guess at the thoughts that lay behind Lady Aline's brown eyes, and almost entirely unable to guess at who she really was underneath all the poise and social charm.

Was that because she'd been railroaded by her father—and by her husband the duke—into a life that she'd never really wanted?

"You never asked Lady Aline about the murder victims," Becky said.

"No, I didn't. We already know that the shoemaker—Samuel Harley—made Lady Aline's wedding shoes. It's quite likely, too, that Lady Aline or her husband have stayed at Martin Goodspeed's hotel at one time or another, they're exactly the sort of clientele that Mrs. Goodspeed would fall all over herself to lure in as paying guests. But no. I didn't want to ask Lady Aline about any of them, or at least not yet."

"Why not?"

"Because if I'd asked, she would know that I'm aware of her connection to the Hyde Park victims. She might have been caught unawares and showed a reaction to Samuel Harley's name or one of the others. But mentioning the murders would have made her suspicious enough of me that she'd have been doubly on her guard from that moment on."

"I suppose you're right."

We were just passing the door of a French pastry shop when Becky stopped abruptly and turned to me. "I just thought of something. What if it's Emmeline?"

"You've lost me. What if what's Emmeline?"

"What if Emmeline is the one who killed all the people in the park?" Becky said. "I know you're going to say she looks like she'd have hysterics if she so much as chipped a fingernail, much less dirtied her hands with actual murder. But I don't think it would trouble her conscience in the slightest to have had Brasher commit the murders on her behalf."

"All right," I said slowly. "And why would she have done that?"

"The man she's going to marry—Stuart whatever-his-name is," Becky said.

"Lord Stuart Kildare."

"Yes. Him. Emmeline said that he was so horrified by the sarcastic article that Miss Cavendish wrote about her aunt's coronation ball that he nearly called off their engagement. He thought that it might reflect badly on him."

"Charming. I suppose that would certainly give Emmeline a motive for wanting Eleanor Cavendish out of the way. But hers was the last in the string of murders. Why would Emmeline have wanted to kill any of the others?"

"I don't know. Maybe they all knew something about her—or about her aunt—that Emmeline didn't want to come out? Something else that would horrify Lord Stuart into giving her the push?"

"That's possible, I suppose," I said slowly. "We know there must be some connection between them all—something beyond mere association, I mean. Obviously neither Lady Aline nor Emmeline would have murdered Samuel Harley just for making her wedding slippers nearly twenty years ago."

"There's that porcelain statue that you told us about, too," Becky said. "The shepherdess that Emma Thompkins' neighbour found in her room? That's exactly the kind of thing that Emmeline would have had to use as a bribe. She's not married, so she definitely doesn't have control of her own money, and I'd bet that her father doesn't give her very much of an allowance.

She wouldn't have money in cash to be able to pay off a black-mailer, so she'd have to take something like that statue and just hope that it wouldn't be missed."

"True." I'd had the identical thought during my conversation with Harriet and Miss Selfridge. "And you mentioned a minute ago that Lady Aline doesn't have an alibi for the time of Miss Cavendish's murder, but neither does Emmeline. If she was alone in the house, no one would have seen her if she went to Hyde Park Wednesday afternoon. It wouldn't have taken very long; she could have slipped out without anyone's being the wiser."

"Unless one of the servants saw her," Becky said. "We ought to ask them."

"We will. And we definitely ought to check on whether the list of Emma Thompkins' former employers includes Emmeline or anyone in her family, too. But we also have the duke's evidence. His account of seeing his wife visit Brasher's shop in order to hire him to commit Martin Goodspeed's murder."

"We don't, though. Not really," Becky said. "All the duke can say definitely is that he saw Lady Aline visit Brasher's shop, and that while she was in there, she mentioned Martin Goodspeed's name. For all we know, Emmeline asked her to go there just so that Lady Aline would look guilty. She could have pretended she wanted Brasher to supply the pork chops for her wedding and asked Lady Aline to have them delivered to Martin Goodspeed's hotel."

"Pork chops?" I raised an eyebrow.

Becky waved a hand. "Well, something like that. You know what I mean."

"I do, actually." I sobered. "In any criminal investigation, some revelations burst on you suddenly while others crept up slowly, like light filtering in through a crack. Right now, I was beginning to get the faintest glimmer. "And you're right," I told Becky. "It's always dangerous to take any eyewitness's account as the absolute truth, when at best all they can tell you is what they think they saw."

CHAPTER 27: FLYNN

"A first-class story," Nellie said. Flynn could see why she'd gone into the reporting business. Right now, he could practically see the excitement crackling under her skin like the electric current between the filaments of a light bulb. "One that the king himself would be interested in seeing revealed."

"And a noble family with a skeleton in the closet," Flynn said. "I know. I heard."

What he was worried about at the moment, though, was that Nellie Bly had just announced to Charles Lightwood that she was in London. And who knew how many other people Lightwood was planning to tell? He hadn't struck Flynn as the sort of fellow who would keep his mouth shut about anything he thought of as newsworthy.

Before he could point that out to Nellie, though, the roar of an oncoming motor car drowned out all the other noise on the street. Automobiles were still new and uncommon enough that people stopped and stared when one passed by, and this one was no different.

Pedestrians turned around or scrambled to get out of the way, paper boys turned to gape, and a couple of horses pulling carriages startled and gave their drivers a nasty moment or two of trying to keep them from bolting in a panic at the noise.

Flynn hadn't studied different types of automobiles much,

but he thought this one was a Daimler, painted black. Instead of having an open top like most motor cars, this one had a tall black cover over the back. Some of the fancy shop owners in the West End used automobiles like that to make deliveries.

Nellie, too, turned at the throbbing roar of the motor and made a face. "I hate those beastly vehicles. Always belching fumes and smoke—"

She broke off as the oncoming motor car suddenly accelerated. Flynn couldn't see the driver's face clearly. The man was dressed in an overcoat and heavy leather driving gloves, and the upper half of his face was covered by an enormous pair of glass and leather driving goggles. But the way he was crouched down low at the wheel, hunched forwards and leaning in towards the wind screen made Flynn's stomach sicken with a nasty feeling.

Flynn made a grab for Nellie Bly's arm, ready to drag her out of the way. But he was too far off to get hold of her, and the next second it was too late.

The driver must have mashed his foot down on the accelerator, because the automobile put on a burst of speed and surged forwards, bumping from the road up onto the pavement as it headed straight for them.

Nellie screamed. Flynn jumped back to avoid getting hit, but the automobile leaped forwards again and he still got clipped by the front fender and went sprawling backwards. His head connected with the pavement, which sent a flash of bright stars dancing across his vision. But through the momentary blurriness, Flynn saw a second man suddenly straighten up from where he must have been hiding in the covered back of the automobile, grab Nellie around the waist, and drag her on board.

It all happened so fast that Flynn barely even had time to blink, much less shake his head to clear it and scramble to his feet. By the time his ears had stopped ringing and he'd got his wits about him again, the automobile had swerved back onto the road and was roaring off.

Flynn still ran after it, pushing himself to go faster until the muscles in his legs burned and his lungs were on fire. But the automobile was faster and easier to manoeuvre around the London traffic than a horse-drawn carriage, and the driver was just ploughing ahead without waiting for anyone to get out of his way. Horses reared, people jumped clear of the motor car's path and shook their fists, but the automobile didn't so much as slow down. Finally Flynn had to drop back as it vanished around the corner of Farringdon Street in a cloud of smoke and petrol fumes.

* * *

"I'm sorry, Mr. Holmes," Flynn said. He stood straight and forced himself to meet Mr. Holmes's keen grey eyes.

There wasn't much that scared him anymore, but he'd rather sleep under a railway bridge in the dead of winter than feel that he'd disappointed Mr. Holmes. There wasn't any help for it, though, so he might as well face it and take his medicine.

"Whoever it was, they took Miss Bly. And I thought I'd better come back here and report it to you, even though I hadn't even got a look at Mr. Fenshaw the editor yet."

He and Mr. Holmes were alone. Becky and Lucy weren't yet back from their visit to the duke's place, and Dr. Watson was seeing patients at his medical practice.

Mr. Holmes was sitting in his favourite arm chair, listening with his eyes half-closed. He was silent long enough for Flynn's stomach to start churning with an unpleasant feeling like he'd accidentally swallowed a nest of snakes.

But then Mr. Holmes said, "You are not to blame yourself. If anything, I am at fault for not having anticipated that Miss Bly would scorn to remain safely in the flat downstairs. In fact, I did anticipate it, but I did not expect that she would disregard my warnings and leave quite so soon. Or that she would take it upon herself to contact Mr. Granby."

"You think he's somehow mixed up in this?" Flynn asked.

"That remains to be seen. We shall have to speak to Mr. Granby, of course. But there are other equally important avenues of investigation to pursue if we are to find Miss Bly."

Flynn swallowed. "You think she's still alive to be found?" That had been the fear sitting in his head like a cold rock, all the while he'd been making his way back to Baker Street: that Nellie Bly was already dead, and they'd be finding her body in Hyde Park next.

"I believe there is at least a seventy per cent chance of it, yes," Mr. Holmes said. "If they had simply wanted to kill her, they could have run her down with the automobile or even used a revolver to shoot her then and there, without bothering with the obvious risks and complications of an abduction. Yet they did abduct her, which means they must have a use for her." He put his fingertips together and his gaze turned distant, the way it did when his thoughts were travelling down some hidden and twisty path. "I believe I might even put the odds of her being alive as high as seventy-five per cent."

That still left a bigger chance of her actually being dead than

Flynn might have liked, but he supposed it was better than nothing.

"What can we do?" he asked.

"Tomorrow is the day of the coronation ball," Mr. Holmes said. "Our time is running short. But I believe there is still a chance for us to discover what this front-page newsworthy story was that Miss Cavendish had uncovered." He nodded, as though he was confirming something inside his own thoughts. Then he said, "I shall have an assignment for you in the morning."

CHAPTER 28: BECKY

August 16

"So our assignment is to look through the Duke of Derrington's carriage house?" Becky said.

It was early morning, so early, in fact, that the sun was barely a glimmer of pink on the horizon and the damp air still held a bit of the night chill. At this hour, the only people awake in Belgravia were the servants. She and Flynn had positioned themselves behind a clump of shrubbery at the edge of Wilton Crescent, which was a half-circle-shaped bit of parkland that stood across the street from Derrington House. So far, Becky had counted four sleepy-looking maids come out to sweep the front steps of the mansions all around them, and three other servants start work at washing front windows.

Derrington House, though, was still entirely dark, with all the curtains drawn.

"Makes sense," Flynn said. "We already know that the bodies are being dumped in Hyde Park by a carriage. Mr. Holmes wants proof that it's Derrington's carriage that's being used." He eyed the marble mansion in front of them. "Looks quiet enough. Do we go around back now?"

"We'd better," Becky agreed. "Before anyone is awake to see us."

The Derrington carriage house was a half-timbered building with a slate roof that looked a bit like a cottage in the country. It stood behind the mansion, part of the row of mews where the wealthy kept their horses and vehicles.

Becky followed Flynn, keeping to the deepest part of the shadows as they crept across the cobblestone courtyard that stood between the mansion and the carriage house. She was dressed like a boy for today's venture. Skirts were all right if you were trying to look innocent enough for someone to discount you as a threat, but they were rubbish if you had to run. And there was every chance that she and Flynn would have to get away from here in a hurry.

The double doors of the carriage house were closed. Flynn gave the handles a quick tug and then shook his head. "Locked."

"Well, we weren't really expecting to be able to get in that way," Becky said.

They were circling around towards the back of the building when across the courtyard the rear door—it was probably the kitchen entrance—of Derrington House opened.

Becky froze and Flynn did the same. She felt as though they might as well have had flashing lights blazing all around them, the way theatres did when advertising the name of a play. But the grey-haired woman—she looked like a scullery maid—who appeared in the doorway didn't even glance in their direction, just sloshed a bucket of dirty wash-water out onto the cobble-stones and went back inside.

Becky released a breath, and they darted around the side of the carriage house. There, an external staircase led up to a small door set under the house's eaves.

"That must be where the coachman sleeps," Becky whispered.

"Let's just hope he's a sound sleeper," Flynn whispered back.

They crept to the back of the carriage house, which proved to have a couple of small windows set high up in the wall.

Becky eyed the distance from the windows to the ground. "Give me a boost up?"

Flynn bent down, cupping his hands, and she stepped into them, letting him propel her up high enough that she could just manage to peer in through the glass.

"Anything?" Flynn asked in a whisper after a second or two.

"It's hard to see." The carriage house was dark inside, and everything looked silent and deserted. Becky could see the hulking shapes of the Derrington carriages. There were two of them, a big black brougham, and an open landau that the duke probably drove about town in fine weather.

"Well, take your time, then," Flynn grunted. "It's not as though we're in a hurry."

"All right, all right." Becky hopped back down onto the ground. "I couldn't quite get high enough to try to open the window," she said. "But the latch doesn't look strong. You can probably force it with a pen knife if we can find something to climb on."

A quick search of the area at the back of the stable produced an empty feed barrel, which they rolled over under the window. Flynn jumped up. Becky wasn't timing him, but it couldn't have taken him more than ten seconds to jimmy open the window latch. He swung the window open and glanced down at her over his shoulder.

"Wish me luck."

"Don't get caught," Becky told him.

"Good thing you said that; I was planning on getting caught right up till now."

Flynn was already scrambling up and over the window ledge, so he didn't see Becky roll her eyes. She heard him drop down to the ground inside with a soft thud, then held her breath, waiting for any sounds of alarm. Nothing happened, except that about half a minute later, one of the carriage house front doors slid back just enough for Flynn to peer out at her and whisper, "Come on."

Becky slipped inside, Flynn slid the door back into place, and then they both turned around to survey the Derrington family carriage house.

CHAPTER 29: FLYNN

The carriage house was dim in the early dawn light coming through the windows, and the air smelled of dust and hay and leather oil. Flynn eyed the feed barrels and coils of rope, the harnesses, bridles, blankets, spare wheels, and all the other assorted gear and tools that packed the space around the Derrington carriages.

"No sign of Miss Bly," he said under his breath.

Becky looked at him quickly. "Did you think she'd be in here?"

Flynn shrugged. He hadn't really been expecting it, but it had been in the back of his mind as possible. Although if they had found her here, it would have meant that she was dead. No one would risk putting a live prisoner in a place as close to the house as this, when any noise would bring someone running to investigate.

"We'll find her," Becky said. "Or Mr. Holmes will."

Flynn nodded without speaking. He didn't get attached to people, and he barely knew Miss Bly. But all the same, he'd be sorry if she came to a bad end, especially after all that they'd been through together in trying to outrun Brasher and his gang. And she'd been grabbed right in front of him, which Flynn took personally.

"You take that side, I'll take this one?" he suggested, jerking his head over towards the left.

"All right," Becky agreed.

They both started to look through the piles of gear. But if this place held any secrets, Flynn wasn't rating their odds of finding them as very high.

"There could be an elephant hiding in here and you'd only know it if he snored," he murmured.

As if on cue, a loud snort came from behind the wall to their left. Flynn almost jumped out of his skin, but Becky whispered, "It's just one of the horses. We'd better leave off searching their stalls until last. They might get spooked and make enough noise that we get caught."

That was all right with Flynn. His rule was that he didn't get within arm's reach of anything bigger than he was, whether human or animal.

"Anything?" Becky said after they'd been searching for a few more minutes.

Flynn shook his head. "We don't even know exactly what we're looking for—"

He broke off suddenly as he lifted a pile of blankets aside and found an oval-shaped metal plaque, painted green at the top and bottom and stamped with a string of numbers in the middle.

Flynn's lips pursed in a silent whistle. "Well, that answers that question."

"What does?" Becky came over to look at what he was holding and drew in her breath at the sight of the metal oval. "That's a cab number badge!"

"Exactly. So someone used the badge to disguise the Derrington carriage—he nodded at the black brougham—as a cab."

"And that's how the bodies were left in Hyde Park?" Becky

nodded slowly, but frowned. "How would Lady Aline have managed to use the carriage without anyone noticing?"

"Well, she could have told Brasher to drive her. You know, had him pretend to be the coachman," Flynn said.

"What would she have told the actual coachman, though—"

Becky stopped short. Footsteps were pounding up the outside steps at the side of the carriage house to the coachman's apartment above. Then a knocking sounded on the coachman's door.

"Hutchins!" A male voice called out. "Hutchins, wake up, man. His grace wants the carriage brought round straight away."

There was a silence. Flynn had frozen, holding absolutely still, so he heard the thump on the floorboards overhead. Hutchins the coachman must have just climbed out of bed.

"What, now?" a deeper male voice that must be the coachman's called back. "Where's he want to go at this hour?"

"Not my business, is it?" answered the first man. "Nor yours. Just get the horses hitched up and bring the coach round. Ten minutes, I told him."

Steps plodded back down the outside steps, and a moment later Flynn heard the sounds of Hutchins moving around the upstairs room. Probably putting on his coachman's livery, maybe splashing cold water on his face to wake up.

He looked at Becky. "We need to get out of here," he whispered soundlessly. "We've got what we came for." He held up the brass number badge.

"Ye-es." Becky drew the word out, making it clear that what she actually meant was the opposite. "Wouldn't it be good to know exactly where the duke is going so early in the morning, though?"

"Sure. It'd be good to get a signed confession from the killer, too," Flynn said. "But I don't see how—" he stopped and held up his hands. "Oh, no."

"Oh, no what?"

"You're about to try and talk me into one of your brilliant ideas. The kind that end with us almost getting either killed or thrown into jail."

"Not this time. I mean, yes, I do have an idea," Becky told him. "But it's a good one. Just listen."

Flynn gave her a sour look. "If it was that good, you wouldn't have to talk me into it."

Above them, the door to the coachman's flat opened and shut with a bang, and Hutchins' heavy footsteps sounded on the stairs, coming down.

Becky darted over to the big black carriage. "Stop arguing and come on," she hissed. "Before it's too late."

CHAPTER 30: LUCY

"More questions?" Lady Aline looked up from a sheaf of what looked like dinner table seating arrangements with a distracted expression. "Of course, anything I can do, but …"

She gestured to the notes and bouquets of fresh flowers and stacks of paper all around her.

I had called at Derrington House still in the persona of a newspaper reporter writing a story about the coronation ball, telling the stiffly correct butler who had answered the front door that I had a few follow-up questions to my original interview and would be grateful for a minute or two of Her Grace's time.

Lady Aline had received me once again in the Derrington House sitting room, which even at this early hour of the morning was a beehive of activity. Servants whisked in and out carrying messages and calling cards and other assorted flower arrangements.

"With the ball tonight, I'm afraid there's a great deal to be done," Lady Aline finished with an apologetic smile. "Three people who had informed me definitely that they were coming have now sent word just this morning that they're not. Two cases of illness, and one death of an aging aunt. All of which I'm sorry for, but it's requiring me to completely rearrange the seating plans I'd made for the dinner!"

The door to the sitting room opened, and her husband, the Duke of Derrington, put his head in. "Good morning, darling."

I'd never seen the duke and duchess together before. Watching the duke's face as his eyes lighted on his wife, I could see faint lines of strain bracketing the corners of his mouth, and his voice had what I thought was a tense, stilted quality.

Lady Aline, though, didn't seem to notice. "Daniel! Good morning. I didn't realise that you were back from your ride in the park."

"Got back a few moments ago. I thought I'd look in before calling at the wine merchants and see how you've been progressing."

"That's good of you," Lady Aline said. The telephone buzzed in the background, followed by the sound of a servant going to answer it. She gave her husband a distracted smile. "I'm coming along quite nicely, thank you."

"Right you are."

Derrington's smile, too, looked more than a little forced, and he gave me an awkward glance as though uncertain whether to acknowledge my presence. I shook my head very slightly, and he nodded again. "Well. I'll be off, then."

Lady Aline sighed as she listened to the sound of the duke's footsteps echoing away down the front hall. "Men. They have absolutely no notion of what it takes to organise an event on this scale!" She gave me a quick, sidelong smile. "To tell you the truth, I think he invented the errand to the wine merchant's shop just to remove himself from all the activity here. But as I was saying, I have my dressmaker coming at ten o'clock for a final fitting of Emmeline's and my gowns for the evening. If you don't mind fitting your questions in before that, though, I'm happy to answer anything that you'd like."

I debated briefly. Maybe Lady Aline's indifference to her husband's going away at this busy time was perfectly genuine. Her tone was certainly convincing. But having him somewhere else, where he could be attacked away from witnesses, could potentially be considered ominous, especially since His Grace wasn't doing an especially convincing job of hiding his suspicions from her.

On the other hand, though, I couldn't see her or anyone else with a stake in the king's attending tonight's ball doing anything to jeopardise the event—and an overt attack on the Duke of Derrington would certainly do that. Even the duke's meeting with an unfortunate accident would result in the ball's being at the very least postponed. And she was immersed in a flurry of activity to enable the ball to take place on schedule.

"Do you recognise the name of Samuel Harley?" I asked.

"Harley?" A faint, puzzled line appeared between Lady Aline's arched brows, but she didn't show any other reaction to the name. "No, I don't believe that I do. Why?"

"He remembers you, that's all. He was a shoemaker, hired to make your wedding slippers when you and His Grace were married. Apparently it was one of the high points of his career."

"Was it really?" Lady Aline looked down at the charts in her hands. "How very sweet of him. Now I feel quite ashamed that I didn't recognise his name. But I'm afraid after all these years …"

"Of course, I understand. I just thought that it might add a bit of human interest to the piece that we're writing: 'The Duchess of Derrington, seen through the eyes of the ordinary men and women who have known her.' Newspaper readers adore that sort of thing."

"Do they?" Lady Aline's expression hadn't changed, but I thought there was a faint note of constraint in her tone.

"Oh yes. Along those same lines, I believe that as a young woman you had a maid by the name of Emma Thompkins?"

"I—oh, goodness, yes. Dear Emma." Lady Aline smiled. "She

ran off and left my employment to be married—so she hoped, at least. I confess I didn't have high hopes for the young man she'd picked. But I gave her a wedding present and hoped for the best. Do you mean to tell me that you've actually found her?"

"Yes, that's right." I didn't mention that technically speaking it was the police who'd found Emma, and that she hadn't been alive to offer any reminiscences. "The wedding present you gave her … it was a Dresden china shepherdess, isn't that right?"

"I—" spots of colour appeared on Lady Aline's cheeks. "Oh, yes, that's right. I'd quite forgotten, it's been so long." She stood up. "And now, I hope you'll forgive me, but I really must go and get ready—"

She was probably about to say, *for my dressmaker's appointment*; even though that was still more than two hours away, it was the most convenient excuse she had at hand. But at that moment, the dignified butler appeared in the doorway, holding a silver salver with a note.

He bowed. "A message has just arrived for you, Your Grace."

"A message?" Frowning, Lady Aline tore the note open and quickly scanned the contents before looking back at me. "I'm sorry. It appears that I'll have to go out. Treadwell." She addressed the butler. "Would you summon a cab for me? I need to go to the Savoy, and there's always such a crush in the street outside, it's not worth asking Hutchins to drive the cab over and find somewhere to park while I'm inside."

"Certainly, Your Grace." Treadwell bowed.

"Was there anything else?" Lady Aline asked me, with something of a return to her usual poised and charming smile. "I apologise for rushing off like this, but if there's anything more you need to know …"

"That's quite all right." I returned her smile. "I think—"

My answer was interrupted by the arrival of Emmeline, who came sailing in from the front hall. Her silvery blond hair and porcelain-fair skin were beautifully set off by the black velvet trim on her green walking suit.

"You're not going out now, are you?" Lady Aline exclaimed at the sight of her.

"Yes, why not? I've a headache and fancied some fresh air. I thought I'd go for a stroll in the park."

"Well, there's the dressmaker's appointment, for one thing," Lady Aline began.

Emmeline interrupted with a wave of her hand. "Just tell her to wait for me. I don't expect I'll be more than an hour or so. And you don't need me for anything around here, do you?"

"Of course not," Lady Aline said. She sounded as though her temper was fraying slightly. "I'd be delighted to attend to all the last-minute details for the ball entirely on my own."

The sarcasm in her answer sailed completely over Emmeline's head. "Good, I thought so. Oh, and Treadwell?"

The butler must have been just outside the sitting room door, because he appeared almost immediately at Emmeline's summons.

"Ask Hutchins to drive by the park to pick me up in about an hour's time?" Emmeline glanced at her aunt. "That way I can be certain that I'll be back in time for the dressmaker's."

CHAPTER 31: BECKY

Becky had already noticed the big, dome-topped trunk strapped to the luggage rack at the rear of the Brougham. As the coachman's footsteps descended the stairs, she tugged Flynn over to it. She'd been prepared to have Flynn force the latch if the trunk was locked, but as it turned out, the lid lifted easily.

Just for a second, Becky's heart skipped as she imagined finding the crumpled and lifeless body of Nellie Bly curled up inside. Then she released a breath as she looked into the velvet-lined interior.

"Empty."

Flynn nodded. "Do you reckon this is where they stashed the dead bodies to bring them to Hyde Park, though?"

"Probably."

Stowing a dead body away inside of the Brougham would have been too dangerous, if someone stuck in traffic alongside the Derrington carriage had happened to glance inside. The trunk, however, would make a perfect spot for concealment.

"It's big enough to hold both of us, though. We can hide inside and see where the duke is going. Easy."

Becky was expecting Flynn to argue. But she should have remembered that whatever other faults he had, he wasn't squeamish. He braced one hand on the edge of the trunk and hoisted himself inside. Becky followed, and they pulled the lid of the trunk back down over their heads.

Just as the double doors of the carriage house slid open with a squeak of wood rubbing against the cobblestones, Flynn whispered, "I'm going to say *I told you so*, if this doesn't go as smooth and easy as you think."

Becky was already having … not quite second thoughts, but her pulse sped up as the full weight of what she'd just led them into struck her. Inside the trunk smelled strongly of mothballs, and it was absolutely pitch black. The close-fitting lid didn't let in so much as a pin-prick of light.

She held perfectly still, barely daring to breathe. The trunk was a tight enough fit for the two of them that she could tell Flynn was doing the same beside her. But although she heard the clump of Hutchins the coachman's footsteps as he came into the carriage house, he didn't come anywhere near to their hiding spot. Instead, she listened to the clink and rustles and soft nickers from the horses as Hutchins led them out of their stalls and hitched them to the carriage. The carriage springs squeaked and the trunk shifted a little as the coachman climbed into the driver's seat. Then with a jolt, the wheels started to roll, hitting the outside cobblestones in the yard with a bump that snapped Becky's teeth together.

For better or for worse, they were past the point of being able to call this off as a bad idea.

A few moments later, the carriage came to a halt at what Becky assumed was the front entrance to Derrington House.

A man's deep voice that must have been the duke's said, "Good morning, Hutchins."

"Morning, your grace. Out early this morning?" Hutchins' voice reached Becky, too, only a little muffled by the trunk's leather walls.

"Yes, Lady Aline asked me to call in at the wine merchant's shop to make certain that everything is in order for tonight. You know how women always worry over everything."

"I do," Hutchins' muffled voice sounded emphatic. "But will we have time, Your Grace? Miss Emmeline has asked to be picked up at the park in about an hour. She's going out for a walk."

"That will be fine," the duke replied.

The trunk lurched and swayed a little as the duke climbed inside the carriage, and then Becky felt them start moving again, picking up speed.

She nudged Flynn and whispered, "Did you hear that? The duchess sent him out on this errand. And then the carriage is going to Hyde Park to fetch Emmeline." She had spent time last night filling Flynn in on her and Lucy's visit yesterday with the duchess and Emmeline. "Who's gone out for a completely trumped-up reason."

"Why trumped-up?"

Becky shifted position in the dark, although there was so little room that there wasn't really any way of getting more comfortable. "She just happened to feel like taking a walk in the park? Emmeline?"

"Why not? It's not far from Derrington House, not even five minutes on foot."

"That's five minutes too long, by Emmeline's standards. The only walking she's interested in doing is down a wedding aisle on her way to marry an extremely rich man, preferably with a title. So why does she want the carriage at the park this morning?"

"I don't know. Do you still think it's really Emmeline who's been having people killed?"

"I think she's a more convincing villainess than Lady Aline," Becky said. "Besides. You said it was a man who was driving the car that abducted Nellie Bly."

"I thought it was a man," Flynn corrected. "But with those driving goggles on, it could have been the king himself and I wouldn't have recognised him."

"But if it was a man, then it might have been Stuart—Emmeline's fiancé," Becky said. "He sounds like exactly the sort of person to have an expensive motor car. They could have used Stuart to kidnap Nellie Bly for them, since they couldn't use Brasher."

"True. Brasher's getting stabbed rules him out. And his pals wouldn't exactly line up for more work. They'd be worried about getting the same treatment," Flynn said.

"But you're not convinced?"

"I don't know. I'm just thinking about Granby."

"Who? Oh, the American," Becky said. "That's true. Nellie did contact him."

"Which makes him one of the few people who knew she was in London."

"She wouldn't have been stupid enough to tell him where she was staying, though. Or that she was going to be visiting Fleet Street yesterday morning."

"I suppose. That sounds more like someone followed her from Baker Street, doesn't it."

Becky considered telling Flynn that what had happened to Nellie wasn't his fault, but she gave up on the idea. Flynn never wanted sympathy. The best she could do was to help him find Nellie Bly, alive and well.

They both fell silent as the carriage bumped and jounced,

jolting Becky's head and knees and elbows painfully against the sides of the trunk. The air was so stuffy that it felt hard to breathe, and the journey seemed to be lasting an eternity. Becky thought that was just her imagination, but then Flynn said, "We're not going to Hyde Park."

"What?" Becky stopped herself from turning to look at him. She'd only bang her head again, and she wouldn't be able to see him anyway. "How can you tell?"

"It's taking too long. Even if we were going all the way across to the Kensington Palace side of the park, we'd have been there five times over by now."

Becky didn't ask where they were going, then. Flynn wouldn't have any more idea than she did.

"Should we risk opening the trunk and taking a look?" she asked instead.

She sensed rather than saw Flynn tilt his head, listening. "We're heading outside of the city. Listen."

He was right. When Becky strained her ears to listen above the creak of the carriage springs and the steady clip-clop of the horses' hooves, she couldn't hear any of the usual sounds of London traffic. No shouts from other drivers, no rumble of wagon wheels or brays from a corn chandler's donkey.

A few moments later, the carriage jolted again, and she realised that the road under them had changed from cobblestones to a beaten earth track. They really were driving out into the country.

Becky didn't know how far they'd come or how many more minutes might have passed before the carriage slowed and then drew to a halt. She strained to listen again, hoping to hear either the duke or Hutchins say something that would give a clue as to where they were.

Instead, the sharp crack of a gunshot punched her eardrums, deafeningly loud even through the muffling walls of the trunk.

Becky was so shocked that for a moment she stayed stock-still, unable even to speak, much less move. Then she breathed, "That was—"

"A gunshot." Flynn spoke in the same soundless whisper. "I know."

Becky reached for the lid of the trunk, ready to push it aside. "We can't—"

Flynn caught hold of her arm. "Unless you woke up this morning hoping to get shot, too, I vote we stay put."

Becky forced herself to gulp another breath of the stuffy, moth-ball scented air. She didn't like it, but Flynn was right. Until they knew who'd fired that shot and why, they were safer where they were.

CHAPTER 32: WATSON

Young Rupert D'Oyly Carte had an apprehensive look about him, as if he thought a sword overhung him and was about to fall at any moment. "Mr. Holmes," he began, "I am entirely willing to cooperate with you, even on this momentous day and at this ungodly hour."

Holmes nodded. "You have had a good season?" he asked.

"Quite good. Despite the King's postponement of the original date for the coronation, we have been at capacity most nights. And our restaurant business has also flourished."

Holmes did not appear to be listening. Rather, he was surveying the great ballroom. Early-morning sunlight streamed through the clerestory windows, igniting the chandeliers in a silent firework display. I wondered what he was looking for. Fleetingly I wondered whether he sought a location where an assassin might hide, although he had not mentioned even a single word of a threat to the King.

"Any news about His Majesty's attendance?" I asked.

D'Oyly Carte gave a tight smile of resignation. "The King keeps his own counsel, I'm afraid. And I wouldn't be at all surprised if he stayed home. Indeed, he was near death only last month, and it's only been a week since he's undergone the strain of the coronation ceremony."

"Why would he make the effort to attend?" I asked.

"To please certain businessmen, both the Imperial Tobacco men from our country and the American Tobacco Company executives. The revenues make up a goodly portion of the economy, both here and in the States. So it is to our country's advantage if both sides survive and prosper." He paused, then shrugged. "Or so it has been explained to me."

"Explained? By whom?" I asked.

"The same man who requested I give you every cooperation. The duke of Derrington."

"Ah. The Imperial Tobacco negotiations."

I looked in vain at Holmes for some sort of direction.

However, he said nothing. His gaze never wavered from its sweep of the great room: the chandeliers, the soft pastels on the wall, the red carpet, the white tables and red-upholstered chairs, all of which had seen better days,

"At the moment, tobacco is king here," D'Oyly Carte replied. Then it seemed he could stand Holmes's inattention no longer. He said, "You seem taken by our decor, Mr. Holmes."

No answer came. I thought Holmes's eyes lingered on the worn cushions of the chairs. I wondered if he suspected some type of bomb had been inserted beneath the red velvet, or somewhere within the white-painted frames.

"My father respected you greatly," D'Oyly Carte went on.

"We remember him fondly," I said, filling the conversational void.

"And my stepmother—she holds you in the same regard. She's at the helm now, steering the Troupe. I'm managing here."

Holmes nodded as if to himself, piecing together a puzzle. "You seem to be contemplating changes here at the hotel."

"What makes you say that?"

"This room wants maintenance. You have had a good season, so you do not lack the resources to bring the décor up to standards fit for royalty. Therefore, you are contemplating something larger, but too large and too time-consuming to complete in time for tonight's event."

The young man's eyes flickered, first with respect, then with indecision. Finally, he appeared to make up his mind. "You are right, Mr. Holmes. As a matter of fact, we are planning a grand expansion and renovation of the entire facility. Financing is already in place. Adjacent land has been acquired and the construction work will commence next year."

He paused and added, "When I say that financing is in place, I mean preliminary arrangements are agreed upon. However, the commitment could be withdrawn."

His next words were laced with a concern that was palpable. "Therefore, nothing adverse must mar tonight's proceedings."

"Would it be an adverse event if His Majesty declined to appear?" Holmes asked.

To my surprise, relief flickered across D'Oyly Carte's face. "To some, that would be a blessing. Yet, the press could see it differently. *King disdains the Savoy,* or some such headline."

"Surely your financial backers would not take that seriously."

"They know the King's health must be his primary concern. But the Americans might feel differently. I understand they are quite flattered that His Majesty has elected to include them in the festivities."

"For the economic reasons you related," Holmes said.

"Tobacco is king," D'Oyly Carte said.

"The Americans are guests here?" Holmes asked.

D'Oyly Carte nodded. "They have taken nearly two floors in the west wing." He gave a quick smile. "They seem a bit rough on occasion, as guests go."

"Rough?" I asked.

"Carryings-on from time to time. Guests with guests, if you take my meaning. Some of the staff refer to the west wing as 'Tobacco Road.'"

"Thank you for that information." Holmes looked at his watch. "You have been most helpful indeed. Now I must depart. As you said, it is a momentous day and there is a great deal of ground to cover."

* * *

We bade our goodbyes and left through the Savoy Lobby. Before we reached the great doorway leading to the Strand outside and the river beyond, Holmes turned to me. "Watson, do you remember the American that Miss Bly told us about?"

"Mr. Granby," I said.

"Perhaps you could gauge his thoughts on the King's attendance."

"Why send me to speak to him, instead of going yourself?"

"I expect he will speak more freely."

"You don't wish to make Mr. Granby unduly wary? You suspect him of something?"

"He may have knowledge that would be useful. You might inquire at the desk. Perhaps he is still in his room."

I nodded. "And do I mention Miss Bly?"

But Holmes was already moving through the great doors that led outside to the Strand.

CHAPTER 33: LUCY

Lady Aline swept out, and a moment later I heard her voice in the hall, asking whether the cab she'd ordered had arrived yet. Emmeline and I were temporarily alone.

"I know that you wanted to go out for a walk," I said. "But would you have just a moment to do me one favour?"

Emmeline regarded me with a definite lack of enthusiasm. "What is it?"

"I was wondering whether you could show me Lady Aline's conservatory?" I asked.

Emmeline blinked. "Why would you want to see that?"

"There will be photographs taken to go along with the article I'm writing, of course. My editor will send a photographer out to take them in a day or two, I expect. But it will be helpful if I can suggest settings that would make a good backdrop for photos. I'm sure he'll want pictures of you as well as Lady Aline. The flowers in the conservatory will make a lovely backdrop for someone with your colouring, if the lighting is right."

Emmeline still didn't look particularly happy about it, but she turned and led the way in silence across the room to the conservatory door.

"Here you are." Emmeline didn't actually enter the glassed-in room, just stood aside and waved a hand in invitation for me to enter. "I suppose this would be as good a place as any for

Aunt Aline to be photographed. Goodness knows she spends a ridiculous amount of time messing about in here."

"She's fond of gardening, then?" I asked. I'd already spotted the distillation apparatus on a long wooden work table that stood against one wall. But I wanted to hear what Emmeline would say.

"That. And brewing her revolting scents." Emmeline's nose wrinkled. "Why she bothers, I can't imagine. You can buy perfumes that are ever so much nicer at Harrods."

"Is that where she produces her extracts?" I gestured to the array of glass bottles and copper tubing.

"Yes, that's right." Emmeline still didn't come into the room, but stood in the doorway with the same expression of distaste. "She hasn't been making any scents lately. With all this fuss about the coronation ball, she's been too busy to come in here much. Although she wanted to provide the roses and lilies for the centrepieces tonight from here, not just order them from a flower shop."

Emmeline gestured to a row of rose bushes that had clearly been stripped of their blossoms; only one bush had more than a few flowers left on it, and the rest had only buds.

"How nice." I took a few steps forward as though to inspect the roses, but I let my gaze travel to the work table, as well.

There was a neat stack of small, paste-board boxes on the end of the table, of the kind found in chemists' shops. The label on the top one was visible: Sodium hydroxide.

Emmeline, looking clearly bored, shifted her weight restlessly. "Now, is that all?" she asked. "Because I really ought to be going."

"Yes, thank you." I gave her a sunny smile, despite the cold prickles that were inching their way across the back of my neck. "I believe I've seen everything I need."

CHAPTER 34: WATSON

"Oh yes, sir. Mr. Granby." The Savoy room clerk was quick to cooperate. "He and his American associates are here for the next several weeks, with the right to extend their stay as may become necessary. How may I help you?"

"Would you please ring his room and say Mr. Sherlock Holmes requests that he come to the lobby to meet Dr. Watson," I said.

"Which room, if you please, Dr. Watson?"

"He has more than one?"

"402 and 316."

I shrugged. "Try 402 first."

The clerk nodded. He reached Granby, made his request as instructed, gave an affirmative nod, and hung up his receiver. I put a shilling into his hand. He said, "Keep an eye on the lift. He'll be down shortly."

I waited, uncertain of how I would approach my interview with Granby. The assignment Holmes had given me had seemed a simple one only moments earlier, when I had approached the reception desk. Now, I was not so sure exactly what line I ought to take. Should I be direct, or more circumspect? Ought I to try to make friends first, establish a common mutuality of interest and then find out what Holmes had asked me to find out? Or should I be more straightforward?

Then Granby, who appeared to be in his early fifties, was

emerging from the lift and heading towards me, hand out-stretched. His voice carried the gentle lilt of the American South. "I'm Granby. Dr. Watson?"

We shook hands and moved to a quieter alcove within the Savoy's opulent lobby.

The American exuded an air of vitality, underscored by his impeccably tailored suit and polished tan boots. His grey hair was neatly trimmed, and his keen brown eyes seemed to take in everything.

When we were seated across from one another he began, a note of bemusement in his tone. "What could Mr. Sherlock Holmes possibly require from an ordinary gentleman such as myself?"

The mention of Holmes's name had clearly sparked his interest.

"We're seeking a missing person," I explained. "A Miss Nellie Bly. It has come to our attention that you might have made her acquaintance."

"Nellie Bly?" he repeated, with a flicker of concern. "She called me here and asked for a meeting. I promised her an exclusive if our deal comes to fruition. She's been a good source of information before. But you're telling me she's gone missing?"

I nodded. "So she didn't come here to meet you?"

Granby shook his head. "Never saw her after she telephoned."

"Did she mention anywhere else she planned to go?"

"No, not a word."

"You've known her how long?"

"About—let me see. We met at her wedding—so about seven years ago. She came to Europe with her husband."

"He's here now?" I asked.

"Oh, no, not as far as I know. He has a lot of business interests in the States. A goodly amount to occupy his time and attention."

Which relieved my mind somewhat. If Miss Bly had deliberately omitted such a significant fact as her husband's being with her in London, that would have cast doubt upon the remainder of her story.

"And your stay at the Savoy?" I continued. "Are you here at her suggestion?"

"Hardly," he chuckled. "It's for convenience's sake. Danny Hinchcliffe arranged it. There's a ball this evening, and the proximity to rooms here afterward is quite advantageous."

"Danny Hinchcliffe?"

"He's the Duke of Derrington. We just call him Danny, out of friendship from his time in America making deals for our tobacco."

"And he suggested you stay here and attend the ball?"

"Got us our rooms and the invitations to the ball as well. He said it would give us something to tell our grandchildren. A lot more exciting for them than the business deal we're here to make with the Imperial Tobacco folks."

"A deal?" I asked.

"You wouldn't know about it, but there's a price war going on that's no good for anyone except the man on the street. We've got to put a stop to it. Danny understands what needs to be done, and he'll do it. I've got to admit he's a superb negotiator, even though he's on the opposite side of the table from us. He'll find a way. Never takes no for an answer, does Danny."

"But he wanted you to attend the ball?"

"Right. As I said, grandchildren can't be expected to care two red cents about a business deal, but they sure do understand gowns and jewels and ceremonial costumes. The duke will have pictures made that we can take back to show at home."

At last I had my opening to pursue the question Holmes had told me to ask.

"So you'll go to the ball even if the King doesn't attend?"

"'Course we will," Granby said. "It's the spectacle. The lords and ladies and all the music and dancing, here in the big ballroom. We Americans don't get to see that every day. And they say nobody does this ceremonial stuff better than the British."

"So, no one among your delegation will complain if the King stays at home?"

A sly smile played on Granby's lips. "Oh, well, some fellows will seize any opportunity to gain an upper hand in negotiations."

"You're saying your colleagues would pretend to take offense?"

"Some of them, yes."

"But would that spoil your meetings with your British tobacco counterparts? And wouldn't that be harmful to the duke?"

"I'm not worried." Granby leaned forwards, hands on his knees. "We are businessmen, after all. And the facts are clear. We need to stop this foolish price undercutting and both sides know it. I'm sure we'll come to an arrangement somehow. As to your second point, Danny has interests in both camps. He's doubly motivated to have a truce in this destructive 'tobacco war,' as some folks call it."

"He stands to gain from a truce?"

"That's why he's paid for this shindig tonight," Granby said. "Spend money, make friends, and make more money."

I pondered this new information. I could see that the businessmen from America, being reasonable, might overlook the absence of the King tonight. But what if the duke's warning was correct and an assassination attempt were to be made? Lestrade's men would be vigilant, of course, but what if the worst were to occur? What if the assassination were to succeed?

It seemed obvious to me that if the event were to end in tragedy, the resulting chaos and police investigation would include all tonight's attendees. Such an investigation would doubtless bring many facets of information about those guests into public view. There was no telling how damaging that information might be to any individual, but those subject to such scrutiny would hardly be in the frame of mind to reach a friendly accord with their business counterparts.

And if this was obvious to me, surely it would be obvious to the duke as well.

Yet the duke had as much as accused his wife of planning the demise of the King. Why would he take the risk of allowing the event to continue, knowing that doing so could have horrible consequences, not only to his personal life but to his business relationships as well?

My mind swirled. Time to pursue other points of inquiry.

I asked, "Do you know a Miss Cavendish, a newspaper columnist?"

"Can't say that I do."

"She calls herself 'Lady Whispers' in her column."

He shrugged.

"She had an appointment with you last week."

"Did someone tell you that?"

"Nellie Bly found your name in Miss Cavendish's appointment book. Then Miss Cavendish was killed."

"How?"

"Murdered. In Hyde Park."

"If my name's in her book, I wonder why the police haven't been around to ask me about that."

"I couldn't say." Already I was wondering whether I had told Granby too much. It seemed unwise, somehow, to let the American know that the appointment book was missing, likely taken by the two thugs who had ransacked Miss Cavendish's room, and that Miss Bly hadn't told the police about the entry but had told Sherlock Holmes instead.

I pondered. Ought I to let Granby know? And should I tell him that in addition to the death of Miss Cavendish there had been five more murders? And that the police had not the slightest inkling as to any thread that might link them all?

Granby interrupted my reverie.

"You look like you could use a good cigar," he said.

From his jacket pocket he produced a fat cigar, dark brown, smooth, and thick with promise beneath its gold band. "For your enjoyment later."

I accepted with a polite nod, slipping the cigar into my pocket. "Thank you."

"You're in for a treat," he said, taking another cigar from his pocket and holding it up with a flourish. "This cigar is not merely tobacco. It's the pinnacle of indulgence. Havana blend on the inside, Connecticut wrapper leaf on the outside. A smoke fit for a king."

CHAPTER 35: FLYNN

Flynn held his breath, straining his ears to listen for any sounds of life from outside the trunk. But so far all he could hear was a whole lot of nothing. Someone had just been shot. He was going to guess that whoever had loosed off the pistol a few seconds ago wasn't just having fun. But which of them had it been? The Duke of Derrington? Or the coachman, Hutchins?

He couldn't think of any reason that either of them could have had for killing the other. But he'd swear that the gunshot had been so close that it couldn't have come from anywhere else but inside the carriage.

Finally, after he'd counted off somewhere around fifty or sixty beats of his own heart, he felt the carriage shift, the springs creaking as though a weight had just been taken off them. One of the two men had just climbed down.

Another hundred or so heartbeats, and Flynn felt Becky shift in the darkness enough that she could put her mouth closer to his ear and breathe in a near-soundless whisper, "Should we risk taking a look out now?"

Flynn hesitated, but then shrugged and reached for the lid of the trunk. "Worst thing that happens is we get shot."

"Well, when you put it that way—" But Becky was reaching up to brace her hands on the lid of the trunk, too. Together, they raised it a bare inch or so, just enough that they could peer out. After the hour they'd just spent in total darkness, even the narrow strip of sunlight that shone in through the crack was almost blinding. Flynn had to blink several times to clear the dazzle from his eyes.

Then what he did see made him suck in a quick breath:

They were surrounded by wooded parkland, deserted as far as the eye could see. No other people, no carriages. Not even any road, Flynn thought. The carriage was resting on a sweep of sandy ground spotted here and there with clumps of grass.

Flynn couldn't guess where they were, but he knew there were areas like this on Hampstead Heath. A figure in coachman's livery was just dragging the lifeless body of the Duke of Derrington into a clump of trees about fifty feet away.

At least, Flynn assumed it was the duke. He was wearing riding breeches and a dark blue coat. His head lolled back, hanging between his extended arms, his tall patent-leather riding boots were making twin furrows in the ground, and a crimson red stain was spreading across the chest of the white shirt that he wore under the riding coat.

"Hutchins!"

The coachman had his back to them, but Becky still spoke in an all-but-silent whisper.

Flynn nodded. "Why'd he want to kill his boss, though?"

Becky shook her head. "Maybe he's working with Lady Aline? Or whoever it is who wants to assassinate the king. Maybe he's a German spy."

That sounded like a plot straight out of sensational fiction to Flynn, but then what did he know?

The figure in green livery disappeared into the trees. Becky swallowed. "We could make a run for it now. We could probably be out of here and find somewhere to hide before he comes back."

The idea had more than a little appeal. But Flynn shook his head. "Better not."

"What?" Becky turned to stare at him. "I can't believe I'm the one trying to convince you to do the sensible thing and get out of here safely while we still can."

Flynn couldn't entirely believe it, either. But he still shook his head again. "Scarper now and we'll lose all hope of keeping track of where Hutchins goes after this. What if we lose sight of him and that's what gives him the chance to try and snuff the king?"

Becky exhaled a long breath, but finally said, "All right. We'll stay where we are. But I'm the one who's going to be saying, I told you so if this lands us in trouble."

Flynn just lowered the lid of the trunk back into place. "I don't think there's any if about it."

He'd be willing to bet this landed them in a whole ocean's worth of trouble. He just didn't see that they had any other choice.

CHAPTER 36: BECKY

Becky startled as the carriage slowed and then drew to a gradual halt. She almost jerked upright, but stopped herself when she remembered that she'd only smack her head against the top of the trunk. She wouldn't have believed it possible, but the darkness and the stuffy air and the rhythmic clip-clop of the horses had all combined to lull her into an almost waking doze. She was fully awake now, though.

"Where are we, do you think?" she whispered to Flynn.

She sensed rather than saw him raise a shoulder in the dark. "I'd guess back in London. Listen."

Now that the carriage was no longer moving, Becky could hear the noise of street traffic again: automobile horns, shouts from street vendors and newspaper boys, the rumble and clatter of other carriage wheels. The threads of tension that had been pulling tight under her ribcage loosened a fraction. They were still hiding in the back of a carriage driven by a murderer, but there was a definite comfort in being back on familiar ground, not to mention being surrounded by other people again.

"So why are we stopping?" she whispered back.

"Search me." Flynn stopped, and Becky pictured him tilting his head to listen.

The carriage springs creaked with the now-familiar sound of weight being lifted off them. A murmur of voices followed, though they were too low for Becky to make out any of the words besides, "Derrington."

Then silence.

"Hutchins must have left the carriage," Flynn murmured. "Come on. We need to find out where he's going."

Becky's heart sped up at the thought of lifting the trunk lid and coming out of hiding, but Flynn was right. Besides, they'd come too far to lose Hutchins now.

Together they pushed the trunk lid open a crack and peered out—straight into the astonished-looking eyes of a young boy dressed in the coarse linen shirt and rough breeches of a stable hand.

"Gorblimey!" The boy jumped back, one hand clapped over his heart. He looked to be about eleven or twelve years old, with a thin, sharp-featured face, watery blue eyes, and a scattering of freckles across his nose and cheeks. "What the dickens are you doing in there?"

Hutchins seemed to have driven the carriage into a large and prosperous-looking stable yard. But it wasn't the stable yard back at Derrington House. This one was built on a far bigger scale, fenced in by tall brick walls and containing space for at least a dozen carriages. Their carriage had been pulled into one of the brick carriage buildings, and the stable boy—to judge by the bucket of curry brushes and combs that he carried—must have been about to unhitch the horses and rub them down.

Outside of the stable building was a large, square cobblestone yard, where another boy led a handsome blue roan horse towards another stall. More workers were pitching hay into feeding racks and mucking out stalls, but none of them had yet noticed Becky and Flynn.

Becky was still trying to think up a plausible explanation for their presence when Flynn pushed the trunk lid fully open and hopped down to the hay-strewn ground.

"We're detectives, keeping watch on the driver of this carriage."

"Detectives?" The stable boy looked them up and down with the beginnings of a sneer. "Go on, pull the other one."

Flynn didn't answer that, just dug into his pocket and came up with a shilling piece, which he handed over to the boy. "That's for not saying anything about us to whoever the boss is around here. And there's another one for you if you can tell me where we are and where the coachman who left this carriage went."

The stable boy looked down at the coin in his hand.

Becky climbed down from the trunk, too, landing beside Flynn just as the stable boy's head lifted and a sly smile spread over his face.

"Bet I'll get rewarded with more than a shilling if I turn the two of you in for trespassing."

Becky suppressed a sigh. She'd been hoping that something about this assignment would turn out to be easy. She shot Flynn a questioning look, and he gave a short fraction of a nod in answer.

He was skinnier than the stable hand, but tougher. Becky didn't doubt that Flynn could trounce the other boy in a fight. But if Flynn made any moves in that direction, the stable boy would see the fight coming—and that would turn into a battle that would last quite a while, right when they were short on time and didn't want to attract anyone else's attention.

The most deadly threat is the one you don't see coming. That was a favourite saying of Lucy's.

"You really don't want to do that," she told the stable boy.

"Oh?" The boy gave her another sneer. "And why's that?"

"Because after I knock you down, I'm going to take all of those curry combs in the bucket you're holding and break them, one by one. Then you'll be the one in trouble for spoiling your boss's property, and you'll have to pay for them out of your wages."

The stable hand stared at her as though he was trying to make up his mind whether she was joking or just plain crazy. Becky didn't give him enough time to decide for sure. She'd been terrified, bumped, bruised, and almost smothered by being inside the trunk for what had to be over an hour. And she was worried about Nellie Bly, besides.

Her hand shot out, seizing hold of the stable boy's wrist and yanking him forward before he had a chance to realise what she was about to do. Then, while he was momentarily off balance, she hooked her ankle around his lower leg so that his foot was pulled out from under him.

Lucy was the one who'd taught her that move, and it worked just like Lucy had always told her it would.

The stable boy fell backwards, landing flat on his back with a whump that vibrated the carriage wheels and made the horses stamp their feet and give a couple of nervous snorts. The bucket of curry brushes flew out of the boy's hand, and Becky picked it up.

"Wait!" The breath had been knocked out of the stable boy when he fell; the word came out more as a croak than anything intelligible.

Becky paused in the act of reaching for one of the combs. "Yes?"

The boy struggled to prop himself up on his elbows and spoke between efforts to catch his breath. "This is the Savoy Hotel."

"The Savoy?" Becky was surprised, although she probably shouldn't have been.

"That's right." The boy jerked his chin in the affirmative, giving her a sullen look from under his brows. "You probably know it already, and if you don't, you should, but this here is the Duke of Derrington's carriage. His coachman just left it here on account of the duke's staying here tonight. His wife's putting on a great fancy to-do for the king's coronation, in case you haven't heard."

CHAPTER 37: WATSON

From the Savoy, I walked along Charlotte Street, intending to walk to the Regent's Park and then to meet Holmes in our rooms at Baker Street so that we could make final preparation for the Coronation Ball this evening.

I could not, however, arrange in my mind the details of the report I would give to Holmes.

Ahead I saw the small park known as Soho Gardens. Sheltered by a green hedge, an empty bench there seemed to beckon me.

I sat, determined to arrange my thoughts.

In my memory, I went over my interview with Granby.

Granby had claimed to know nothing about the entry Miss Cavendish had made in her appointment book concerning a meeting that was to take place last week. He had said he did not even know her.

Yet he had readily acknowledged making an appointment with Miss Bly for yesterday, an appointment which she had not kept.

Two appointments, neither of which had taken place.

Had there been a connection?

Flynn had been with Miss Bly when she had been abducted in a motorised vehicle near Fleet Street, nearly a mile from the Savoy.

How could Granby have been involved in the abduction?

Could he have told someone about the upcoming appointment with Miss Bly? A difficult task, though, to find her near Fleet Street and be ready with a vehicle.

Something still bothered me about Granby. Something I could not put my finger on.

I retreated into my memory again. Granby had not seemed distressed about the possibility that the King might not attend the Coronation Ball. He had seemed confident that a mutually beneficial arrangement would be made between the two giant tobacco conglomerates, whether the King attended or not.

Business was business, after all.

But something was wrong somewhere.

I cast my mind back to the start of the interview. When Granby had appeared at the elevator, I had been waiting and he had recognised me. We had introduced ourselves and walked over to the lobby alcove. We had sat and conducted a perfectly congenial conversation.

And what had been the result?

In my imagination, the voice of Holmes suddenly made itself heard.

The result of the meeting, Watson?

I replied, "Granby showed no concern for the King's attendance or non-attendance at the Coronation Ball. And Granby gave me a cigar. 'A cigar fit for a king,' he had called it."

So the only thing that happened, Watson, is that you received a cigar?

"No, Holmes. I did get information. But I judge it to be unimportant. I heard nothing that presented a motive for an attack on the king, or—"

Or what, Watson?

I shook my head. "I simply do not feel right about it."

I suggest we take that as a point of inquiry. You received information, and yet you felt you were missing something. What did Mr. Granby say that first gave you this feeling? When did you first have this feeling?

At Holmes's last imagined question, I felt a rush of embarrassment, mingled with relief. I recalled that I had felt unease even before I first laid eyes on Mr. Granby.

"I must go back to the Savoy at once," I said.

Then I stood up from the park bench, hoping no one nearby had been listening to my one-sided dialogue.

CHAPTER 38: LUCY

After the dignified butler had showed me out and closed the front door to Derrington House behind me, I stood for a moment on the front step, deliberating.

My visit had taken long enough that Flynn and Becky ought to have been long since done with their search of the duke and duchess's stables. And if they'd been caught, I would surely have heard the uproar, which should mean that they'd come away cleanly. But I still had to fight against the impulse to invent an excuse for strolling past the stables, just to be certain.

I was still debating with myself when an amiable looking old man dressed in the black coat and wide-brimmed black hat of a nonconformist clergyman strolled past the house, making for Wilton Crescent.

He wasn't moving terribly quickly; I caught up with him just as he was removing a bag of breadcrumbs from his coat pocket to scatter for the pigeons that were flocking on the stretch of green lawn.

"Revisiting old favourites among your disguises?" The clergyman persona was one he had used before.

Holmes brushed crumbs from his fingers and turned to regard me calmly from behind the lenses of the pair of round-rimmed spectacles that went with the costume. "I wanted to be certain that you would recognise me."

I didn't mention that he could have chosen a more auspicious disguise. The most memorable occasion on which he'd worn his present garb had been when he was recognised and outwitted by Irene Adler.

"What's happened?" I asked instead. Clearly the matter must be urgent, otherwise Holmes would have simply waited until I returned to Baker Street.

"The duke left in the carriage a short while ago," Holmes said. "I have been keeping watch on the house from a distance, and observed him drive away in the company of his coachman."

"Yes, he told his wife he was going to call at the wine merchant's shop. Was there any sign of Flynn and Becky?" I asked.

"His Grace was alone in the carriage," Holmes said. "However, I believe an examination of the trunk strapped to the luggage rack of the carriage might have shown an additional two passengers."

"Let's hope that the same thought doesn't occur to either the coachman or the duke."

It was difficult not to let my mind jump immediately to the worst possible scenario of their having stowed away on the duke's carriage. But if Flynn and Becky seemed to bounce into one danger after another like a pair of India rubber balls, they also tended to bounce out again unscathed.

"Do you think they'll be all right?" I asked Holmes.

Holmes' gaze was abstracted, as though he were thinking of something else, but he said, "I give them at least a seventy-eight per cent chance of ending today without coming to harm."

There were times when I wished my father were a little less rigorous in his scientific commitment to the truth. But there was very little I could do to help Flynn and Becky now, beyond solving the case before us.

"Lady Aline received a message a short while ago, summoning her to the Savoy."

"Did she indeed." I had the impression that my announcement was merely confirming something that Holmes had already been expecting, an impression which was proved accurate a moment later when he went on, "It is fortunate, in that case, that I took the precaution of asking Watson to remain at the Savoy."

"And you and I are going … where?"

Holmes tossed the remaining bread crumbs to the birds and folded the paper bag. "To Buckingham Palace. It is no surprise that our sovereign's schedule is exceedingly full. But I have been informed that if we can be at the palace within the next twenty minutes, we may have a brief audience with the king."

CHAPTER 39: FLYNN

"Do you know where the Duke of Derrington's coachman went after he left the carriage here?" Becky asked the stable boy.

His encounter with the ground hadn't put the stable hand in a better mood. He was back on his feet again, but he gave Becky a withering look. He snorted. "He handed me the reins, told me to be sure and see that the horses got a good rub-down. I said, Right you are, gov, and he walked away. That's as much as I know."

And it was all that they were likely to get out of him.

Becky thought so, too, because she put down the bucket of curry combs and brushes.

The stable boy flinched at the movement as if he was scared that she was going to dump him on his backside again. Then his lip curled. "I could still get you thrown out of here for trespassing. Maybe even arrested."

Becky must have been expecting him to say something along those lines, because she didn't miss a beat. "You'd have to catch us, first."

As she spoke, she toed over the bucket, scattering the combs and brushes all over the stable floor. The stable boy gave a yell of surprise, but by that time Becky had already bolted out the stable door. Flynn followed close on her heels, although he took the time to toss another shilling over his shoulder. He saw the coin hit the stable boy square in the middle of the forehead. Then he turned and ran after Becky.

Together, they tore across the courtyard and into the narrow lane that ran along the back of the hotel, then turned a corner, and from there entered the Strand.

Becky slowed to a walk. "You must be getting soft."

Flynn knew she was talking about his giving the stable boy another shilling. He shrugged. "He's going to be in trouble with his boss for letting the brushes get all muddy. There's a better chance he'll keep his mouth shut about us if he at least makes a profit on the afternoon."

"He'd do that anyway. He'd sound crazy if he tried to tell the head of the stables that a pair of stowaways in the Duke of Derrington's carriage kicked all of his tools into the mud," Becky said. "But fine. He's probably having a worse day than we are."

Flynn wasn't going to put money on that, but he said, "Where to now?"

They'd circled around to the front of the hotel, where a fountain was splashing in the middle of a bed of flowers. Becky looked up at the terraced balconies that decorated the upper windows and doorways. Cream coloured pillars with gilded capitals supported the terraces, and more flowers spilled out of boxes at each window.

"Hutchins must have a had a reason for coming here, of all places. I mean, he could have left the carriage anywhere—but he drove straight here."

"The coronation ball is tonight," Flynn said. "If he's planning to take a pot shot at the king, he'd have to be here."

"So he's probably here now. Hiding somewhere," Becky said,

still looking up at the Savoy's glazed white brick walls. "The question is where."

"The real question's how do we find him," Flynn corrected.

"True." Becky tapped her chin with the tip of one finger. "We have to do this carefully. If he's already committed at least one murder; he's not going to hesitate to commit more if he thinks we're onto him."

Flynn nodded. He wasn't squeamish, and he'd never known the Duke of Derrington. But he didn't like recalling the way the duke's head had flopped lifelessly while Hutchins dragged his body away into the trees.

Becky frowned a moment longer. Then she started towards the hotel entrance. "We need to get a look at the register."

"You're not going to get very far into the Savoy looking like that," Flynn pointed out. Neither of them was.

Becky might be dressed up like a street urchin, but she wasn't used to thinking about how many doors got slammed in your face when everyone believed that you actually were one.

"You're right." Becky looked down at her ragged jacket and dirty trousers, which didn't look any better for having been stuffed into a musty trunk for the past couple of hours. "Bother. Well, we'll just have to think of something else, then."

"Like what?"

"Like …" Becky's gaze wandered over the street, the fountain, and the front of the hotel, then finally lighted on an elderly flower vendor who had stopped to sit down on a bench and rest her feet. The woman's tray, filled with bunches of violets and pansies, sat on the bench beside her. "Like that!" Becky said. "How much money do we have left?"

Flynn dug in his pockets, coming up with a handful of coins, which he rapidly counted. "One shilling, sixpence."

"And I've got half a crown," Becky said. "That makes four shillings all together."

Her jaw was set with a determined look that always gave Flynn a bad feeling about what was coming, but she started towards the grey-haired flower vendor before he could argue or ask exactly what she had in mind. "Well, that will just have to be enough."

CHAPTER 40: BECKY

Becky balanced the tray of flowers carefully, trying to look well-behaved and respectable as she approached the doorman who was guarding the main entrance to the Savoy.

The flower vendor had wanted to haggle a bit, but in the end she had accepted the four shillings that Becky offered her in exchange for all of her flowers and the tray to carry them, besides. It was probably more money than she saw in an entire week, so Becky didn't wonder that the old woman had agreed to the bargain.

She and Flynn had divided the flowers between them. The tray was big enough to hold all of the bouquets, really. But if Becky had carried them into the hotel alone, that would have left Flynn without a convincing reason for coming along. They'd used a couple of handfuls of water from the hotel fountain to splash water on their faces and neaten up Flynn's hair. Becky's braids were still tucked up under her cap, but she'd done her best to make sure that her hands and face were clean.

Now she just had to talk her way inside the Savoy.

She smiled at the doorman as she stopped in front of the entrance. He was a big, burly man with dark hair and side whiskers, and he didn't give her so much as a flicker of a smile in return, just stared stolidly straight ahead as though he were looking straight through her.

Not a very promising start, but Becky didn't let herself feel daunted. The doorman wasn't likely to pull out a gun and try to shoot them, which in her book made him the least intimidating character they'd encountered this morning.

"Good day," she said. "We've got a delivery for the Duke of Derrington."

The doorman's expression didn't change, but he did transfer the flat stare from the middle distance to focus on her. Becky did her best not to squirm while he studied her for a long moment.

Finally he said, "Flowers? I wasn't told about another delivery."

"They're not for the ball," Becky said. "They told me at the flower shop that the duke ordered them to be sent here as a surprise for his wife. They're to be taken straight up to the duchess's suite."

She was hoping that Lady Aline did, in fact, have a suite of rooms reserved at the hotel. Or that if she didn't, the doorman didn't know it.

The doorman's eyes narrowed. "Why would His Grace send Her Grace the Duchess posies of violets?"

That was the drawback to this plan. Violets weren't exactly rich people's sort of flowers, not when you could buy them on the street for a penny a bunch. Or four shillings for an entire tray.

Becky shrugged, trying to look unconcerned. "Search me, gov. Maybe violets are her favourite?"

She had the feeling that the doorman might have argued or asked more probing questions—like which florists' shop they'd come from—but at that moment, a stout white-haired woman came sweeping up to the Savoy's entrance like a galleon in full sail, her nose in the air. Three servants, all of them laden down with parcels and bags and packages, trailed along in her wake.

Becky had no idea who the woman might be, but she was clearly Somebody—and evidently the doorman agreed. He jerked his head in an impatient motion for Flynn and Becky to get inside and out of the way, then bowed to the stout woman.

"Your ladyship. I hope you had an agreeable morning of shopping?"

Becky didn't wait to find out whether Her Ladyship had. Clutching the tray of violets, she scuttled inside and across the hotel lobby, with Flynn following close at her heels. Hurdle number one was over and done with. Now hurdle number two.

The lobby of the Savoy was built on even grander lines than the fountained courtyard outside. The walls were panelled in two shades of dark green stamped velvet, with a marble frieze that ran all the way around the room. Gold pillars reached up to the ceiling, which was painted in white and gold. Orange shades to the electric globes that hung from the ceiling cast a soft warm light over the groups of hotel guests sitting on the green velvet chairs and sofas, sipping tea and reading newspapers.

Becky made straight for the long mahogany desk at the back of the lobby.

"We're here with a delivery for the Duchess of Derrington," she told the clerk. "We're supposed to bring these flowers up to her room."

The clerk was a weedy-looking young man with heavily brilliantined hair parted in the centre and a few sparse hairs on his upper lip that could optimistically be called a moustache. He squinted down at them through a pair of horn-rimmed spectacles. But apparently he had a far less suspicious nature than the doorman, because he just pulled the big leather-bound hotel ledger towards him and ran his finger down the list of entries.

As he was looking, Becky turned to Flynn and said, under her breath, "Distract him."

"What?"

"Distract him!"

Flynn gave her a look, but at least he didn't hesitate. He pretended to stumble, dropping several of his bouquets of flowers all over the marble tiled floor. Petals scattered everywhere.

The clerk's head jerked up, his eyes widening at the mess. "Look here, watch what you're doing!"

"Sorry about that." Flynn bent to gather up the flowers. "Just slipped out of my hands."

He tried to scoop up the fallen bouquets, but in the process managed to drop several more. People were beginning to stop and stare.

"Stop!" The clerk came around to their side of the desk and started to help pick up the scattered flowers. He said something else—scolding Flynn for clumsiness, most likely. But Becky wasn't paying attention.

Flynn managed to bump heads with the clerk, making it look like another accident. The clerk let out a yelp, followed by another growl at Flynn to watch what he was doing.

And while they were both crawling around on the floor, Becky stood on her tip-toes and scanned the entries in the hotel ledger. Reading upside-down wasn't easy, but she'd been practicing for situations exactly like this one. She even managed to flip back a page or two and read the earlier entries before the clerk finally dumped the now slightly crumpled violets into Flynn's arms and with a huff returned to his place behind the desk.

"The Duchess of Derrington is in room"—he ran his eyes down the page—"Room 311."

He didn't actually add, *Now get out and stay out*. But from his tone of voice the implication was clear.

Becky turned and started towards the corridor marked *Lift* at the back of the lobby.

"You could have told me what you were planning," Flynn muttered as they walked away.

"I did."

"I meant telling me with more than about two second's notice."

"It worked, didn't it? You distracted him perfectly. And I got a look at the list of guests staying here."

"Anything interesting?" Flynn asked.

"I think so." Becky paused to let a mother shepherding two small children get into the electric lift ahead of them, then lowered her voice, though it was hard to contain her excitement. "I didn't see Hutchins' name anywhere."

"Not likely he'd book a room under his own name," Flynn pointed out.

"No. Obviously not, but I had to be certain. That's not the interesting part. What I did see was two separate entries for that American tobacco baron that Nellie Bly knew about. The one Mr. Holmes sent Dr. Watson to talk to?"

Flynn looked at her, suddenly more alert. "George Granby? And he had two entries in the hotel register?"

"That's the one. And yes. He's reserved both Room 402 and Room 316. He signed into room 402 a few days ago, but Room 316 was only reserved for him yesterday."

Flynn pursed his lips in a silent whistle. "We hadn't thought about him for a suspect. But he's someone who might not like the Duke of Derrington, if they're business rivals."

"I'd be willing to bet that Mr. Holmes has considered him

as a suspect all right, otherwise why send Dr. Watson?" Becky said. "But I agree. We don't know any reason why this Granby might want to assassinate the king."

"So we need to get inside the room—the one that was only booked yesterday," Flynn said.

"Exactly." A hotel page boy in a brass buttoned jacket and pill box hat was hurrying towards them along the hall. Becky didn't know whether page boys carried pass keys to the hotel rooms, but surely they could find some employee of the Savoy who did. She glanced at Flynn. "I hope you haven't forgotten how to pick pockets since coming to work for Mr. Holmes."

CHAPTER 41: LUCY

The royal residence of Buckingham Palace stood at the far east end of St. James Park, stately and impressive with its classical white columned portico at the centre of the edifice. Holmes and I arrived just at the finish of the changing of the Guard, and had to stand to one side and wait while the stiffly erect guardsman in their famous red tunics and tall black bearskin hats marched in time to the brass military band.

"I suppose we can hope that his ascension to the throne has had a sobering effect on His Majesty?" I said as we watched the ranks of soldiers finish the ceremony and assume their appointed places in front of the palace.

"You are pointing out that we are once again risking our own lives for the sake of a man who is notoriously—some might even say flagrantly—unfaithful to his wife the queen, and whose tastes for expensive wines, cigars, and cuisine verge on the hedonistic?"

"I might not have put it quite that way, but yes." This wasn't by any means the first time we had encountered our sovereign King Edward VII, as he was now styling himself, although it was our first meeting with him since he had assumed the throne. Our last encounter had been at Ascot, when he was still Prince Albert, the oldest son of the late queen.

Holmes waited for the band to stop playing and then started

up the wide marble steps at the front of the palace. We were evidently expected; none of the guard moved to stop us.

"The death of Queen Victoria unsettled the country—indeed, the entirety of the British Empire," he said. "One might call it the end of an era. And at such times, people need a symbol of stability to cling to. A promise of hope and security for the future."

"Such as the institution of the monarchy—no matter how flawed the human face of that institution may be?"

"As you say. Also, all talk of institutions and symbols aside, our king is a mortal man, with a mortal man's life to be saved, as we would save any other life that was threatened by criminal treachery or greed."

He was right, of course.

Upon our entrance, we were shown into the Green Drawing-room at the eastern front of the palace. The long, high-ceilinged room was hung with green satin, striped and relieved with gilding, and the door and shutter panels were filled with mirrors that reflected the morning sun. Gilt-framed portraits in oils adorned the walls, and crystal chandeliers hung from the ceiling.

The uniformed servant who had ushered us in announced our names and retired, leaving us to the heavyset bearded man who was sitting on one of the green satin sofas that were grouped around the vast marble fireplace.

"Your Majesty." Holmes bowed, and I followed suit with a curtsy.

King Edward waved the gestures aside. "Please. No formality here. The two of you have saved me from being blown up, shot, and poisoned. That surely entitles a certain degree of familiarity. Besides which, I find I have small patience for ceremony at the moment." The king shifted position and grimaced. "As you know, I have escaped death before. And two years ago, a wretched Belgian boy attempted to shoot me as I was on my way to Denmark. That was a near miss if ever there was one. But I have never realised my own mortality so fully as I did while listening to the surgeons discuss my chances of survival if they did not risk operating."

"We're happy to find that the operation was a success," I said.

King Edward's gaze moved from Holmes to me. I could see at first glance the stamp that his recent bout with appendicitis had left on him: his face had an unhealthy, yellowish pallor, and there were pouches under his eyes and lines on his face that hadn't been there before. "Thank you, Miss James. Or rather I should say Mrs. Kelly. You're looking as lovely as ever."

I smiled. At one point, the king—he had been the Prince of Wales then—had made it clear that he wouldn't be at all averse to adding me to the ranks of his many dalliances. Although he'd shortly thereafter decided that he didn't entirely know what to make of me, since I was capable of firing a gun, defending myself in close combat, and unlike many women didn't trip over myself with eagerness at the thought of becoming a royal mistress. His attitude towards me had in the end arrived at something approaching respect, which I suspected was rather a novelty for him.

"I hope your husband realises what a fortunate man he is," King Edward finished.

"Don't worry, I make sure that he does."

"Capital, capital." King Edward's focus shifted once more to include us both. "This rather puts me in mind of Shakespeare: When shall we three meet again? In thunder, lightning, or in rain?" He coughed, winced, but then went on, "Or on the occasion of a coronation ball, eh?"

"That is precisely the matter on which I had hoped to engage your attention," Holmes said. "If you are still feeling well enough to attend?"

"Oh, indeed. I would not miss such an occasion."

King Edward waved a hand as though to dispel the impression that his recent brush with death had produced in him anything like sobriety. I remembered that according to rumour, within twenty-four hours of the operation for appendicitis, he'd been sitting up in bed and smoking a cigar.

Despite—or perhaps because of—his royal position, he could with some justification claim a difficult upbringing. From birth, he'd had the burden of his parents' high expectations heaped up on him, expectations to which he could never fully measure up. He'd been thwarted by his mother the queen in his one desire for an active career in the army, then blamed by her for his father Prince Albert's death, when Albert had travelled to Cambridge to issue a reprimand to his son over an affair with an actress and died of typhoid fever two weeks later. And throughout his life, King Edward had also possessed both the means and the opportunity to indulge his every desire and whim.

The result was the genial, often selfish, frequently kind, and always complex man who now sat before us.

"Eat, drink, and be merry, for tomorrow we may die," King Edward finished. He stopped and fixed Holmes with a keen look that reminded me that, for all his love of luxury, the king was not a stupid man. "Or perhaps tonight? That is what you are come to tell me, are you not? That there is some threat in the offing at tonight's ball?"

"I fear so, your majesty. Although there is as yet some question as to from what direction that threat may arise."

King Edward's scrutiny of Holmes's expression intensified. "But you suspect?"

"I do."

King Edward made another expansive gesture. "In that case, I put myself entirely in your hands. I have trusted you with my life before this and you've not led me awry. Tell me what you would have me do."

CHAPTER 42: FLYNN

Flynn stood at the door to room 316 and hesitated, the pass key in his hand.

Getting the key hadn't been any challenge. He didn't pick pockets too often these days—only when Mr. Holmes needed him to—but he hadn't lost the knack. A walk down the hotel corridor had given him three separate chances to bump into hotel employees, and on the third try he'd been able to lift the ring of keys off a middle-aged woman in a housekeeper's uniform.

She'd sent him away with a flea in his ear, but she'd never even noticed that her keys were gone.

Still, Flynn looked up at Becky before inserting the key into the lock. "What happens if this is the wrong room? I mean to say, what if this is the room where George Granby is actually staying?"

"Then we pretend to be delivering him some flowers?"

Flynn's bouquets had been too bruised and crumpled by their encounter with the lobby floor to pass for a believable delivery anymore, but Becky was still carrying her tray of violets.

The story sounded thin to Flynn, but it wasn't as if he had any better ideas—which Becky was no doubt about to point out to him. So he just slid the key into the lock and opened the hotel room door.

The room inside was dim, the lights out and the curtains

drawn, which relieved Flynn's mind somewhat. George Granby wasn't likely to be sitting here alone in the dark.

The relief only lasted a couple of seconds, though, before Becky gave a small, startled exclamation and pointed to the bed. Flynn's stomach dropped. A woman's motionless figure was lying stretched out on top of the coverlet. She wasn't asleep. Flynn couldn't have said how he knew that for certain, except that there was something unnatural in how still she was lying, her feet together, her arms straight at her sides.

Flynn's first thought was that it was Nellie Bly, and that she was dead. But then he saw that this woman had blond hair.

Becky drew in a quick breath as she stepped over to the side of the bed. "That's Lady Aline!"

She reached to feel for a pulse in the duchess's neck, then lifted one of her eyelids. Lady Aline didn't move or even stir. "She's still alive," Becky said. "But I think she's been drugged with some sort of narcotic—a powerful one."

Flynn came over to stand beside her. "Why? And by who?"

Becky shook her head. "I have no idea. But this makes it look more likely that Lady Aline really is innocent."

"Unless she and whoever she was working with had a falling—"

Out, Flynn was about to say. But at that moment, someone seized him from behind in a vise grip. A rough cloth sack was yanked down over his head, so that he couldn't see anything. He still tried to kick out at his attacker, but he felt a sharp prick like an insect's sting in his neck. Cool numbness flooded his body, turning his muscles into rubber.

His last conscious thought was that the inside of the burlap sack over his head smelled familiar. Then everything stopped.

PART FOUR

CHAPTER 43: BECKY

Becky woke up with throbbing pain in her shoulders and her neck, and a feeling like her head had been stuffed with tangled-up skeins of Mrs. Hudson's yarn. She managed to pry open her eyes and discovered that her shoulders hurt because her hands were tied behind her back. She also found that she was lying on her side on a carpeted floor, and that Flynn was just a few feet away.

"Flynn!"

Flynn's hands were tied like hers, and his eyes were closed, but his lashes fluttered at the sound of her voice.

"Flynn! Wake up!"

His eyes opened, focusing on her, and then he groaned. "What happened?"

"I don't remember." The memory of how they'd come to be here and what had happened to them would probably come back to her sooner or later, but for now it kept slithering out of her grasp. "Do you?"

Flynn's brows knitted together in effort. "I remember smell-ing … smoke? And I think tobacco."

"Oh, well, mystery solved then." Becky tried to move her legs and discovered that her feet were tied together at the ankles, too. "We were attacked by a packet of cigarettes."

She raised her head enough that she could at least take a look around them.

They were in what seemed to be a bathing chamber: a small, square room with a single window, a vanity table with a row of small glass bottles arranged in front of the mirror, and a deep cast iron bath tub that stood against one wall. The floor was white and black tile, and the walls were painted in pale green.

Memory—and the realisation of where they were—finally hit Becky like a sledge-hammer blow. "The Savoy!"

Flynn must have remembered at exactly the same time, because her words collided in mid-air with Flynn's. "The Duchess of Derrington!"

Becky nodded. When she turned her head, she could see the door of the bathing chamber: a solid panel of dark mahogany. Lady Aline—assuming that no one had moved her—must be on the other side of that door. The Savoy Hotel prided itself on the modern convenience of providing private bath rooms for the hotel suites; it was a selling point for their richest guests. That must be where she and Flynn were now: stashed in the bathing chamber attached to room number 316.

Though that realisation raised more questions than it answered.

"We were drugged," she said. "Injected with something."

She couldn't reach up to feel with her fingers, but there was a sore spot on the side of her neck.

"Probably the same stuff that someone gave the duchess," Flynn said with a grimace. "What I'd like to know is, Why bother? Whoever shut us up in here could just as easily have killed us."

That wasn't a comforting thought, but he was right. "Obviously they have plans for us and for Lady Aline."

Plans that Becky would bet didn't involve their living to a ripe old age.

"How long do you think we were unconscious?" she asked.

"Had to be hours," Flynn said. "Look."

He nodded to the window, which was fitted with glazed, opaque glass for privacy's sake. Becky couldn't see any details of the view outside, but all the same she could tell that Flynn was right. The light slanting in on them had the purple, dusky quality of early evening, with a yellow-tinged glow that had to be the streetlights coming on.

Becky threw her weight to the side, trying to lever her way up into a sitting position, but all she managed to accomplish was to grind her cheek harder against the grout between the floor tiles.

"The ball will probably be starting soon," she said.

"Probably."

"So how do we get ourselves untied and away?" Whoever had drugged them and tied them up was bound to be back, and more probably sooner than later.

Flynn's gaze travelled around the room, then lighted on the vanity with its row of glass bottles. "What would it take to smash a couple of those?"

Becky looked at him. "Having the use of our hands and feet, for starters."

"Not if we can knock them over and onto the floor. Watch yourself; you might want to cover your face for this."

It took some effort, but Flynn managed to wriggle and slide his way over to the bottom of the vanity. He drew back, then slammed his shoulder against the wooden base. The glass bottles rattled in their places, but didn't fall. Still, the idea had promise.

"Move over," Becky said.

She set her jaw and manoeuvered herself around, scrabbling

and pushing with her heels against the tiles until she could position herself next to Flynn.

"On three?"

Flynn nodded. "One. Two."

On three, both of them threw their weight hard against the base of the vanity. Becky heard the clatter of at least one glass bottle falling over, then rolling towards the edge. For what seemed like an endless second, it paused there, suspended. Then came the glorious smash of glass against the floor.

Becky felt the sting of a small shard striking her cheek, but she didn't care. The glass bottle now lay in broken fragments. Picking one of the biggest pieces up with her hands tied together wasn't easy, but she managed it.

"Now," she said. "Let's cut these ropes and get out of here."

CHAPTER 44: WATSON

Inside the Savoy lobby, I watched the reception desk.

"402 or 316?" the clerk had asked. He had rung 402, received his reply right away, and Granby had come down less than three minutes after the call,

So, why 316? Why would an American businessman need a second room on a different floor?

One way to find out.

I walked up the side stairs to the West Wing rather than taking the lift. I did not wish to have my movements known.

Three flights up, I opened the door to the hallway and saw a sign with room numbers. To the right were 300 to 305; to the left were 306-321.

I strode in the direction of 316, I reached it, and stepped forwards to knock.

But then the door opened.

Before me stood Flynn and Becky. Just behind them was an open door leading into a bathing chamber, and a pile of ropes.

"How did you find us?" Becky asked. She was rubbing her wrist.

"No time to explain," I said. "I'm looking for Mr. Granby."

"The tobacco man?" Becky asked. "Miss Bly said she had an appointment with him. Was he the one who brought us here and knocked us out?"

"The man himself was in the lobby about an hour ago, talking with me. But he could have hired someone."

"Well, there's no sign of anyone else here. No suitcases, no clothes in the closets. We can show you if you like," Becky said.

"I believe you. Do you think whoever did this will come back?"

She was about to answer when, from the room next door, we heard a high-pitched, shuddering moan.

CHAPTER 45: LUCY

Holmes and I stood on the steps of Buckingham Palace, looking out towards St. James Park. Boys on bicycles raced to and fro. A man with a donkey was giving rides to children in exchange for a penny.

"I didn't have the chance to tell you earlier," I said. "But Lady Aline confirmed that Emma Thompkins was a former maid of hers. She says that she gave the Dresden statue to Emma as a parting gift when Emma left her service years ago. Or rather, I suggested that was the case, and Lady Aline agreed."

"Did she indeed." Holmes' gaze was both distant and speculative. If I had to guess, I would say that he was meticulously plotting out possible scenarios for tonight's ball in the way that chess players anticipated the moves and counter moves of a game.

"Yes. Also, I got a look into her conservatory. Her hobby is distilling flower essences into various perfumes, apparently. One of the chemicals that she has on her worktable is sodium hydroxide."

"Ah. That makes things simpler," Holmes said.

"Does it?"

"It at least gives us confirmation of the form that the threat to his majesty's life will most likely take."

I didn't mention what would happen if we—and the advice that Holmes had just given to King Edward—turned out to be wrong. Holmes knew that as well as I.

"What now?" I asked instead.

"I believe that something in the nature of definitive proof would not go amiss. Theories are all well and good, but the Hyde Park murders show a high degree of cold calculation and total lack of regard for human life. The mind behind those crimes will not be easily panicked into a confession."

"No. I could pay a visit to the murder victims' family members," I said. "Well, not Emma Thompkins' friends; I doubt that they could help. But I imagine that a talk with the Colonnade Hotel proprietor, Mrs. Goodspeed, might be productive."

Down at the foot of the palace steps, a little boy in a sailor suit ran up to one of the guardsmen, shouting and making faces in an effort to attract the soldier's attention. The guardsman continued to stare straight ahead, his face impassive under the tall black fur helmet, as though the boy wasn't there. After a moment, the boy ran back to his nursemaid, giggling.

"You might also pay a call at the Church of St. Augustin, in Kensington," Holmes said. "That is where the Reverend Wyatt spent years as a junior clergyman."

"I see. You'd like me to get a look at the marriage registry?"

"Indeed. I have a few inquiries of my own to make, which will likely take up most of the afternoon." Holmes glanced down at his watch. "However, I shall see you tonight at the Savoy, if not before."

* * *

Mrs. Goodspeed was clearly no happier to see me today than she had been before.

The Colonnade's front lobby was busier than it was yesterday, with a group of ladies sitting in arm chairs and drinking tea, and an elderly woman sitting in front of the fireplace and feeding bites of cake to a white Pomeranian dog.

Mrs. Goodspeed's frizz of red hair stood out like a halo around her head, and she had a pair of pince-nez perched on the end of her nose. She was standing behind the Colonnade's front desk, talking to a middle-aged couple who appeared to be asking for a room. At the sight of me, her lips pinched, her nose wrinkled, and I had the distinct impression that if it would not have created a disturbance in the presence of her guests, she would have attempted to make me walk straight back out the door.

As it was, she handed over keys to the middle-aged husband and wife, then faced me with a look that suggested she was wishing with every fibre of her being that I would drop dead.

"I am extremely busy just now, and I really don't think I can help you—" she began.

"I won't take up too much of your time," I interrupted her. "I promise. I just have two questions for you."

I could almost see the debate taking place in Mrs. Goodspeed's private thoughts. On the one hand, she was loathe to answer anything I asked out of sheer principle. On the other, agreeing to hear the questions would almost certainly get me out of here faster.

"Very well." She lowered her voice so that none of the guests in the lobby would overhear. "What was it that you wished to know?"

"Did the Duchess of Derrington stay here before her wedding to the duke? Her maiden name would have been Zachary. Aline Zachary."

Mrs. Goodspeed's lips pinched even more tightly shut. "I really couldn't say—" she began.

"Please, try to remember, if you can," I said. "I know it's quite a long time ago—"

Hostile Mrs. Goodspeed might be, but she wasn't at all difficult to manipulate. The mere implication that she might not be able to recollect had her visibly bristling.

"There's nothing the matter with my memory!" she snapped. "Just let me think." She took off the pince-nez and tapped the wire frame against the edge of the desk, frowning. "Yes, that's right," she said at last. "That would have been in 1884. No, it was in '85. Lady Aline stayed here with her father for the week before the wedding. An odd character, her father. Most peculiar in his way of speaking. But then, what can you expect from an American?" Mrs. Goodspeed sniffed. "Besides, I seem to recall that he was in poor health. Something the matter with his heart. We'd just had the electric lift installed." She nodded towards the back of the lobby. "Which was a lucky thing for him, because he'd been strictly forbidden to climb stairs."

"That's very helpful," I told her. "Just one thing more."

Mrs. Goodspeed looked wary. "And what might that be?"

"Would you look at this picture of the duke and duchess?" I reached into my bag.

The photograph I had brought with me hadn't been easy to come by. Lady Aline seemed to avoid being caught in front of the photographer's lens. But on a hunch, I had asked Jack last night to look through the evidence that had been boxed up and brought to Scotland Yard from Eleanor Cavendish's apartment.

The hunch had paid off, in that I'd found among her papers a small clipping of a newspaper story two years ago. The story was about a luncheon put on by the Royal Horticultural Society, and the featured picture attached to the story showed a picture of Lady Aline and her husband, shaking hands with one of the society's founding members.

Mrs. Goodspeed gave a martyred sigh, but bent to study the newspaper clipping as I set it down on the desk between us. Then she started, frowned, and put on her pince-nez again to peer more closely.

Finally she looked up at me, a puzzled frown creasing her forehead—almost the first expression besides annoyance I had yet seen from her.

"What is the meaning of this?" she asked.

"I don't know yet," I told her honestly. "But I would be very surprised if by the end of the day, I haven't found out."

CHAPTER 46: FLYNN

"Did you hear that?" Becky ran to the wall and the connecting door between their room and the room next door.

Flynn nodded and tried the door. "Locked from the other side." He eyed the lock. "Doesn't look like it would be hard to get it open, though."

He didn't have lock picks, but he was betting that Becky did. She almost never left Baker Street without them.

"Wait a moment." Dr. Watson held up a hand. "I heard what sounded like someone in distress over in the next room, as well. But there's nothing to show that whoever is next door has anything to do with this room or with Mr. Granby. Granby is paying for rooms 316 and 402. The room next door is 318. We can't simply break into someone's private hotel room—"

"But it might be Lady Aline," Becky interrupted.

Dr. Watson blinked. "Lady Aline? Why should it be Lady Aline?"

"Because she's not here! That is, she was here." Becky gestured to the bed, which they'd already noticed was empty. That had been the first thing they'd done as soon as they'd pulled the ropes off and opened the door to the bathing chamber: run to the outer bedroom to check. The covers on the bed were still rumpled, but the room was empty. "She was drugged—unconscious," Becky said. "Then Flynn and I got locked up in the bathing chamber, and … oh, it's too much to explain everything! We need to get in there." She stepped closer to the connecting door. "Can't you claim that as a doctor, you thought that there might be someone ill in there and had a duty to investigate?"

Dr. Watson's expression was still dubious, but then most people had that reaction to hearing one of Becky's plans. He at least didn't object when Becky took out her lock picks and started to work.

Becky's hands weren't quite as steady as usual. Flynn reckoned she was still feeling the effect of the injections they'd been given. His own head ached, when he let himself think about it. But even still, no more than half a minute after Becky had slid in the first lock pick, Flynn heard the tumblers click over to open.

"Got it," Becky said. She pushed open the door and they stepped through into the next room.

Number 318 was dark, the curtains all drawn. But there was light enough for Flynn to make out the woman's crumpled body lying on the floor with her wrists and ankles tied.

Becky spoke first. "That's not Lady Aline—it's Nellie Bly!"

CHAPTER 47: LUCY

My visit to the Church of St. Augustin seemed at first as though it would be far less of a success than my trip to see Mrs. Goodspeed. The church curate who greeted me in the vestry was a cheerful young man by the name of Simmons who both looked and sounded more like a rugby player than a part of the clergy. He had fair hair and a round, cherubic face, and he informed me that unfortunately I wouldn't be able to look at the church's marriage registry for the year of 1885.

"Burned up in the fire we had a few years back, you see," Simmons said. "I thought Reverend Wyatt would cry, I really did. Though between ourselves, it wouldn't surprise me if he'd been the one who started the fire. Accidentally, of course," he hastened to add. "But poor old Mr. Wyatt was a bit of an old dodderer, always forgetting to snuff out the candles on the altar when he took early morning service. Though I shouldn't speak ill of the dead." Simmons' expression clouded over. "I just heard a few days ago that Reverend Wyatt had been attacked and killed in Hyde Park."

I let my eyes widen. "You don't mean that he was one of the Hyde Park victims? I read about them in the paper. I've not wanted to go into Hyde Park ever since."

"Yes. Grim, no question," Simmons agreed. "Must have been some madman. Can't think of any other reason why someone would have wanted to kill Reverend Wyatt. He was a bumbler, as I say, but as kind as they make 'em. Still, I don't suppose you want to hear all about that. What I started out to say is that we lost all our records from 1897 back—births, deaths, marriages, christenings. All burned up in one go."

"That is unlucky." Unluckier than Simmons knew, but I smiled. "Well, thank you for your time."

I was about to turn away, when Simmons said, "You know, it's funny your coming in here to ask about marriage records." He was frowning as though he'd just thought of something.

I stopped. "How so?"

"Not funny, really, I shouldn't have said that. It's just that you're the second person to come in here asking to look at our marriage registry in the past week."

"Really? Who was the other?"

"A man. Came in here wanting to see the marriage records. And when I told him about the fire, he asked whether I could put him in touch with Reverend Wyatt. Seems that Reverend Wyatt was the officiant at the wedding this fellow was interested in."

My pulse had quickened, though I did my best to keep my expression toned down to mere polite interest. "And were you able to tell him where to find the reverend?"

"Oh yes. Reverend Wyatt retired about a year ago, but I had his address all right. He rented lodgings not too far from here. Wanted to be close by the church so that he could still come in for early morning services. Once a clergyman, always a clergyman."

Simmons still spoke cheerfully. But then, he had no idea that in giving away the reverend's place of residence, he had probably signed Wyatt's death warrant.

"What a coincidence," I said. "I wonder whether it was anyone I know. Do you think you could describe what this man looked like?"

CHAPTER 48: BECKY

Becky didn't know exactly what sedative whoever had attacked her and Flynn had used, but getting dosed with it was currently at the top of her list of things she hoped never to experience again.

They were back in the Baker Street sitting room. Night had fallen outside, the noise of traffic in the street quieting to just the occasional clip clop of a passing carriage. A tea tray that Mrs. Hudson had brought up was being largely ignored in favour of preparing for the coronation ball that would begin in under two hours.

Or rather, the adults were preparing and hashing out plans. Becky was sitting on the sofa. She'd been all right at the Savoy, when she'd had to force herself to be alert enough to untie those scratchy ropes and get out of the bathing chamber. Now a reaction had set in, and she was wishing that her muscles didn't feel like leaden weights and that her head didn't still feel as though it were stuffed with soggy cotton wool. Flynn was beside her, and her one consolation was that he didn't look as though he felt much better.

"Have you spoken to Miss Bly?" Mr. Holmes asked Lucy.

Lucy had come into the room just a moment ago, looking radiantly beautiful in an emerald green satin gown. A pearl necklace encircled her throat, and she had a matching pearl comb in her dark hair.

"I've just left her," she told Holmes. "She's downstairs lying down at the moment. But she's insisting that she'll be able to come tonight."

Becky was expecting Mr. Holmes to refuse, but he nodded. "That may be all to the good, so long as she is willing." Mr. Holmes, too, was in formal evening dress. He was standing in front of the mirror, tying his white bow tie, but glanced at Lucy to add, "And you have the proof we discussed?"

"Proof enough. At least, I hope it will be," Lucy said. "And of course, the king is prepared." She smiled faintly. "This will be quite an interesting ball, with neither the host or the hostess likely to be present, and His Majesty the King expected to attend."

Holmes returned her smile, though Becky thought that his was tinged with grimness. "We must do what we can to step into the breech. I have already spoken to Mr. D'Oyly Carte."

"That's just as well, since we can't entirely predict what will happen. Although I think our best chance is still to get a confession in front of witnesses," Lucy said.

Becky wished she had the energy to ask what they were talking about. But before she could manage to make her lips move, Dr. Watson entered the sitting room, slightly out of breath.

"I didn't have any atropine on hand at my surgery. I had to make a special trip to the dispensary at St. Bart's hospital. But I got it." He held up his black leather medical bag.

"Well done." Mr. Holmes finished tying his bow tie and allowed himself a small smile. "I believe that will significantly increase our odds of eliciting that confession."

Somewhere in the back of Becky's mind, she knew that she'd heard about atropine and its medicinal uses. But she couldn't untangle her thoughts enough to call up the memory.

She did, though, manage to sit up straighter and ask Mr. Holmes the questions that had been troubling her ever since they'd left the Savoy.

"What about Hutchins, the coachman? He shot the duke, and he's still out there somewhere. And Lady Aline? We never found her at the hotel, which means she's probably still a prisoner of whoever drugged her—"

Mr. Holmes held up a hand. He wasn't usually the sympathetic sort, but the look he gave Becky now was almost kind.

"You need not trouble yourself about Lady Aline," he said. "Or about Hutchins. I promise you, I have the matter well in hand."

CHAPTER 49: LUCY

The Savoy's ballroom was decorated in gold and white: gilded trim on the ceiling and on the walls, gilt-framed mirrors, and white satin upholstered benches around the perimeter. The ball had only just begun, but already the room was crowded with men in white ties and tailcoats, and ladies like a flock of brightly coloured birds in their satin and taffeta gowns.

Watson had already pointed out Mr. Granby to me. The American was standing on the opposite side of the ballroom, puffing on a cigar and speaking to a group that I assumed were his fellow American businessmen. Granby seemed to be the one doing most of the talking, gesturing emphatically and stabbing the air with the end of his cigar when he wanted to make a point.

So far, no one seemed unduly troubled by the absence of the duke and duchess. People laughed and chatted and sipped from the gold-rimmed champagne flutes that the Savoy's waiters carried on trays through the crowd. A string quartet was playing on a raised dais at one end of the room, and a few couples were already circling the dance floor to the strains of "By the Beautiful Blue Danube."

Jack, standing beside me, eyed them warily. "You don't think we'll have to dance, do you?"

Jack, too, wore formal evening dress: a tailcoat, white tie, and white gloves. He looked as much at home in the ballroom as any of the other men, with the black jacket perfectly tailored to his broad shoulders and his dark hair combed back from his face. But he'd grown up alone on the London streets, without any sort of schooling at all, much less dancing lessons.

I glanced up at him. "You deal with thieves and murderers for a living, but the idea of having to waltz is—"

"Terrifying," Jack finished for me. He grinned. I laughed and leaned against him, but only for a moment.

A flurry of activity was taking place near the door. Jack saw it, too, and straightened. His expression didn't exactly change, but his energy shifted, somehow, becoming instantly alert and ready to react in a moment to any threat or danger.

"The royal entourage?"

"It looks that way," I agreed.

In addition to his personal attendants and guards, King Edward had brought with him an elderly bearded man carrying a doctor's kit, and a woman in a nurse's severe white uniform, the white veil covering her hair like the habit of a nun.

The king was answering someone's question as Jack and I arrived at the edges of the crowd that had immediately grown to surround him upon his entrance.

"Yes, still not feeling quite up to snuff. Doctors insisted I bring along a couple of medicos with me, just in case." He gestured to the elderly man and the nurse. "Dr. Henshaw and Nurse Seaman. Here to take care of things if I need them. Though I promise not to let them spoil all my fun." He winked.

Despite the wink and the lightness of his tone, King Edward still looked pale and drawn; it wasn't hard to understand why his private physicians would have insisted that he bring medical specialists along to tonight's ball.

Mr. Granby had somehow contrived to push himself to the front of the crowd and now stepped up to address the king.

"Your Highness." He bowed. "Or is it, Your Majesty? I'm afraid in my country, we don't always understand the niceties of royal etiquette." He laughed heartily, then gestured to a servant in the uniform of the hotel waitstaff who was hovering behind him. "Still, speaking on behalf of my fellow countrymen, it's my honour to present to you this small token of our esteem and the hope that tonight will mark a new era of cooperation between the American and Imperial Tobacco alliances."

Looking distinctly nervous, the Savoy waiter ducked his head and stepped forward. He was a middle-aged man with stooped shoulders, spectacles, and a head of thick grey hair, and he walked with an arthritic limp. But he shuffled forwards, bearing a gold-foil-wrapped cigar box in white-gloved hands, and with a deep bow, he presented it to the king.

CHAPTER 50: BECKY

"Flynn!" Becky hissed.

They were still in the Baker Street sitting room, where the clock over the mantel had just struck ten o'clock. The ball would have started just a short while ago.

Mrs. Hudson had given them tea and toast with marmalade for supper, then retired to bed for the night, so 221B was entirely quiet save for the occasional soft creaks and settling noises of a house at night. Everyone else had already gone off to the Savoy, but Flynn and Becky were still resting from the effects of the opiate that they'd been given. At least, they were supposed to be resting.

Becky had curled herself up in Dr. Watson's favourite armchair with a rug over her. But she hadn't been able to shut off the questions that kept churning through her mind, until finally she'd given up and decided that she had to talk them over with someone.

"Flynn!" she hissed again. "Are you awake?"

Flynn was lying on the sofa, which proved that he'd felt just as awful after the injection as Becky had. Usually for him to agree to spend even a portion of a night under a roof and inside four walls meant that he was practically at death's door.

Now he said, without rolling over, "No. I'm asleep."

"Fine. You can listen to me in your sleep, then." Becky ignored the sour look Flynn gave her as he sat up and turned to face her.

This was important, or she was nearly certain that it was. "I've been thinking: why bother to bring the Derrington carriage to the Savoy?"

"What?" Still looking out of sorts, Flynn blinked and rubbed his hands down his face as though trying to wake himself up. "I suppose someone wanted an excuse for being at the Savoy. That's what Lucy and Mr. Holmes said."

"Ye-es," Becky stretched out the word dubiously. She'd overheard Lucy, Jack, and Mr. Holmes discussing the case before they'd left, just as Flynn had. But the various pieces hadn't fully come together in her own mind until now. "But why bother to park the carriage in the Savoy's stables? The Savoy's not Buckingham Palace. It's not particularly well guarded. I suppose there'll be guards on duty tonight, with the king expected to put in an appearance, but this morning ... nearly anyone could have walked straight in, pretending to be a guest or a servant of a guest or someone wanting to eat at the restaurant on the first floor. So why bother with the carriage?"

Flynn frowned. Now that he had woken up a bit, he didn't look annoyed anymore, just thoughtful. Becky could almost see him thinking it all through and coming to exactly the same conclusion that she had come to.

"We need to get over to the Savoy straight away," Flynn said.

Becky had already thrown off the rug and jumped up, hopping as she struggled to put on her shoes as fast as possible. "I'll telephone for a cab."

CHAPTER 51: WATSON

"Cigars, then?" King Edward VII mused.

The king's beard was impeccably sculpted, a testament to the precision and care that went into royal grooming, but the tale told by the heavy pouches beneath his eyes was of a different sort. So, too, was the evidence of the crinkled skin bulging over his starched white collar.

I had heard the whispers in medical circles: in Buckingham Palace on the date originally scheduled for the king's coronation, surgeons had anesthetized the king on a makeshift operating table in his dressing room. They had penetrated a layer of fatty tissue more than four inches deep before they could lance open a large sixteen-ounce abscess that had been first mistaken for appendicitis.

I briefly wondered whether this brush with mortality might steer the king towards a healthier path. I thought not, recalling his earlier, futile health crusades in German spas that I had witnessed six years earlier.

Yet, my duty was not to ponder his future wellness but to safeguard his life today—a commitment ingrained from my days in uniform. My military days might be behind me, but the resolve they had forged remained strong.

I hovered at his elbow as with a shaking hand he took the box from Granby. Pinching the gold foil between his forefinger and thumb, he pulled at a corner of the wrapping, tearing away a long swath. He crumpled the shiny material into a ball and tossed it aside.

The box, crafted from Spanish cedar, was a testament to fine craftsmanship, chosen for its aromatic qualities, moisture regulation, and resistance to pests and decay. The king lifted the lid, unveiling a dozen six-inch cigars, each tipped with a gold wrapper that caught the light.

Then he looked at me, as if for guidance.

I leaned in, my gaze scrutinising the wrappers, mentally comparing them to the one Granby had presented with such grandeur a few hours earlier.

The king's eyes held a hint of curiosity.

"Just admiring the workmanship, Your Majesty," I assured him.

"Very well." His gaze shifted to Granby. "Am I to sample one?"

Granby responded in his now-familiar courtly tones of the American south, "It would be an immense honour, Your Majesty, should you choose to indulge." I could tell that Granby was trying to say the right thing, despite his earlier statement that he knew little of royal protocol.

The king gave me a knowing look. "All right," he said. "Let us sit over here and have a cigar."

He deposited his bulk at the end of a nearby settee and motioned for me to take the seat alongside, on a red-upholstered cushion. I obeyed.

He handed me the cigar box, now with its gold foil torn off and the branded emblem of the American Tobacco Company fully visible, burned into the Spanish cedar lid.

Glancing up, I caught sight of Lucy, radiant in her emerald satin dress, with Jack steadfast by her side, making their way towards us. Beyond them, a small assembly of Granby's colleagues and a handful of guests seemed drawn by curiosity towards the royal spectacle.

The musicians played on, seemingly detached from the royal engagement.

Lucy and Jack came to a halt a short distance away. They turned their backs to us, effectively shielding our little gathering from curious eyes.

Flanking our now-secluded spot were the king's medical companions—an elder physician and a veiled nurse. To our right stood Granby, embodying the American entrepreneurial spirit. To our left, an old white-haired Savoy waiter bent forward slightly, a box of safety matches in hand, poised to strike one alight the moment the king signalled his readiness.

I cradled the cigar box on my knees, its lid fully open, presenting the assortment to the king. With a tentative forefinger, he probed at the tightly packed row of cigars, finally coaxing one free. Clasping the golden wrapper between thumb and forefinger, he lifted it, only for his grip to falter.

The cigar tumbled onto my lap. I felt its weight as it meandered down between my legs.

"Just a moment, Your Majesty," I offered, my voice steady. I moved swiftly to retrieve the wayward cigar.

"Clumsy of me," he said.

"Not at all, Your Majesty." I added, "I have my pocket knife with me, so I may as well cut the head." I did so, removing the top layer of the outer tobacco wrapper, to allow the cigar to draw properly.

Within moments, the king had the cigar I had prepared. He brought it to his lips with a firm grip.

He nodded at the white-haired Savoy waiter.

With a swift movement the match was struck. A moment later, when the phosphorous of the match head had burned away, the waiter stepped forward, proffering the yellow flame.

The flame touched the tobacco at the foot of the cigar. The lit end glowed. The king puffed, twirled the cigar, and puffed again. Then he bent over, giving a small, choking cough.

The eyes of the surrounding crowd were on King Edward, all attention focused on him as he gave another wheezing cough. Several people even took anxious steps forwards, exchanging worried murmurs.

But I saw the white-haired Savoy waiter take first one surreptitious step backwards, then another.

The king's elderly physician stepped forward, as though out of concern for the king. But at the last second, he turned, swivelling in the waiter's direction.

"Hold him!" commanded Sherlock Holmes.

CHAPTER 52: FLYNN

The Savoy stables were comparatively quiet at this hour of the night. With the stables reserved for guests at the hotel, most people attending the ball had parked out in the street outside. Flynn could hear music playing, and light streamed out of the hotel windows, illuminating the courtyard and the horse's stalls. But it wasn't too difficult for him and Becky to make their way into the stable yard without being spotted.

"This way," Becky whispered.

She led the way to the stall where they'd seen the Duke of Derrington's carriage parked earlier today. Flynn heard her let out a quick breath of relief when they saw that the big black vehicle was still there.

"We're not too late."

"Or we're wrong and nothing's going to happen here after all," Flynn said.

"We've been over this," Becky whispered. She tiptoed across the straw-strewn cobblestones to the carriage. "There's only one reason that makes any sense for leaving the carriage here."

"Because the carriage is going to be used to carry something—or someone—away from the Savoy," Flynn said. "I know."

It was just that at the moment he was wishing that Becky's reasoning didn't make so much sense.

"Exactly." Becky approached the trunk, which was still mounted on the luggage rack at the back, and opened the lid.

Flynn grimaced. "Again?"

"It worked once before, didn't it?"

Again, Flynn wished he could argue, but he didn't bother. For one, arguing with Becky when she'd got one of her ideas was a waste of breath.

For another, he heard the sound of heavy footsteps coming towards them across the cobbled stable yard.

"Quick!" Becky whispered soundlessly.

Flynn gave her a boost up so that she could get into the trunk without making too much noise, then hoisted himself up, as well. They'd just lowered the lid of the trunk back down over their heads when the footsteps reached the entrance to their stall, then stopped.

Flynn held his breath, his heart beating hard enough that he almost thought whoever was out there would hear it. The footsteps came nearer, but didn't approach their hiding spot. Instead, Flynn heard a grunt as though someone was struggling under a heavy weight. Then the carriage dipped, the springs squeaking as something was deposited inside.

Becky nudged him, and Flynn nodded in the dark. She'd been right. Someone was trying to smuggle something away from the Savoy under cover of night. He was ready to stay where they were for now, waiting to see where that same someone was planning to go. But at that moment, there was a low groan from inside the carriage, followed by a gasp.

Then a woman's voice said, "Where am I? What's happening?" The carriage shifted as though she were trying to climb out. "Who are you?"

Becky's hand tightened on Flynn's arm. "That's Lady Aline!" she whispered into his ear.

Flynn had never heard the duchess speak, but he believed her.

A man's voice—more of a growl than anything—cursed, then said, "Should have given you another dose of the drugs before I brought you out here."

"Drugs?" Lady Aline sounded dazed. "What—"

The man's voice interrupted. "Stop right there and get back in that carriage. Your loving husband wants your death to look like a suicide. But don't think I won't take my chances and shoot you straight through the heart if you make any trouble for me."

"My husband?" Lady Aline's voice faltered. "Daniel? What are you talking about? What do you mean?"

The man's voice growled something else, but Flynn didn't catch whatever it was. Without having to talk about it, he and Becky had started to slowly and soundlessly raise the lid of the trunk. There was no reaction, which meant that they and the back of the carriage must be out of the nameless man's line of sight.

"Why are you doing this?" Lady Aline's voice was shaky, bewildered-sounding.

The man laughed harshly. "For money, chiefly. A great deal of it. Now get into that carriage and sit down."

"No."

"What?" Now it was the man who sounded like he had no idea what to make of the situation.

Flynn eased himself over the side of the trunk and onto the ground. Becky did the same.

"I said no." Lady Aline's voice was firmer, now. "You're clearly going to kill me. I'm not going to allow myself to be shut up in here and carried off somewhere like a lamb to the slaughter.

If you want to shoot me, it's going to have to be right here and right now."

Flynn started to search around for a weapon. There wasn't much at hand. The best he could come up with was a bit of board that looked like it had broken off from a crate of feed. He picked it up, hefting it like a club in one hand, then glanced at Becky, who nodded.

Slowly, they started to inch their way around the carriage. Flynn spotted the man, who wasn't much more than a dark shadow in the dim light. He wore a long black overcoat and a cloth cap, which made him even harder to recognise.

"You really want to play that game?" he growled. He raised his hand, and even in the darkness, Flynn caught the metallic glint of a revolver as the man took aim.

Lady Aline was half in, half out of the carriage, holding onto the door. Her face was a pale smudge surrounded by fair hair. She made some kind of wordless sound, but didn't draw back even at the sight of the gun.

Flynn charged, bringing the board down in a hard swing at the man's head. He should have connected with the back of the man's head, but the man must have heard him coming, because at the last second, he spun around. The board glanced off the man's forehead, and he staggered back, losing his grip on the revolver, but he didn't fall.

A ray of light from the courtyard outside fell across his face, and Flynn stared. He'd never seen the man in person before, but he recognised the description Mr. Holmes had given him: tall and thin, with a narrow face, grey hair, and dark eyes that glittered behind octagonal spectacles.

For a second, Flynn was so stunned that he just gaped at

Mr. Fenshaw, editor in chief of *The Tatler*. He didn't even make a dive for the revolver that Fenshaw had dropped when he stumbled. Luckily, though, Becky scooped the gun up and jumped back so that she was out of Fenshaw's reach.

Fenshaw looked from one of them to the other, a look of calculation in his eyes. Then he spun around and bolted out of the stable. Flynn heard his footsteps pounding away across the cobblestones.

"Do we chase him?" he asked Becky.

She hesitated, but then shook her head. "Let him go. We're not likely to catch up, and I don't want to leave Lady Aline." She nodded to the duchess, who was leaning heavily against the door of the carriage. Lady Aline had put on a brave show for Fenshaw, but now her face was white enough to be mistaken for a ghost. Flynn thought she looked to be on the verge of fainting. "Come on," Becky said. "We need to make sure that she's safely inside with Mr. Holmes."

CHAPTER 53: LUCY

Jack reacted at once, seizing hold of the waiter and twisting his arms behind his back.

The assembled crowd looked in confusion from him to the king to the elderly physician who had just revealed himself to be Sherlock Holmes.

King Edward waved away the looks of concern. "I'm all right. Quite all right, no need for concern."

"We are delighted to hear it, Your Majesty," Holmes said. He had already removed the elderly-physician disguise and now straightened up, revealing his full height. He stepped forwards, addressing the waiter, who was struggling in Jack's grasp.

"That will be quite enough of that, Your Grace. Might I add that the outline of your ducal signet ring is quite visible beneath the white gloves you are wearing."

For a moment, the Savoy waiter merely gaped at him, his expression gone slack with shock. Holmes took the opportunity to yank off both the wig of grizzled hair and the spectacles, revealing the Duke of Derrington.

A stir ran through the crowd: mingled expressions of confusion and alarm.

"You have no right to hold me!" Derrington continued to struggle in Jack's grasp. Jack held him firmly. As strong and fit as the duke was, Jack was stronger.

"You might find this useful." Holmes removed a silk scarf from his pocket, holding it by the corner. Jack took it and tied Derrington's wrists together.

"I demand that you release me at once!" Derrington stopped struggling, but continued to glower at Holmes. "Dressing up as one of the hotel wait staff isn't a crime."

"Perhaps not." Holmes' expression was as calm as always. "Unfortunately for you, the same cannot be said for murder."

"Murder?" Derrington's face flushed a dull, ruddy colour. "What are you talking about? Whose murder?"

Another stir ran through the crowd of listeners. Holmes held up a hand, silencing them all. As always on these occasions, he had taken command of the room as thoroughly and as effortlessly as a general takes command of his army. He was addressing Derrington, but he raised his voice enough to be heard by all.

"To begin, we must go back to the start of this case: the bodies found in Hyde Park. Samuel Harley, the Reverend John Wyatt, George Pennythwaite, KC, Emma Thompkins, and Martin Goodspeed."

"I've already told you!" The duke's voice rose. "My wife—"

Holmes cut him off. His voice didn't grow any louder, but his tone cut straight through the duke's angry bluster and reduced him to silence. "I am well aware of the story you told to me about your wife Lady Aline—a story that was from start to finish, an exercise in absurdity, with one blatantly glaring lie heaped upon the other."

"What do you mean?" a hint of uncertainty crept into Derrington's tone.

"First, you claimed that your wife purloined money from the

drawer of your desk in order to hire Brasher, a known killer, to commit a string of murders on her instruction."

"That's right! I—"

"Silence, if you please." Holmes once again held up a hand. "The notion that your wife would abstract cash from your desk—where it was an almost certainty that it would be missed—was absurd. No woman of your wife's rank and station in life is without a piece of jewellery or two that she could either sell or pawn for a hundred pounds. Nor would Brasher have scrupled to accept such a piece in lieu of ready cash if it had been offered. That is absurdity number one in the preposterous story you told. Absurdity number two was your account of finding your wife burning a paper with German words on it—words which, when translated, hinted at a plot to kill the king." Holmes paused. "There are enough flaws in that story to sink the proverbial battleship. Beginning with the idea of your wife kindling a fire in the grate of her bedroom on a warm morning in August. Such an action would have been practically guaranteed to attract the interest and curiosity of your household servants—which was precisely what anyone plotting against the king would wish to avoid. Likewise, the notion that anyone planning as devious and risky a plot as the assassination of His Majesty would invite potential discovery by committing the details of the plan to paper—and in German, no less—is equally an insult to the intelligence of any listener whom you ask to believe such a tale."

Derrington, still red in the face, swallowed, but didn't answer.

"Then we come to your account of seeing Mr. Brasher driving a carriage—undisguised and in broad daylight—to Hyde Park in order to deposit the body of Emma Thompkins there." Holmes raised an eyebrow. "Need I point out that a man of Brasher's considerable criminal experience would be far more likely to conduct such an operation stealthily and under cover of night?"

The duke's face worked, but he cleared his throat and managed to speak with an effort at sounding nonchalant. "None of this is evidence, Mr. Holmes. If you are implying that I myself had something to do with the deaths of the Hyde Park victims—"

"Oh, I am doing considerably more than implying," Holmes said. "I am stating outright that you are the man responsible for their deaths, and that in at least one case, you yourself committed the actual killing, for reasons that I will shortly make plain."

"Reasons?" The duke's handsome face was almost unrecognisable now, flushed and sweating, his teeth bared in a sneer. "And what reasons would those be?"

Holmes' expression remained calm. "To answer that, we must travel further back. Back to the occasion of your marriage to Lady Aline. Or Aline Zachary, as she then was. Daughter of Zebulon Zachary, an American tobacco baron." Holmes paused again, eyeing Derrington. "I believe that upon your marriage and following the death of your father-in-law you took control of Zachary's tobacco estates and his business affairs?"

"What of it?" the duke demanded.

"I am merely pointing out that from your point of view, the marriage was an advantageous one in the financial sense. A look back into the state of your own financial affairs would reveal that you were in dire straits, due to some unfortunate speculations and rash investments. You needed a large infusion of cash in order to right the ship—which your marriage to Lady Aline provided."

Derrington swallowed again, but said nothing.

"You also, at the time of your marriage, had a mistress," Holmes continued. Both his expression and his tone had hardened, somehow. "A young woman by the name of Cynthia Reynolds."

The duke gave a forced laugh. "Really, Mr. Holmes. My private affairs—"

"Are scarcely private, when they affect King and Country," Holmes said. "You and Lady Aline spent your honeymoon in the Caribbean, ostensibly because you wished to show her your estates in Jamaica. In reality, Jamaica was a convenient place for you to commit the first in the string of murders of which you stand accused: that of your wife."

Several people around us gasped. Some exclaimed.

The duke stared, then forced another harsh laugh. "Have you quite taken leave of your senses, Mr. Holmes? My wife has been alive and well these twenty years."

"A woman calling herself Lady Aline has been alive and well," Holmes said. "Your mistress, Cynthia Reynolds, was several years older than Aline Zachary, but she bore a strong resemblance to her in terms of colouring and height. After you killed Lady Aline in Jamaica, disposing of her body somewhere on your private estate, it was quite a simple matter for Cynthia to step into the role of Lady Aline, your wife. I doubt whether even your servants on the estate were aware of what had occurred. You could have killed the genuine Aline within hours of your arrival, before anyone had more than a passing look at her. Perhaps you invited her to come with you on a private walk or ride around the estate? A ride from which she never returned?"

"I did no such thing."

"Of course you would say that. At any rate, you had Cynthia already in position and waiting to become the new Duchess of Derrington. As such, she travelled back with you to this country, and has been playing the role with flawless execution ever since. Since Aline was American by birth, only a handful of people in England had ever met her before your marriage. You were relatively safe from exposure. Until your ambitions to step into a more prominent role in the world tobacco trade brought you more into the public limelight—and thus into danger that someone would uncover your secret."

The duke's expression now resembled the snarl of a cornered dog. "You cannot prove any of this nonsense!"

I had been quiet until now, but at that I stepped forward. "We can, actually. All the Hyde Park murder victims were people who had met with Lady Aline—the real Lady Aline—during the short time she was in London before your marriage. Emma Thompkins was her lady's maid. Samuel Harley made her wedding slippers and delivered them to her personally. He told the story often to his daughter, who repeated it to me. And if I'd been paying proper attention, I would have realised that the woman calling herself your wife and the woman whom you married nearly twenty years ago were two different people."

"Preposterous."

"Not at all. Samuel Harley spoke of how pretty Aline Zachary was when he met her, wearing a dress that matched the colour of her eyes. The woman whom the world has known as Lady Aline has brown eyes. It's a rare bride who will shop for her wedding trousseau in a brown-coloured dress. I should have realised sooner that Samuel Harley's story suggested that the real Aline's eyes were green or blue."

"Trivial detail."

"Not if he could identify the real Aline. And another victim, Martin Goodspeed, hosted the real Aline at his hotel. Yet another victim, George Pennythwaite, KC, was your own private solicitor years ago—the same lawyer who drew up a will for Zebulon Zachary, leaving everything to Aline, and naming you as executor and trustee. He would have known the real Aline as well."

"You're clutching at straws."

"Finally, and we would need an exhumation order to prove it, but I would wager a significant amount that you helped your father-in-law along into the next world. He had heart trouble already. An extra dose of digitalis in his medication would have resulted in a death that looked natural. And if you doctored the medicine before leaving for your honeymoon, you would appear to be above suspicion, since you were out of the country when Zachary died."

Derrington stared at me, his chest rising and falling rapidly. "None of this is—"

"True?" I finished. "If you're going to continue to lie, you could at least be more creative with your denials. The only Hyde Park victim whom we can't absolutely prove was connected to Lady Aline was the Reverend Wyatt. I imagine he was either the officiant or one of the witnesses at your wedding, but the church records that would show it were lost in a fire a few years ago."

The duke started to speak, but I went on without giving him time for an interruption. "What we can prove, though, is that you visited Reverend Wyatt's former church, asking for the reverend's current address. The curate there remembers you. I'm sure he would be able to identify you as the man who came in. There's also Mrs. Goodspeed. It was an oversight on your part not to put her out of the way, as well. She remembers the real Aline Zachary. I showed her a photograph of the woman calling herself your wife. She was ready to swear straight away that they weren't the same woman."

Derrington faced us, continuing to breathe heavily. "This means nothing," he ground out. "To achieve a verdict against a man of my station—a peer of the realm—the Crown will need to pursue a legal case in the House of Lords, and follow up with appeal after appeal until we're all old and grey."

"That is perhaps open to some debate." Holmes spoke once again. "However, there is no question that a confession would be significantly more efficient."

"A confession?" The duke's harsh bark of incredulous laughter rang out over the surprised murmurs of the crowd. "Are you quite mad, Mr. Holmes?"

"Not mad," Holmes said. "I simply have the advantage of knowing that the scarf which Sergeant Kelly used to tie your wrists a few minutes ago was saturated with a solution of nicotine. The same nicotine with which you were attempting to frame your wife for the attempted murder of the king. You have a weakness for heavy-handed clues, Your Grace," he added. "If your wife had truly conceived of a plot to assassinate His Majesty, do you seriously imagine that she would leave her solution of sodium hydroxide—the chemical used for extracting nicotine from tobacco leaves—out in the open on her worktable for all to see?"

Derrington gaped at him, his mouth hanging open. His face was still flushed an unhealthy, mottled red, and his breath came in harsh gasps. "Nicotine?"

"Indeed." Holmes' voice remained as calm as before. "If you receive the antidote—a solution of atropine—sometime in the next ten to fifteen minutes, I believe that your odds of survival are quite high. Without the atropine ... well. Were I in your position, I should be wary of making long-term plans."

"Nicotine poisoning?" The duke continued to stare at Holmes as though struggling to absorb the sense of the words. Then he passed his tongue across his lips and said, in a harsh voice, "What do you want?"

"As I said earlier, Your Grace. A confession. For the murder of your wife, Aline Zachary, and for your part in the Hyde Park killings."

Derrington opened his mouth, but Holmes once again spoke over him. "And you will tell us the location of Cynthia Reynolds," he said. "Otherwise known as the Duchess of Derrington."

Holmes' expression had turned granite hard. He took a step towards the duke, his voice quiet, but tinged with steel all the same. "Since you have gone to such elabourate lengths to frame Cynthia for the attempted murder of our king—a creative means of disposing of one's wife; I must congratulate you on your originality, if nothing else—I believe it highly likely that she was an innocent dupe in all of this. What did you tell her? That the original Aline had betrayed and abandoned you? Run off with another man? And that by stepping into her role as your wife, she, Cynthia, could ensure that the legacy of Mr. Zachary's tobacco industry did not suffer by passing into a strangers' hands after Zachary's death?"

Derrington licked his lips again, but said nothing.

Holmes took another step forwards. "Having shot Hutchins, your own coachman, you came here disguised as him, so that you could enter the Savoy without anyone's being aware of your true identity. Still in the guise of Hutchins, you drugged your wife, putting her in a room which you had taken under the name of George Granby, your competitor in the tobacco trade."

At that, Granby made a shocked, strangled noise. "What?"

Holmes spared him a glance. "I fear so, Mr. Granby. If his plan to incriminate his wife failed, he hoped to make you his scapegoat. It was for that reason that he invited you to tonight's ball."

Granby paled visibly, but Holmes had already turned his attention back to Derrington. "Where is Cynthia Reynolds?" he commanded. "You will tell us where she is at once, if you wish to live!"

Utter silence claimed the room; even the astonished murmurings and exclamations of the crowd had died away.

The duke stared at Holmes for another long moment. Then his knees buckled. If Jack hadn't been holding him, he would have fallen to the ballroom floor.

"Please," Derrington gasped. His voice was a wheezing rattle, his eyes rolling back in his head as he sagged helplessly in Jack's grasp.

Holmes watched him a moment, then turned, found Watson in the crowd, and nodded. Watson stepped forward, already reaching into his black medical bag for a syringe, the needle of which he skillfully injected into the duke's neck.

The duke gave a shudder as Watson depressed the plunger. Then another shudder rippled through the duke's frame. He breathed once, twice, and then raised his head, looking up at Holmes. Then, abruptly, he started to laugh, a scraping, ugly sound in the room's quiet.

"You're too late, Mr. Holmes. You've given me the cure. I'll live. But Cynthia is already—"

The door to the ballroom burst open, and Becky and Flynn

stumbled in, their hair and clothes windblown and dishevelled with what had clearly been a headlong run. "It's all right, Mr. Holmes," Flynn managed to gasp out between breaths.

Becky nodded as he paused for air. "We found Lady Cynthia in time," she said. "She's still alive."

CHAPTER 54: WATSON

The Duke of Derrington stared at Flynn and Becky. His face was still flushed a mottled red, but it was clear that he had been exaggerating his earlier symptoms, because he now stood upright under his own power, albeit in Jack's grasp.

He gave a harsh bark of a laugh. "I don't know what tales my wife has been telling, Mr. Holmes—" he began. "But I categorically deny all of them. And the same goes for the wild imaginings you have been spewing for the past quarter hour. Since you appear to be unable to present us all with anything remotely resembling definite proof of your fantastical claims, I demand that you unhand me at once. And you had better pray that I will not bring legal action against you for your attempt to poison me with nicotine!"

The crowd around us murmured, people shifting uneasily. Holmes's expression remained impassive as he regarded Derrington from under half-lidded eyes.

"Oh, I believe we can bring more than theoretical claims," he said.

I saw the shadow of uneasiness creep into Derrington's gaze, although his expression remained defiant. "What do you mean?"

"He means me." The woman in the white nurse's uniform stepped forward. She'd been so quiet and inconspicuous up until this moment, standing in the background behind King

Edward, that more than one person in the crowd startled at hearing her speak.

Derrington stared, as though he'd not until this moment registered her existence.

In a swift, smooth movement, the nurse reached up and removed the white veil, revealing the unruly dark curls of Nellie Bly. She had already taken out the pads in her cheeks that had altered the shape of her face, and now stepped forward to confront the duke with an air of confident assurance.

"You really should have told your associates to go more heavily on the chloroform when they kidnapped me off the street," she told Derrington. "I'm sure that you were hoping to incriminate Mr. Granby as well as your wife in this scheme. But I saw your face clearly after you'd brought me up to the hotel room. And I am perfectly willing to swear to that in a court of law."

For an instant, as silence once more claimed the room, it looked as though the duke might try to continue with his act of brazen defiance. But then a spasm of rage twisted his face. He lunged at Nellie, but was brought up short by Jack's restraining grasp.

"Curse you!" he shouted. "Curse you all!"

Then a woman's shrill voice called into the room.

"Daniel?"

The woman's voice came from the entry door. "Daniel? Does your far-reaching curse also include me?"

All eyes turned to her.

She entered the room, accompanied by Inspector Lestrade. Her blonde hair was dishevelled, her wide eyes gaunt with fatigue, and her even white teeth were bared in a wide, obviously forced smile. "After all these years as your beloved? After

I served you and did your bidding, am I, too, to be cursed? Surely not!"

Derrington raised his eyes to her and stared. "They are telling lies about me, my dear."

"Are they, now?" She advanced closer. "And they have you trussed up as well. What a pity!"

She moved behind him and reached out as if to untie the purple scarf that still bound his white-gloved hands.

"Don't touch it, Lady Cynthia," Holmes said.

She gave him a brief glance. "You know my name?"

"We know your name and your history."

She looked at her husband. He was perspiring now. "You're in disguise, Daniel? White gloves and all?"

"I can explain."

"Something to do with Fenshaw, then?"

"Who's Fenshaw?"

I saw Becky was about to speak, but Holmes held up a warning finger.

"Oh, he's the nice gentleman," she began, her voice laden with sarcasm, "who drugged me and dragged me to your carriage a few minutes ago. He said you'd paid him to kill me."

A murmur ran through the crowd. I saw Lestrade move closer.

But then a hush fell as Derrington raised his gaze even higher. "You see, Mr. Holmes, there is no limit to my wife's treachery. She has clearly fabricated her story—"

"Not true!" Becky interjected. "I heard Mr. Fenshaw. So did Flynn, here!"

"—and paid a pair of street urchins to support her accusations."

"Not true," Becky repeated.

But Holmes raised a finger again, and she did not continue.

"So, Your Grace," he said, "you insist that everyone who testifies against you is lying. Is that your defence?"

"It's up to the Crown to prove they're not. My peers in the House of Lords will judge the truth. I am innocent until proven guilty."

"So you've said." Holmes appeared to consider the duke's position.

The duke went on, confident. "Miss Bly will, of course, relish her moment in the sun, testifying before nobility and being published in newspapers on both sides of the Atlantic. But my barrister will make mincemeat of her publicity-seeking fantasies, just as they will discredit my traitorous wife's sanctimonious tales."

Holmes's gaze found mine. "Dr. Watson," he said, "would you kindly use your knife to remove the scarf binding His Grace's wrists?"

I did so, carefully, and dropped the poisoned silk fabric into my medical bag.

Jack still held the duke by his collar, however.

"So I'm free to go, then?" the duke enquired.

"By no means," Holmes replied. "I merely had the scarf removed so we might observe your white gloves and recall that you were wearing them when you handed His Majesty the box of cigars."

"What of it?"

"The cigars were poisoned, coated with the same type of nicotine solution as was used to soak the scarf."

"And you're suggesting that's why I wore the gloves?"

"If you were called upon to open the box, remove a cigar and prepare it, you knew you would be far safer wearing gloves."

"Balderdash."

"You wouldn't fear handling the cigars without gloves, then?"

"The cigars aren't poisoned."

"Indeed?"

"We all saw the king light one up and smoke it."

"A stroke of good fortune for him, perhaps. Yet you stand here before witnesses, including His Majesty himself, and all will testify that you handed over the box of cigars and lit the one the King was holding. You were then making your way from the room when I stopped you."

"Hardly incriminating, Mr. Holmes. My job was done. The King had his cigar."

"So, I return to my question. You would not be afraid to handle the cigars without gloves?"

A quirk of a smile flashed across the duke's belligerent features. Wordlessly, he peeled off his gloves, first one, then the other, and dropped them with a theatrical gesture onto the carpeted floor.

"You are prepared, then? The antidote Dr. Watson provided may have worn off by now. Or the quantity may not be sufficient to neutralise the effects of the nicotine that could be coating the surface of a dozen cigars."

The duke nodded. "Bring them on, and we'll find out."

The King looked down at the box of Spanish cedar beside him on the settee, then up at Holmes.

Holmes shook his head. "I merely wish to point out that the cigars remain in their box, and since Derrington here handed them to you, they have not left Your Majesty's side. We shall have them analysed. The poison found on their surface will convict you, Derrington, and no barrister, including yours, will 'make mincemeat' of a king's testimony. The trial will be for high treason. Attempting the life of the sovereign, to be precise."

Derrington stared. "I demand to see—"

Holmes cut him off. "Your demands are of no consequence. As you may know, the crime of high treason carries with it a different set of regulations and procedures, created to protect the Crown over the centuries. Quite different from the relatively benevolent due process afforded to those whose crimes are of a lesser nature. You will be thrown into prison, in solitary confinement if the king wishes it, and the conditions of your confinement could be most debilitating. Your trial before those you consider your peers may not take place for quite some time, and when you do appear before the public, you may have changed considerably. We shall all see you in your debased and degraded condition. You will be humiliated over a protracted period before your peers during your trial, during your sentencing, during your subsequent appeals, if you have funds to pay for any, and during your remaining imprisonment, until your ultimate execution."

The King tapped the cigar box with a fat forefinger. "How long for the chemical analysis?"

"By noon tomorrow," Holmes replied.

The King said, "We'll decide where to put him when the chemical analysis is done."

Holmes nodded.

"Your analysis be damned," the duke said. "Those cigars are perfectly safe. As I said, the King himself is living proof."

"He is proof that the cigar he smoked was not poisoned. However, the cigar he smoked was not from the box in question."

Holmes nodded to me.

I stepped forwards. "We had anticipated the contingency," I said. "I had a similar cigar given to me earlier by Mr. Granby here. I substituted that one when I cut the tip. The other lies in the cigar box."

Derrington stared, and this time his expression was filled with pure hatred.

"Inspector Lestrade," Holmes said. "Do you have a set of handcuffs on your person?"

Lestrade stepped forward. "Daniel, Duke of Derrington, I arrest you—" he began.

But then, in a swift, cat-like gesture, Derrington's left hand jerked upwards to his mouth. He bit down. Lestrade pulled his hand away, but Derrington was already chewing on something from his now-opened signet ring. White foam issued from the corner of his twisted mouth.

"No antidote for cyanide, Mr. Holmes," he gasped. "You won't see me humiliated. No one will!"

The colour drained from his face. His hand clawed at the air, lashing out in Holmes's direction. He leaned forwards, twisting away from Lestrade's attempt to support him. Very deliberately, he bared his teeth in a grotesque smile, which, I thought, had an air of triumph about it.

Then a great convulsion shook him, and he fell.

"You goaded him," said Lady Aline.

"He prepared his ring and chose to use it," Holmes replied.

"Coward's way out," said the King.

Then he took Holmes aside, coming towards me, speaking quietly.

I heard him clearly.

"You saved the Crown a good deal of time, expense, and embarrassment, Mr. Holmes."

"No more than my duty."

The King nodded. "Matter of fact, you saved the Crown. Again."

CHAPTER 55: BECKY

August 18

"Truly, I don't know how I can ever thank you," Nellie Bly said.

Two days had passed since the nearly disastrous coronation ball. Nellie was dressed for travelling in a herringbone tweed skirt and jacket, and looked as though she'd entirely recovered from her ordeal. She was addressing everyone in the Baker Street sitting room—Mr. Holmes and Dr. Watson, Lucy and Jack, but her gaze was particularly focused on Flynn, who looked the way he always did when anyone tried to praise or thank him: about as comfortable as someone who had just sat down on a hedgehog.

He shuffled his feet and muttered something about, "That's all right," before Becky decided to rescue him.

"So you'll be going back to America, then?" she asked Nellie.

"That's right." Nellie Bly's lips quirked wryly. "I think I've had enough investigative reporting to last me for a while. Helping my husband to run the Ironclad Manufacturing Company will seem a positive holiday after the last few days."

"Speaking of companies," Dr. Watson said, "What's going to happen to the Duke of Derrington's tobacco estates?"

"The duke's legal affairs will take some time to untangle," Holmes said. "But it appears likely that Cynthia Reynolds will inherit the duke's money and his Jamaican holdings, at least."

"Really?" Lucy looked incredulous.

"The duke's will leaves everything to his niece, Emmeline. I understand that Emmeline, however, is sufficiently horrified by all that has come out into the open about her uncle that she wants nothing to do with any of it."

Lucy laughed. "No, I suppose Emmeline wouldn't want her own reputation besmirched by association. She'd be too terrified of having her illustrious fiancé call off the wedding for fear that it might tarnish his family name."

"So she's handing the money and the estates over to Cynthia?" Becky asked.

Mr. Holmes smiled faintly. "Cynthia offered, and I understand that Emmeline could scarcely sign her name to the documents quickly enough."

"I'm glad," Becky said.

"So am I," Lucy agreed. "You were exactly right about her being innocent in the murder of the original Aline Zachary, by the way," she added, speaking to Mr. Holmes. "The duke told her that Aline had run off with the low-born boy she'd been in love with as a girl. Aline's father was dead and she had no other family to mourn her or even realise that she was gone. Derrington persuaded Cynthia to step into his wife's shoes because he told her that the shame of losing a wife would be hard for his reputation, and might harm the business he was building with his tobacco estates. He never told her that Aline had an inheritance, or that he'd been made the trustee for Aline's money."

"Precisely," Mr. Holmes said. "Zachary's will left everything to Aline, and named the Duke as executor and trustee, with control of all assets until Aline was thirty, though required to pay a generous monthly allowance from the income. Soon after the wedding, however, Derrington liquidated the assets under his care and transferred them to his own account. There is a British court which oversees trust arrangements, but since the public believed that Aline was happy and content with her position as Duchess, there were no questions—which of course was the duke's real intent in persuading Cynthia to play the part of Aline."

"Cynthia will do an excellent job of managing the business side of things, I think," Lucy said.

"And the value of the tobacco shares is likely to rise if the agreement with Mr. Granby and his fellow Americans goes through," Holmes added. "I'm sure Miss Reynolds is canny enough to realise the wisdom of such an alliance."

"A very satisfactory outcome all around, then, Holmes," Dr. Watson said.

"In all but one regard."

"Oh? And what is that?"

"The editor of *The Tatler*. Mr. Fenshaw." Mr. Holmes's brows drew together. "It was he who informed the Duke of Derrington that Eleanor Cavendish suspected that the current duchess was not the real Aline Zachary but rather Cynthia, the duke's French mistress. Poor Miss Cavendish informed her editor of what she thought would be a front-page story, thinking only that it would be enough to allow her to return to serious journalism again rather than vapid society pieces. She little thought that Mr. Fenshaw would try to turn her story to his own advantage by selling the information to the duke."

"I'm surprised that the duke didn't simply kill Fenshaw, as he had all the others who suspected the truth," Lucy said.

"Indeed." There was an odd note in Mr. Holmes' voice that Becky didn't entirely understand.

"His escaping doesn't negate the success of capturing the duke, though," Dr. Watson said. "After all, Fenshaw is only one man."

"Is he?" The strange note in Mr. Holmes' voice was more pronounced. "According to Lestrade, Fenshaw was spotted on a train to Dover in the early hours of yesterday morning, but from there he appears to have vanished without a trace."

"I don't understand." Dr. Watson frowned.

It was Lucy who answered. "Mr. Fenshaw was likely a German spy. Only a major European power would have the ability to help a man get out of the country so quickly. I think it's safe to say that the assassination plot was, in fact, his idea, which he suggested to Derrington as a way to not only get rid of Cynthia but also curry favour with the Kaiser—who notoriously hates King Edward and England."

Dr. Watson drew back, looking shocked.

But Mr. Holmes inclined his head. "That is my meaning, yes." He stopped, his gaze fixed on the middle distance. "I may be wrong, of course. But I doubt that we have seen the last of Mr. Fenshaw."

THE END

HISTORICAL NOTES

This is a work of fiction, and the authors make no claim whatsoever that any historical locations or historical figures who appear in this story were even remotely connected with the adventures and events recounted herein.

However …

1. The postponement of King Edward VII's original coronation and his medical condition at the time have been accurately described here, insofar as the authors are able to determine. However, the authors have found no evidence of a coronation ball held after the August 9 coronation ceremony at Westminster Cathedral. Nor have they found evidence of a serial killer operating in Hyde Park at that time.

2. After protracted negotiations in London, on September 27, 1902, about one month after the fictional Coronation Ball, the 'tobacco war' between the British Imperial Tobacco Company and the American Tobacco Company ended with the formation of a joint venture: the British-American Tobacco Company Ltd. The parent companies agreed not to trade in each other's domestic territory and to assign trademarks, export businesses, and overseas subsidiaries to the joint venture. The company remains headquartered in London. As of 2021, its net sales were the largest of any tobacco company in the world.

3. The Connecticut Valley has been compared for its quality cigar-wrap tobacco to what the Médoc region of Bordeaux is to fine wine. A combination of good soil, adequate rainfall and abundant sunshine has made it one of the world's premium tobacco growing regions for several centuries.

4. The region also played a role in American history which would have been unforeseen at the time of this story. In 1944, a 15-year-old freshman at Atlanta's Morehouse College named Martin Luther King spent the summer of 1944 working as a farmhand at the Cullman Brothers shade tobacco farm in Simsbury as part of a tuition fund-raising seasonal employment program. In 1947, he ventured north again alongside a group of fellow students to work those same tobacco fields. Although Connecticut was still rife with inequality and prejudice, these summers afforded King and his companion-labourers with basic freedoms–such as dining in non-segregated restaurants–that they had never before experienced.

5. Richard D'Oyly Carte, who features in the first two adventures of Sherlock and Lucy, passed away in 1901. His son, Rupert, succeeded him as the new Chairman of the Board for the Savoy Hotel enterprises. After a decade acquiring a block of land next to the Savoy Theatre, and north of the original hotel, the company demolished the buildings thereon in 1903 and designed the Strand blocks, turning the hotel to face forward in its present location, squarely towards the Strand.

6. Under the pseudonym Nellie Bly, American reporter

Elizabeth Cochrane shattered records by circling the globe in just 72 days, outpacing Jules Verne's fictional Phileas Fogg and capturing imaginations far and wide. This fearless American journalist also plunged into the heart of darkness at a mental institution, not merely to observe but also to experience and expose its inner workings from within. She later wrote eleven serial novels and then, at age 31, married 73-year-old American millionaire industrialist Robert Seaman. Bly still ranks as a superhero in the world of words.

Lucy James will return. Nellie Bly and Mr. Fenshaw will also return, in the *Becky & Flynn World War I Mystery Series* by Anna Elliott.

A NOTE OF THANKS

Thank you for reading *The Affair of the Coronation Ball*. We hope you've enjoyed it.

As you probably know, reviews make a big difference! So, we also hope you'll consider going back to the Amazon page where you bought the story and uploading a quick review. You can get to that page by going to this link on our website and scrolling down:

sherlockandlucy.com

You can also sign up for our mailing list to receive updates on new stories, special discounts, and 'free days' for some of our other books: www.SherlockandLucy.com

About the Authors

Anna Elliott is the author of the *Twilight of Avalon* trilogy, and *The Pride and Prejudice Chronicles*. She was delighted to lend a hand in giving the character of Lucy James her own voice, firstly because she loves Sherlock Holmes as much as her father, Charles Veley, and second because it almost never happens that someone with a dilemma shouts, "Quick, we need an author of historical fiction!" She lives in Pennsylvania with her husband and five children.

Charles Veley is the author of the first two books in this series of fresh Sherlock Holmes adventures. He is thrilled to be contributing Dr. Watson's chapters for the series, and delighted beyond words to be collaborating with Anna Elliott.

Printed in Great Britain
by Amazon